# DARKER STILL

A NOVEL OF
MAGIC MOST FOUL

# DARKER STILL

### A NOVEL OF
### MAGIC MOST FOUL

# LEANNA RENEE HIEBER

SCHOLASTIC INC.
New York Toronto London Auckland
Sydney Mexico City New Delhi Hong Kong

ISBN 978-0-545-43409-6

12 11 10 9 8 7 6 5 4 3 2 1          12 13 14 15 16 17/0

Printed in the U.S.A.                                        23

First Scholastic printing, January 2012

*To all who have struggled to make their voices heard,*
*historically and presently*

New York County, Municipal Jurisdiction
Manhattan, July 31, 1880

New York City Police Record Case File: 1306

To whoever should have the misfortune to review this closed—but still unresolved—case, I extend my condolences. I tell you truly that all persons involved have been insufferably *odd*.

All we know directly of Miss Natalie Stewart, disappeared at age seventeen, is what you will read here in what was left behind as an absurd testimonial.

Herein you shall find pertinent newspaper articles enclosed by Miss Stewart regarding Lord Denbury and his infamous portrait. There are also letters from involved parties.

I am left to conclude that everyone involved is a certifiable lunatic. Should you wish to indulge yourself and read a young lady's foolish reveries on such highly improbable events, so be it. Should you *believe* any of it, I hope you have no business with the New York Police Department now or in the future.

Regards,
Sergeant James Patt

THIS JOURNAL IS THE SOLE PROPERTY OF:

*Miss Natalie Stewart*

AS A GIFT TO MARK THIS, HER EXIT FROM

*The Connecticut Asylum*

# June 1, 1880

Sister Theresa handed me this farewell gift with such relief that it might as well have been a key to her shackles. I'm a burden to her no more. Someone else will have to glue her desk drawers closed and exchange her communion wine for whiskey.

But now I trade the prison of the asylum for another. The prison of home.

Oh, I suppose I ought to clarify the word *asylum*, as it has its connotations.

The only illnesses the students of the Connecticut Asylum have are those of the ears and the tongue. The mute, or the deaf, are not the mentally ill. Those poor souls are cloistered someplace else, thank God. We had enough troubles on our own.

But now that I'm home, a prison undercurrent is here too. The desperate question of what is to be *done* with me lingers like dark damask curtains, dimming the happy light of our dear little East Side town house. For unfortunates like me, firstly, a girl and, secondly, a mute girl, life is made up of different types of prisons, I've learned. If I were a man, the world could be at my command. At least it would be if I were a man and could speak.

Every night I pray the same prayer: that I may go back to that year of Mother's death and startle my young self to shake the sound right out of that scared little girl. Maybe I'd have screamed. A beautiful, loud, and unending scream that could carry me to this day. A shout that could send a call to someone, anyone, who could help me find my purpose in this world. But since that trauma, I've yet to utter a word. Not for lack of trying, though. I simply cannot seem to get my voice through my throat.

I've often thought of joining a traveling freak show. At least there I wouldn't have to deal with the ugliness of people who at first think I'm normal and then realize I can't speak. I *hate* that moment and the terrible expression that comes over the person's face like a grotesque mask. The apologetic look that thinly veils pity but cannot disguise distaste, or worse, fear. If I were already in a freak show, people would be forewarned, and I could avoid that moment I've grown to despise more than anything in the world. But would I belong beside snake charmers and strong men, albinos and conjoined twins? And if not, where do I belong, if anywhere?

As a child, I heard a Whisper, a sound at the corner of

my ear, and saw a rustle of white at the corner of my eye. I used to think it was Mother. I used to hope she would show me how to speak again or explain that the shadows I see in this world are just tricks of the eyes. But she never revealed herself or any answers. And I stopped believing in her. I stopped hearing the Whisper. But what *does* remain are the shadows that come to me at night. There are terrible things in this world.

I don't have pleasant dreams. Only nightmares. Blood, terror, impending apocalypse. Great fun, I assure you. (Perhaps it's good I can't speak; I'd share dreams at some normal girl's debutante ball and send her away screaming or fainting.) There are times when I feel I need to scream. But I can't.

I've so much to say but don't dare open my mouth. The sounds aren't there. I tried, years ago. Therapists soon gave up on me, saying I was too stubborn. But it wasn't me being *stubborn*. I was anxious, nerve-racked, afraid; I hated the foreign, unwieldy sound that crept out from behind my lips so much so that I haven't dared try since. Perhaps someday.

That's why I was given this diary. Other girls were given lockets or trinkets. When I've nothing to occupy my mind or my hands, I resort to mischief. Now if the asylum had just had more books (I'd read them all, *twice*, within my first two years), I'd never have bothered with the communion wine. I wouldn't have had the time for glue, tacks, or spiders.

I'd have been reading about trade routes to India, the impossible worlds of Gothic novels, or even the tedious wonders of jungle botany—*anything* other than this boring, dreary world we live in. And so, dear diary, you'll bear my written screams as I yearn for a more industrious, exciting life.

Unless I find an occupation or a husband, which in my condition is laughable, I'm destined to languish in solitary silence. Most men of Father's station would have whisked me off to some country ward upstate never to be seen again. (I've been continually reminded of this by scolding teachers who insist I ought to be more grateful for a doting father.)

And I *am* grateful for sentimentality on Father's part. I look too much like Mother for him to have sent me off, and goodness, if my sprightly nature doesn't remind him of her. So I've always felt a certain security in my place here a few blocks from Father's employer, the ten-year-old Metropolitan Museum of Art. A building and an institution I've come to adore.

Tonight, Father's having a dinner party with his art scholar friends. They're quite boring, save for his young protégé, Edgar. I could suffer Edgar Fourte's presence under *any* circumstance. But make no mistake, I positively hate that wench he proposed to. If only I could have fashioned some mad plot and sent Father away, I would have thrown myself at Edgar's mercy and become his lovely, tragic young ward. I'd have made myself so indispensable to him, not to mention irresistible, he'd never have considered another woman.

I've been told I'm pretty. And he's a man who likes quiet. What could be more perfect than a pretty wife who doesn't speak? But alas, I'll have to find some other handsome young scholar with a penchant for unfortunates since Edgar stupidly went and got himself engaged to one. So what if she's blind? She can't see how beautiful he is. What a waste!

Ah, the clock strikes. I must help Father with preparations and then make myself *particularly* presentable, if nothing else than for Edgar's punishment. I'll return with any notable gossip or interesting thoughts.

## LATER...

They've clustered into Father's study for a cigar, having stuffed themselves as scholars do at a meal they didn't pay for themselves, leaving me a few moments with these dear pages.

We're in luck; they *did* discuss something fascinating at dinner.

An odd painting is coming to town. An exquisite

life-sized oil of a young English lord named Denbury is about to arrive for a bid. And they say it's haunted.

Now if there's one thing I can't help but adore more than Edgar Fourte's face, it's a ghost story. Perhaps it stems from that long-ago Whisper. Or the shadows I see at night. Wherever the thrill comes from, I can't deny my obsession.

Evidently Lord Denbury simply disappeared one day. Locals assume that it was suicide, that he was overcome with despair at losing his family. But it was odd, for he was so well loved by everyone in town. Such a tragedy! Only eighteen years old with no siblings, he lost his parents when they died in a sudden accident. Having to take on such a mantle of responsibility must have weighed heavily upon him, or so everyone supposed. He inherited money and lands with his title, but with no surviving family to help him, he simply went and drowned. A fine piece of clothing bearing a pin with his crest washed onto the bank of a quieter part of the Thames. A damaged body was later found farther downriver and assumed to be his, but was that conclusive?

In such a troubling case, people tend to seek a reason. Once they find one suitable, they'll close the matter in their minds and hearts for their own comfort. But I wonder…

He was devilishly handsome, they say, and studied medicine. Supposedly he helped open a clinic for the underprivileged in the heart of London. So absorbed in learning medicine, he hadn't taken the time to court anyone, though he was continually sought after. He attended a Greenwich hospital nearly round the clock, absorbing all the knowledge he could. I should like to have known him and commended him for being a credit to his class. They say he was a good-natured fellow, if not a bit mischievous, as most clever boys are, and had a way of talking to all sorts of people. Perhaps he could have found a way to help me.

All that survives him is a grand portrait by an artist who remains unknown despite the vast sum paid for the commission, as recorded in Denbury's personal ledger. Considering the portrait is of such fine quality, it's odd that no one sought attribution. Discovered behind a curtain by surprised housekeepers after Denbury's disappearance, the painting is said to appear nearly alive with the soul of its subject.

How a group of men like Father's friends managed to absorb and retain this fantastic gossip is beyond me, but since it involves art, it comes into their territory. Mr. Weiss suggested that when the item makes its way to New York, where the estate broker plans to sell the piece, my father and the Metropolitan ought to consider buying it.

I desperately want to see it. To see *him*. I must convince Father he ought to at least put in a bid, so that "the Met" seems fashionable. The supernatural *is* all the rage these days, and America's foremost art museum must stay ahead of the times.

Dear me, I've forgotten their coffee, and they'll be clamoring for it. I'll return once I've served them and given Edgar an unbearably sweet smile. Did I mention that his cheeks went red when I descended the staircase and waved? Perhaps there's something about a girl back from boarding school that makes a man see her differently. Too late, Edgar, too late. Not that I'd fault you for breaking off your engagement…maybe there's a way I can assure it… Drat. Coffee first. Schemes later.

## LATER…

I hate them. All of them. Especially Edgar. Don't they know I might be at the door at any moment? I may be mute, but I am *not* dumb.

I'd hesitated outside the study, the coffee tray carefully balanced in my hands. Their cigar smoke wafted beneath the door, acrid tendrils making that threshold a foreign passage where women are forbidden to go—unless, of course, they are there in service. And then I heard my father say something he'd recently said directly to my face:

"I don't have the foggiest idea what to do with her. I've no idea what would be best…"

Which was, sadly, the truth. It was the subsequent

response from Edgar, of all people—I'd know his voice anywhere—that shocked me:

"Why don't you just send her off to a convent, where you wouldn't have to worry about her, Gareth? She could become a nun and change out her own communion wine for whiskey for a change. A vow of silence certainly wouldn't be difficult!"

Before any of them had a chance to laugh or snigger at the insult, I threw wide the door, sending coffee spilling onto the tray. My nostrils flared as I narrowed my eyes and looked right at Edgar. He blushed again, this time not because he thought me pretty. Let him rot with guilt for everything he's done to cause me misery. He's never known how much I care—no, *cared*—for him, but surely now he knows I'll never respect him again.

I may be an unfortunate, but Father taught me never to stand for being made fun of.

"Edgar, shame on you," Father muttered.

There was deathly silence in the room as I served each of the men: first, Father, who was looking up at me apologetically, second, Mr. Weiss, who couldn't look at me out of embarrassment, and then finally Mr. Nillis, who never has a single interesting thing to say but always has a grandfatherly way of patting my hand, which I'll take over being teased any day. Mr. Nillis beamed up at me, entirely oblivious of the awkward moment, and patted me on the hand. I managed to offer him a grateful smile for his small, unwitting courtesy.

I turned and walked back out the door with the last cup of coffee, Edgar's, in my hand. He would not be served. Now I sit sipping it myself as I write this account and stare out the window at Eighty-Third Street three stories below, golden and dappled beneath patches of shade in summer's setting sun. Men in top hats and women in light shawls and bonnets stroll slowly along the cobbled street toward the gem that is our beloved Central Park for one last promenade before dusk. They have a slow but sure purpose to their movement, to their existence, which is more than I have. What *am* I going to do with myself?

Oh, Mother. If you hadn't died, I'm sure this wouldn't have happened. I'd speak. And *you'd* know what to do with me.

# June 3

I was secretly terrified that Father would actually take Edgar's advice and I'd wake to find my bags packed, a train ticket purchased, and a position in a convent secured. But perhaps the incident gave me leverage, for Father knew I was upset, and he hates it when I'm upset.

He came to me this morning in the parlor, where I sat in a patch of sunlight at the reading table by the window, enraptured by a newspaper article discussing the recent subject of intrigue, that of the mysterious—and delicious—Lord Denbury painting.

Now, Father doesn't rightly know how to deal with me, it's true. I must resort to writing notes as he still hasn't grasped the particulars of sign language. But thankfully, he gives me money for newspapers. Any paper, every paper, and has always encouraged my reading and education. So I was the first in the household to see the etching of Lord Denbury himself. I was thoroughly engrossed in staring at it when Father interrupted.

"Natalie, my dear girl, I apologize for what Edgar said. Perhaps he forgets that you can hear very clearly—"

My eyes surely must have flashed with anger, for Father was quick to clarify. "Not that it would have been an appropriate comment under any circumstance."

I turned away. He sat across from me and waited until I decided to return his gaze.

"Tell me," he began a bit nervously, "what would you like to do? I'll try my best. Anything. What would you wish for in your adult life that a girl…in your condition…could reliably attain?"

I studied my father for a moment, as if weighing my options. But I knew what I wanted. The morning paper had made it clear. I scrawled capital letters on the blank end of the opposite page: ACQUISITIONS. Big, bold, and expectant.

Father blinked a moment. "Acquisitions," he repeated slowly. "At the museum?"

I gave him an expression as if he were daft. Where else?

"Indeed…" After a moment, he nodded. "I think you'd make a fine consultant." I nodded enthusiastically. He eyed me and then added, "Tell me. Is there something you'd like to acquire?"

Offering my most pleased smile—why, how lovely of him to ask—I pointed directly to the hasty charcoal likeness of Lord Denbury's painting in the paper. The sketch alone was engaging so I could only imagine the piece in the flesh, or rather, the canvas. Something about that young lord called to me.

According to the paper, Mrs. Evelyn Northe, a wealthy spiritualist known for keeping interesting friends (wealth has a way of allowing you to be "interesting" when in other circles you'd be denounced as scandalous or mad), was closing in on the purchase of the Denbury painting. We simply couldn't let her have it over the Metropolitan.

"The Lord Denbury nonsense?" Father's nose wrinkled in disapproval. I nodded, undaunted. He examined the article.

"Well indeed," he sighed. "If Mrs. Northe is considering it so seriously, I'd be called a curmudgeon, not to mention incredibly out of fashion, if we didn't at least stake a claim…" Father rose, straightened his suit coat, and nodded crisply, as he always did when sealing a decision.

"Good then. We'll go call upon Mrs. Northe. If she's hell-bent on buying it, I'll press her to offer it to us on loan. I wouldn't wish to make an enemy of her. Charms aside, I hear she always gets her way. Let's hope it works out the best for all of us."

He kissed me lightly on the head and left for the museum offices.

Grinning, I jumped to my feet, too excited to sit still. How I longed to join the bustle of the city I could see through the window: the people striding swiftly to their destinations, the carriages jockeying for place on such a fine day, the shopkeepers calling to passersby. But now I had purpose. Perhaps I might become part of their world after all.

Then again, there are always shadows in the back of my mind. Those lovely people down below move effortlessly in carefree sunlight, far from nightmares, while this haunted painting is the stuff of nightmares. And yet *this* is what calls to me most strongly. As if it's where I belong. I turned away from the window.

I have included the article about the portrait herein for my future reference and for commemoration.

The *Tribune*, June 4, 1880

A portrait recently arrived at the vault of the Art Association on Twenty-Third Street has become such a sensation in various circles that public viewing is now prohibited.

No one can deny the appeal of the portrait's eighteen-year-old subject, Jonathon Whitby, Lord Denbury, who is said to have perished by drowning in Greenwich, England. The promising young medical scholar suffered what appeared to be a most devastating loss of both parents in a tragic accident. He soon followed with his own demise, when a body surfacing downriver was hastily assumed to be his.

However, the young lord is survived by a startling likeness in a life-sized portrait mysteriously commissioned just before his death. Those who have seen it report that the air around the painting is impossibly chilly and that the eyes are *too* life-like, as if Denbury's ghost hovers in the very room. Some of a more delicate nature have even fainted at the sight.

Mrs. Evelyn Northe, wife of the late industrialist Peter Northe, an acclaimed collector and no stranger to a poltergeist or séance, oddly rejects the idea of the painting being haunted but offers no alternate explanation. She's among the elite who have been courted to purchase the piece by the estate's creditors. As for the reported fainting spells of some women who have viewed the portrait, Mrs. Northe had this swift retort: "He's devastatingly handsome, this Lord Denbury. I daresay they fainted for love of his looks, not fright."

If not purchased directly into private ownership, the painting will go to public auction next week. Due to the insatiable curiosity surrounding the piece, it has now been closed off from viewing as the Art Association has stated that they do not employ enough guards to manage the task of keeping the public from touching the young Lord's likeness.

# June 5

Father wasted no time in obtaining an invitation during Mrs. Northe's calling hours. I write this even now as our carriage jostles downtown toward her Fifth Avenue home. So forgive me if the pen slips when we clatter over a bump.

I've never been inside a Fifth Avenue home, though I can see the street from my window. That avenue sometimes feels like the boundary line with another country. Father is distinctly middle class, and while he runs in intelligent and well-respected circles, they're far from the richest in the city. He may steer decisions at the Met, but wealthier power makes them reality.

By all accounts, Mrs. Northe cuts a figure that will be intimidating to a man like Father and utterly fascinating to me. I only wish I could talk to her. I write very quickly and carry a pad of paper with me wherever I go. Perhaps she'll have the patience to indulge me.

## LATER…

What an afternoon!

Firstly, let me say that Mrs. Northe is a most gracious and charming woman. And I daresay she and my father got along better than could be expected. Almost too well for a daughter not to feel a bit awkward, as I often do anyway, let alone if I sense *flirtation* could be afoot…

And I believe I may have a new friend! Her name is Margaret Hathorn, Mrs. Northe's niece, who immediately insisted I call her Maggie. She was dressed exquisitely in a green satin dress of doubled skirts and capped sleeves. I found myself staring at the lace detailing on nearly every gathered fold. I didn't think I much cared about fine dresses, though Maggie certainly does. I'm reminded I've not spent much time in fine society. And she only gave me one of *those* looks for just a moment. I forgave her easily for that.

Mrs. Northe's house was splendid—everything I could have expected and more, trimmed with the finest Oriental rugs and lavish marble pieces, and that was just the foyer. The interior architecture had grand staircases and chandeliers reminiscent of what I've seen in pictures of European opera houses. Several windows featured richly colored stained glass by a son of the Tiffany family, which Mrs. Northe proudly said would be all the rage in the next decade and we ought to invest in the man's work now.

Evelyn Northe, of course, was splendid too, a woman I

would guess to be nearly forty. She was dressed in the latest French fashion with fitted sleeves tapering with countless buttons and gathered skirts of mauve satin drawn into a cascading bustle, all trimmed in seed pearls that I would have thought suitable for a ball gown. But amid the opulence of the home, the ensemble appeared somewhat mundane.

I glanced into a beveled, bejeweled mirror at my side, my green eyes wide with drinking in the sights, and couldn't help comparing myself. My blouse and skirts were neat and trimmed with lace, and I'd put my nicest pearl hairpins up into my thick locks of auburn hair, allowing a few ringlets to fall against my cheeks. I knew I wasn't terrible to look at, but I did feel awkward in such surroundings.

I was soon surprised by a comfort I could not possibly have expected.

As Father introduced me, he gave the practiced, cursory explanation that I could hear perfectly well but could not speak, to which Maggie gave that slightly pitying look. Mrs. Northe did not bat an eyelash but instead offered me a "Pleasure to meet you" in standard sign. At this, I confess, my mouth dropped in an uncouth fashion and I had to recover a moment before signing "Thank you" in response.

"I speak six languages," Mrs. Northe explained casually. "I found that learning a seventh with my hands was *thoroughly* rewarding."

Father looked away, put to shame by the woman when

he hadn't bothered to learn to sign himself. I can't blame Father. He's always hoped that one day I'll just open my mouth and all will be well. But I did appreciate a woman of such fine taste who could make me feel so welcome in such a personal way, when society never would have required it of her. Maggie seemed suitably impressed by her aunt; clearly this was a new discovery for her as well.

As Mrs. Northe swept us into the parlor, a maid in a crisply starched uniform was instantly upon us with tea and confections.

"So, Mr. and Miss Stewart," Mrs. Northe began, tea in hand. "I understand you are here in regards to the Denbury portrait."

We nodded.

"Oh, he is beyond words!" Maggie cooed, fluffing her emerald skirts. "I'm positively in love with him." My father blinked at Maggie. "Denbury," she clarified. "He's beautiful. Natalie—may I call you Natalie?—you'll positively *die* when you see him. He is unparalleled."

"I plan to purchase, Mr. Stewart," Mrs. Northe interrupted smoothly. "So if you are here to outbid me, I do hope the board of your decade-young Metropolitan has a *considerable* sum in their budget," she said with an affable smile, leaning toward him a bit.

Father's tense lips flickered into a small smile and he coughed a little. I knew he was far more nervous about being in a room with her than he was about talking business. "I would never presume to outbid you, Mrs. Northe, and I have the utmost respect for your taste and wishes. Might I propose that you graciously allow the Metropolitan to have the portrait upon loan for a brief while? With full recognition of your ownership, of course. I believe that my superiors would chastise me if I let something so…talked about…go entirely without a request to include it in an upcoming exhibition."

"Indeed. I will certainly consider such a proposal. I'd hate to deprive you and your institution of so striking a man as Lord Denbury," Mrs. Northe said.

Maggie's face fell. "You mean you won't have him always at the house?"

"Margaret, hush. Your family lives a block from the museum. You can visit."

I couldn't help it. My hands flew out to ask if the painting was, indeed, haunted, despite her protestation in the paper. Maggie stared at me intently, curiously, as if she thought that by just watching my fingers, she might understand them too.

Mrs. Northe's smile remained as she registered my question. I was pleased that she did not exhibit any of the cold distance the upper echelons of society feel necessary when dealing with the merchant class. And I credit that she had influenced her niece similarly.

"I am a spiritualist, Miss Stewart. I believe that certain objects can retain a bit of living energy and that death is just one veil away from our earthly home. It isn't that I believe the picture is haunted, per se, but that it could quite possibly have a connection with a lost part of Denbury's soul."

She turned to my father. Maggie was listening, rapt, clearly as intrigued by spiritualism as I was. "And *that*, Mr. Stewart, is something to be regarded carefully and reverently. That particular aspect is priceless. I don't trust the painting with just anyone. But I wasn't about to tell that to the papers."

My expression surely betrayed my eagerness, for Mrs. Northe added, "I shall take you to see him, if you like, Miss Stewart. The Art Association has him locked away all to himself in a side room."

I nodded, too taken with the idea and with Mrs. Northe to think about asking Father for permission.

Maggie clapped her hands. "I tell you, Natalie, you'll just *die!*"

To my father, Mrs. Northe declared, "The sooner we are able to secure the portrait from his broker, the better."

"Why's that?" Father asked.

"I fear the man is mad. It's as if he were an inmate at Bedlam the day prior to setting sail with the portrait. He keeps shuffling about the association and mumbling something about a master. I daresay that when people get uneasy around the painting, it has less to do with Denbury and everything to do with Crenfall." Mrs. Northe turned to me. "So, shall I take you tomorrow, Miss Stewart?" she asked.

Here I turned to Father. He evidently had been watching Mrs. Northe with somewhat of a dazed look, for he had to shake his head a bit, as if waking from a reverie. "I'm sorry."

"Ah, our gossip bores you, Mr. Stewart. Quite all right." Mrs. Northe laughed.

"No, no, it wasn't at all that I was bored…" My father fumbled. "I was…very interested in you, I assure you. I mean, in what you were saying. Interested. Yes."

Could it be that my father blushed? Maggie seemed to catch it too, and we shared a smile.

"Indeed. I'll have a carriage fetch you in the morning, Miss Stewart. Let's make a day of it. You did mention, Mr. Stewart, that your daughter has just returned from her schooling. I'd like to take her somewhere nice to celebrate her return before she examines this work of art for herself."

"That's too kind of you—" I began to sign, blushing at her generosity. But she interrupted me.

"Not at all," she signed in return. "I've no daughters. I always wanted one. It would be as much for me as for you."

But she has her niece, Maggie, I thought. And I looked at Maggie for a moment, puzzled. Something in Mrs.

23

Northe's eyes stilled me. I didn't understand. Maggie seemed kind and engaging enough…

I tell you, there was something knowing in Mrs. Northe's eyes that went beyond mere hospitality. It was as if she saw something I couldn't understand. In that moment, I had the distinct sense that being acquainted with Mrs. Evelyn Northe would be one of the most important things ever to happen to me.

# June 6

My life shall never again be the same. Something is irrevocably changed. But, alas, let me start at the beginning and not skip over how the day began. I'm told I'm good with details.

How is it that, in one mere day, Mrs. Northe and Maggie have come to feel so much like family? Despite any social differences, we all fell in so naturally.

Maggie is the sort of girl I always wished I had as a friend. At the asylum, I was surrounded by deaf and mute girls, as well as some blind ones. All of them were lovely, of course, but to be around a pretty girl my age, a girl of society in fine dresses and immaculate gloves…I almost felt like I could fit in among the world at large, a world where there is *possibility*.

Mrs. Northe took me to the finest of teas downtown before insisting that she have me sit in a photography studio for a portrait session.

"All pretty young ladies need a portrait to offer a beau," Maggie explained. When I protested in clumsy signing that I'd never had nor would I ever have a beau, Mrs. Northe scoffed at me as Maggie fluttered around me, primping my dress for the photograph. I was set down in the vast room filled with drapes and milling onlookers and told to stay put.

"I'll not have you say such a thing. I had a premonition," Mrs. Northe scolded. "And my premonitions are rarely wrong. I saw you teaching at a school with some handsome doctor looking in on you."

"Ooh!" Maggie cooed. "A doctor. That's noble!"

I smiled at the thought. I'd have to teach other unfortunates like myself, but I found I rather liked the idea. It sounded right. Perfect, in fact. I'd make sure other girls like me had as many books as their hearts desired and no one to tell them they were merely stubborn.

Sitting for a portrait takes a great deal of patience, and I don't think the gentleman taking it was very fond of me, for I have a hard time keeping my knees from bouncing. That made me wonder how long Denbury had had to pose for his portrait. How had he withstood it? And what would he look like in person?

It didn't help that Maggie kept trying to make me blush and laugh. Goodness, the girl does like to chatter. Thankfully, I'm a very good listener. Even if I could talk, I'm not sure I could have gotten in a word edgewise. She related every last detail she'd recently gathered about the goings-on of New York City's foremost elite, telling all the juicy, amusing bits. I got quite a colorful education. Mrs. Northe didn't weigh in for a second, so I assume the topics were of no interest to her. The Hathorns and the Northes seem to have different priorities.

While we were en route to the Art Association, I confessed to Mrs. Northe that I wanted to know more about spiritualism.

"It would only do to introduce you to one experience at a time," she replied aloud to my signed inquiry as we jostled up Broadway, eyeing Maggie as she spoke. "It has been an intensely personal journey for me, and you must look at it the same way if you want to create a lasting experience of faith and belief. This is a concept I keep stressing to Margaret, but she won't leave me be about it."

"I'm obsessed. I want to know *everything* there is to know about spiritualism!" Maggie cried, not realizing she was echoing what I had just signed. "I want to go to séances and talk to the dead. I want to comprehend that sort of power and then to wield it—can you imagine what you could do—"

"For the last time, Margaret Hathorn, there is no *power* in spiritualism. And those who are interested in it for the sake of power quickly become my *former* friends," Mrs. Northe said sharply. Maggie snapped her mouth shut. "Not to mention that your mother would never forgive me for teaching you anything about it in the first place. She already is convinced I'm going to Hell."

"She is not…" Maggie rallied, but unconvincingly.

Mrs. Northe turned to me with a smirk, signing: "But I'm rich enough to be considered redeemable. Amazing how wealth buys salvation."

I bit my lip to keep from grinning. I didn't want Maggie to feel left out of the joke, but she was looking out the window and pouting about having been put in her place in front of me. Mrs. Northe's jovial honesty about her position, her money, and her faith was quite refreshing.

I recalled Sister Theresa at the asylum once railing about spiritualism being the Devil's work, which had made me immediately curious as to how and why. Father isn't much of a churchgoer, being descended from lapsed New England Congregationalists, but Mother, a devout German Lutheran, never missed a Sunday at Immanuel near our home. In her honor, I attend services regularly.

I find the ritual of faith a comfort, and thankfully the Lutheran congregation is rather stoic. They don't much care that I can't speak, and the service is almost all in German. Is it more tragic that I understand *two* languages that I don't speak? Regardless, if Sister Theresa was right about the Devil's work, I can't have Mother turning in her grave.

Perhaps Mrs. Northe read my mind, for she was quick to

clarify. "Now to be sure, I am an Episcopalian Christian. But my experiences in spiritualism have only expanded my faith, strengthened my commitment to the Lord, women's rights, and the rights of all people, and enriched my delight in the Divine Mystery of the universe."

That sounded grand.

"What you may have guessed," she added, her tone suddenly weary, "is that not all persons interested in the discipline come to it purely for spiritual growth, enlightenment, or education. Some become involved because they think somehow they will gain power. Influence. An other-worldly advantage," Mrs. Northe said bitterly. "And these people quickly fall away from spiritualism to make their own orders and sects as their egos see fit."

"Do you know such people?" I signed.

"Unfortunately, I do," Mrs. Northe said. "Ah. We have arrived. Come, dear, are you ready to meet him?"

I grinned.

"You'll just *die*, I tell you!" Maggie crowed, and she took me by the hand and dragged me into the building.

The Art Association was a lovely edifice on Twenty-Third Street with floors full of fine art, though the grandiose Metropolitan had spoiled me to the extent that nothing could possibly compare. Mrs. Northe swept me expertly through the various rooms, passing under numerous carved wooden arches. She nodded to all she passed in cordial greeting, and Maggie parroted her with the same firm confidence, though she did so with a bit more haughtiness to her step and her head held slightly higher. Clearly they were in familiar territory here, and my task was to keep up.

We at last came to an unassuming back room where the lamps were trimmed low and a distinct chill hung in the air.

Mrs. Northe gestured for me to go ahead.

I turned the corner and held my breath.

Would it be a horribly clever redundancy to say I was speechless?

If Mrs. Northe spoke to me in those first moments, I never heard her. I was lost in the music of *him*.

I'd never seen anything so beautiful in all my life. His eyes were impossibly real. Bright, shocking blue, they burned with cerulean light. They cried out from the canvas, desperate for more show of life than brushstrokes, as if simply two dimensions were an insult.

He was tall and sure, broad shouldered and fit, with his hands clasped behind his back. He had jet-black hair that was neat around his ears but fell in gentle curls. He looked firm and authoritative, master of his domain.

The masculine lines of his face were beautifully composed, as one would expect in the perfection of a dark seraphim. Tiny traces between his nose and the corners of his pursed and perfect lips indicated that his mouth would grow lines of an often wide smile as he aged. But no such trace of gladness could be seen in his portrait's expression. His lips were set in a stern expression of young defiance, his perfect nostrils flared.

His suit was fine and charcoal gray, something perhaps for sporting or hunt, something masculine but youthful and unpretentious. He was posed in a study filled with books and well-appointed items: a desk stacked with fresh paper and a blotter, fountain pens and golden trinkets of measure and study, and a high-backed chair before a fireplace bedecked with treasures from around the world.

A verdant pastoral scene could be glimpsed out the bay window, his Greenwich estate, surely. Everything about the painting drew me in. Perhaps it *was* haunted after all—the life in those eyes…the slight chill that I couldn't quite shake. The flare of his nostrils was that of an animal smelling blood.

Mrs. Northe leaned in to murmur, not wishing to distract me from his gaze. "A shame. Such a handsome youth to be lost at eighteen."

"Heartbreaking," Maggie sighed.

I could only nod, though I couldn't help feeling that Denbury wasn't really gone. He was so unbelievably *present*. As Mrs. Northe had alluded, some part of that man's soul was surely in the room with us.

A gangly, sharp-nosed man with an affable smile poked his head around the corner.

"Why, my dear Mrs. Northe and Miss Hathorn, you didn't mention you'd be stopping by again so soon."

Mrs. Northe gestured at the painting. "He's hard to resist. I had to bring Miss Natalie Stewart by to see him. You know Gareth Stewart of the Metropolitan? This is his daughter." Mrs. Northe turned and signed his name to me—Mr. Sullivan—before he could say anything. I took the cue and inclined my head in greeting.

Mr. Sullivan stared at us, confused by Mrs. Northe's gesticulations. I was quite used to that response. Lest he make some social mistake, he ignored the exchange entirely, inclined his head to me, and turned back to Mrs. Northe with pressing urgency, his affable smile fading.

"May I have a word with you alone? About the buyers."

"Ah. Yes. And?"

Mr. Sullivan glanced over at me nervously. I smiled a bit too broadly, as if the lamps weren't quite on in my attic. It couldn't hurt to appear nonthreatening in this case, considering that Denbury seemed to make most people nervous.

Mr. Sullivan continued with hesitancy, holding out a paper. "Shall we discuss it somewhere apart from the young ladies?"

"Oh, it's all right. Miss Stewart can't hear a thing you say, and I daresay Maggie here has demanded I share *every* particular of her beau," Mrs. Northe said, winking so that only I could see. Maggie sighed at the word "beau." Mrs. Northe turned back to Mr. Sullivan, and I continued to stare at the painting as if I hadn't heard a word. "You go right ahead, Mr. Sullivan. What's odd about the list?"

I could feel Mr. Sullivan glancing at me, embarrassed. "Oh, poor dear," he said, offering me that all too familiar pitying look. "All right then. Just look at the list of buyers here."

Out of the corner of my eye, I watched the color slip from Mrs. Northe's face as she perused the list. To have somehow earned her confidence like this was a great honor. I pledged to do my best to deserve it.

"Good God, Mortimer," Mrs. Northe gasped, letting slip his familiar name. She was on a decidedly familiar standing with nearly everyone involved in this operation. Including now my father. Hopefully that would bode well for Lord Denbury.

"I was just thinking of these, dare I say, *gentlemen*," she said in dismay. "These men are all…"

"Spiritualists. I know. Isn't that odd?"

Maggie was instantly alert, her nostrils flaring like Denbury's, as if she too smelled blood. Or in Maggie's case, excitement and perhaps scandal, things she deemed delicious.

"No, Mortimer, let's be clear," Mrs. Northe began sharply. "The men on this list are not spiritualists. Not anymore. They've become downright dangerous. Bentrop especially. They dabble in the pure occult through secretive sects that practice Dark Arts. We can't let Denbury fall into their hands."

"What harm could they possibly do with a painting?"

"I'm not certain. But I would rather not find out." Mrs. Northe squared her shoulders. "Mr. Sullivan, will you help me draw up purchase documents?"

Mr. Sullivan looked baffled. "Surely it's not...an emergency?"

"I'm not a woman to take chances. I'll not have this piece in hands I would not trust to touch a dog."

Mrs. Northe excused herself to tend to the particulars, and Maggie followed along uninvited.

I was left alone with the painting. I took a step closer, absorbing every detail. Then a movement out of the corner of my eye had me turning my gaze...

And then my heart stopped. I choked and questioned my sanity in one fell swoop.

As I live and breathe, and upon my beloved mother's grave, I swear that Denbury himself walked by the alcove where the painting was kept and glided toward the hallway beyond. It had to be him! I screamed within, my eyes darting madly to the painting and then to the figure who bore the same elegant lines and the same dark curls, though wearing a different fine suit of deepest red...

And then he stopped. He turned to me. I saw the only thing that was different: his eyes were off. He was so beautiful, and yet with his eyes not quite as you'd expect, he was unsettling. And, I remembered, he was dead.

"Hello, pretty," he murmured, glancing around as if to make sure we were alone. "What's your name?"

His accented voice sounded normal enough, for a ghost. It was young, male, British...

I gestured to my throat and opened my mouth, but no sound came out.

"Oh, you can't tell me." He frowned, and the terrible look of pity I expected was instead delight. "How fascinating." His clouded eyes seemed to sparkle, and I realized what was odd about them: they reflected strangely in the light, the orbs glowing, like those of an animal at night if a lamp was flashed before them. "And how lucky. If you resisted me...who would know?"

I stood there staring, knowing I should be offended by such a brazen comment, and yet one doesn't think about how manners should be when chatting with the dead. He gestured up at his own image. "Amazing, isn't it? It's like he's alive. He's watching you. I don't blame him. I'd watch you too, pretty thing. I daresay we'd be beautiful together..."

His lilting British accent was underscored with something that was both enticing and alarming. We both heard a rustle from another room. He put his finger to his mouth but then laughed. "Oh, but of course you'll keep our little secret. You've no choice. Brilliant. Ta." And he moved into the hall and disappeared.

That ghost was nothing like what I'd imagined Denbury—a young genius and reportedly a perfect *gentleman*—would be like. That was not how one, dead or alive, spoke to a lady. And yet, there was something terribly compelling about him. Ghosts, I supposed, had their thrall, their ways about things. Yet why would a ghost refer to his own likeness not as himself, but as another entity? And why am I now trying to make sense of that?

As if my sanity weren't tested enough, dear diary, I was then strained even further. I turned back to the painting, and my heart went again into spasms.

And here I swear to you, as I looked up again at Denbury, I realized…

The painting had changed.

I'd intimately catalogued the piece so I knew something was different. It took me a while to realize what, but when I saw it, the change was undeniable. The retreating perspective line of the woodwork and floor along the bottom of Denbury's bookshelf was now interrupted. By a book.

One of the books on the lowest shelf was tilted out from the bookshelf so that part of the title was just barely visible. *The Girl…*

It was a good thing I could not squeal, for I might have

made a scene. First his ghost—a rude one at that—and now this? My blood was alternately hot with excitement and cool with fear. What did that mean, *The Girl*? Was this image of Denbury asking for help? And did the book title mean anything at all other than a sign that the painting was somehow *alive*? Haunted after all! How many ghosts could one young man have?

Before I could clear my head and decide whether I would tell Mrs. Northe and Maggie of these developments, a small and beady-eyed man entered the room. It would seem all bad omens come in threes.

The man wore an ugly tweed suit, and his hair was plastered with some sort of unappealing agent that reeked of sour mint. His gaze went right to me, and he leered. I returned my attention to the painting, suitably offended. He seemed to remember himself and bowed after a moment, but not before I felt the keen desire to plunge myself into a hot bath to rid myself of his stare. I shuddered. After already having been improperly chatted up by a ghost, I determined that this man was decidedly hateful. He took a step closer and stared at the painting with a sort of triumph, an uncanny look.

"Mr. Crenfall," Mr. Sullivan boomed suddenly, sweeping into the room and stepping directly between us, for which I gave him a thankful glance that he received with an apologetic grimace. I couldn't imagine anyone wanting to be alone in a room with that man, and Mr. Sullivan seemed quite aware of it. "There you are indeed, sneaking in and out. What sort of businessman does so?" Mr. Sullivan scolded. "Mrs. Northe and I were just discussing Lord Denbury here, and she has made you an offer you *cannot* refuse."

Mrs. Northe eyed me with concern for a moment before moving into the room a step, with Maggie triumphantly behind her. "Backed, of course, by the Metropolitan Museum of Art. And the very City of New York," Mrs. Northe added for good measure.

I raised an eyebrow but then remembered I wasn't supposed to be hearing this.

Crenfall's piggish eyes flickered from the painting to Mr. Sullivan and then to Mrs. Northe. He leered at Maggie, and then he laughed nervously. "But Mr. Bentrop has confided to me the highest purchase price. He plans to return early from his trip to Egypt just to procure the portrait."

"Bentrop does not have the resources to outbid me and the Metropolitan together." Mrs. Northe stepped closer. Even from a distance, she towered over Crenfall. "Come now, Mr. Crenfall, I'm not a dullard. You've been showing strange favoritism, and that won't do in my circle. I've a *wide* circle. You don't want the press, the wealthy patrons who have built this fine temple of art, and indeed the *city* getting any more involved, do you?"

Crenfall opened his mouth as if to protest, but Mrs. Northe drove her point further. "Tell Bentrop not to bother coming home from Egypt. He may continue his grave-robbing in peace."

The broker was wholly out of his league. Maggie was beaming. Clearly she relished the power and privilege her aunt wielded so effortlessly. Crenfall's shoulders, tight with worry, fell and he shrugged as if acquiescing defeat when he should have been kissing Mrs. Northe's feet for the sum she would pay.

Muttering, he left the room. The sale of the painting evidently wasn't about money after all. For any of them. And I now knew why. Unnatural happenings were afoot.

"Well," Mrs. Northe said brightly, turning to Denbury's portrait. "My fine chap, you've got yourself a new mistress!"

Maggie sighed again, staring up at him with fawning eyes.

I'm sure it was my imagination, but there seemed to be a certain relaxing of Denbury's brow, as if he'd narrowly escaped certain doom. His blue eyes looked relieved, so unlike the disturbing onyx gaze of his ghost. I found myself wanting to reassure him, to speak words of comfort and friendship.

Where was all this coming from? These two Denburys caused distinct reactions within me. My heart reeled, and I felt sick to my stomach. Were these two different echoes of the man, one his better half, a noble soul with angelic eyes immortalized on canvas, and the other left to wander the earth with darker intent? Had the occult somehow gained what was left of him? The painting remained changed, with that book's spine and the gilded letters out in plain sight, but there was no further sign of the corporeal form that moved and spoke.

Mrs. Northe kept eyeing me. Could she tell what I was thinking? Could I possibly tell her what had happened?

Father came at his appointed time, and both Mr. Sullivan and Mrs. Northe greeted him warmly.

"Alas, I've forced your hand, Mr. Stewart. If I hadn't intervened, this incredible piece would have fallen into hands as good as thieves'. I've signed off on the purchase of the work just now to put a swift end to this circus. But I'll need the backing of the Metropolitan and its connections to lawyers, creditors, and civil servants of New York, should Crenfall seek to fight me on this."

"And why should he do that?"

"I don't know that he will. But something about his handling of this sale is highly suspicious. He seemed in quite a hurry to rush the portrait out of England," Mrs. Northe replied. "Come, let us be off to dinner. Natalie, ride with me."

Father trotted along after the three of us, baffled but happy to be invited.

Once in the privacy of the carriage, Mrs. Northe wasted

no time. "I kept you in that room, Natalie, to hear it all. Have you ever met someone you feel, in the instant, you were meant to meet?"

I nodded.

"Well, I feel that way about you, Natalie. God brings people into our lives precisely when we need them."

All I could do was nod again, suddenly quite pleased to be "needed." Not only did I feel the same way about her, but the impossible had unveiled itself and I could not deny it. Maggie was compelled by her aunt's urgency, and I was surprised she didn't edge herself into the conversation.

Mrs. Northe continued. "Earlier I mentioned that some persons associated with occult dealings seek powers beyond themselves. By this I mean all matter of spells, witchcraft, and imbuing of objects."

"To what end?" I asked. My hands shook as I signed, and I was helpless to control the tremors.

"Most often, immortality. I fear this painting has, in part, something to do with that very desire."

"Immortality!" Maggie exclaimed as if she were about to burst. "You see, this is the stuff I *live* to hear about!"

Mrs. Northe ignored her, instead eyeing me.

My heart leaped as I signed. "You think Denbury might still be alive? Because I…"

And here I stopped. I was not ready to confess anything. I didn't want to be shipped to a *real* asylum.

Mrs. Northe again eyed me, now with a knowing look that was both comforting and unnerving. She ignored that I'd stopped midstream. "All I know is this portrait cannot fall into the wrong hands. I'll have Sullivan transport it to my house tonight." She looked at me apologetically. "Unfortunately, I do believe I've given the Metropolitan more than a beautiful painting's worth of trouble."

"I'll take him off your hands," Maggie offered eagerly. Mrs. Northe glanced at her with a smirk that showed she wouldn't consider it for a minute.

Dinner was finer than we'd perhaps ever eaten, thanks to Mrs. Northe, but I had no appetite. Denbury's eyes—both sets of them—kept searing into my soul. I kept reliving what his ghost had said. My body was warm, tingling in a way I was not at all proud of, but I was flattered that something related to Denbury thought me pretty, that perhaps something of him had indeed chosen to watch me as I watched him. Beautiful together...

I wondered what *The Girl* meant and how I might explain it to Mrs. Northe. Or if I'd even seen what I thought I saw in the first place. Could it possibly have been wishful thinking? Willing the sort of intrigue found only in wild Gothic novels to a mere canvas? Maggie would, in her words, surely die if she found out.

Mrs. Northe was doing me the honor of trusting my confidence. I know I ought to return the courtesy, even at the risk of sounding like a madwoman. But I am, quite frankly, afraid.

## LATER...

*(Watching a bright moon rise in the sky
from my bedroom's bay window)*

And here, these diary pages serving as a true friend, I hereby confess what I used to believe, what I rejected, and what I may be forced to believe again in regards to ghost stories.

I have mentioned the Whisper. My childhood world was painfully quiet, of course, as you can well imagine. I did not make noise, and no one made noise around me. Father and I developed our vaguely comfortable silence long ago.

He had me educated as if nothing were wrong with me, bringing in tutors and academics. As my hearing and relative temperament seemed fine, I was taught to read and write from an early age, and I received a very fine education for a young girl, though I could not speak of it. I had made noise until the day Mother died. Evidently I had been quite the chatterer.

Father had just kept waiting for the day I would start back up again. As if nothing had ever happened.

But because I never did simply chatter away again,

Father had sent me off, as there was no use pretending that I might.

I assumed that, because of this preternatural quiet, my hearing must be hypersensitive, an overcompensation.

There was often a Whisper at my ear, gentle and subtle. While it was a human voice, I could never decipher words. I heard occasional familiar English syllables and was sure I often heard my name. But if it was a message on the wind, like some paper in a bottle sent to wash ashore, the communication failed because I could determine no meaning. I closed my eyes, straining when I heard her—it was most certainly a *her*.

Once I was old enough, I understood that the vague "mother" I faintly recalled no longer existed. Yet it isn't beyond the pale for a child, like I was, to hope that an inexplicable, disembodied voice at her ear is that of her lost parent.

A movement would follow the sound, something out of the corner of my eye. A rustle of white like the corner of a lace curtain billowing in a soft breeze. It indulged every fantasy of a ghost without ever producing an actual image of one. I would turn, squint, and strain but never quite grasp hold of it.

No vision, no message. It was infuriating.

Devoted to such authors as Wilkie Collins, Edgar Allan Poe, and Charles Dickens, I wished to escape into their worlds where ghosts could be seen and addressed. I wondered what good speaking in this world was if I couldn't even hear the most important words being said from beyond. What good was speaking when I'd determined none of the world listened to one another, especially not when a woman was speaking. I dreamed that were I to step into Mr. Collins's or Mr. Dickens's world, I would be able to speak freely. Then I'd turn and greet the specter that had haunted me ever since I could remember.

But the pain of adoring a world that I could never touch grew too great for me.

At thirteen, I rejected it all, with all the vehemence that year of my life produced, and refused to entertain the idea of a ghost story.

Until Denbury.

He has brought back that old familiar pull, the pining ache of those dear old stories. He is water on parched lips. I've missed the sweet longing for those worlds, the titillating sense of magic that courses down my spine with delicious possibility, and the sense that the veil to another existence is very thin near me…the sense that I am gifted. I've missed that thought.

However, as that feeling returns to me now, it is drastically altered. There is, of course, the excitement of a ghost story. But if the tale proves true, it's suddenly not as alluring. It is, in fact, terrifying.

## 3 A.M.

I woke from a dream and must recount the details. There was the Whisper. Mother's whisper, surely. I saw a flicker of white at the corner of my room as I lay in my bed. I struggled to move, to crane my neck to see her, but I was pinned. The Whisper was insistent, that female voice. In the dream, I could understand it. It called my name. I opened my mouth to respond. But even in my dream I couldn't. How cruel to be denied the faculty of speech even by my own unconscious state!

"Natalie…" came another voice. One with a British accent. A delectable voice that sent shivers down my spine.

I turned my head toward that familiar voice. And there in my room was Denbury, striking and compelling Denbury the painting, filling my wall and staring down at me. His blue eyes were wide and searching. "You are the girl…the girl to help me. Please, help me, Natalie…" The lips of his painting did not move, yet I heard him clearly.

My body was heavy, weighted, but I reached out my hand. My back arched. I did want to help him. I wanted to go to him, to be *with* him…

And then he turned. His eyes went glowing black. The lips of his painting moved, and his was the voice of his lascivious shade. "Pretty thing."

His image peeled from the canvas, and his body stepped down from his painting, down onto my bed, as if entering through a door. He fell upon me, and a hand like a claw closed over my throat.

I shot awake with a small choking gurgle. An ugly sound.

I write this while the moon is again bright. I'm hoping its silver rays can banish the shadows. I rub my throat and still feel the pain. Knowing that a bruise is only in my mind is small comfort.

From the Desk of Mrs. Evelyn Northe

June 7 (at an hour earlier than anyone should be writing letters)

Dear Mr. and Miss Stewart,

Alas, it seems we are now waging a dangerous war. I'm terribly sorry if I've escalated the situation improperly, but I'll set aside blame for the greater issue of safety.

Last night my house was quite nearly ransacked and my two guards overcome, and I had the opportunity to reassert that I'm a damn good shot with a pistol.

It would seem burglars wished to take Denbury. I did inform the police, but now I'm beginning to regret it, for they simply do not understand the finer points of the darker forces at work here. However, they will post guards at my home. And perhaps at the Metropolitan, where, my dear Mr. Stewart, I hope you won't mind keeping Lord Denbury from this point on.

Keep your eye open for a man with a limp around the

painting. In the darkness, I couldn't make out the identity of the intruders as I fired a shot and they scrambled for the exit. One took a bullet of mine as a souvenir in his thigh.

Respectfully,
Mrs. Evelyn Northe

# June 8

Father knocked on my door before breakfast, handing the above letter to me and having lost what little color he possessed. Once at the breakfast table, he was irate in a way I'd never seen, hardly touched his eggs, and jumped up as I placed the last of my bread into my mouth.

"I'm going to see her. I don't like that she's there alone. All this over a silly portrait."

The fact was that Mrs. Northe wasn't there alone. She had staff. But Father suddenly wanted to play the hero, and I tried not to smile at his uncharacteristic concern.

He was on his feet and ready for departure more quickly than I'd seen him move in some time, whereupon I took up Mrs. Northe's letter and have enclosed it in these pages. I shall keep all evidence I find in this curious case. Someday someone might thank me for it.

Father told me I was to remain at the house while he checked on Mrs. Northe. I shook my head. I hailed a carriage and was seated inside before he was. He stared at me with his usual mixture of sentiment: always impressed by my initiative and always wondering why it never initiated my speech. Alas, I never had an answer to offer him.

I write this en route to Mrs. Northe's residence, my mind whirling and my stomach in a knot. A dark cloud hangs about this painting and about all those who come across it. Will all of us end up like Crenfall, odd and inept and slave to this beautiful man? Or am I the only slave among us? I cannot get Lord Denbury out of my mind's eye for a second, even in sleep.

Though I find Denbury a handsome, dashing man, I can only liken his effect to a siren as in the myths of old, meant to lure a hero toward danger. And I've arrived at his threshold once more.

## LATER...

Can you tell from my script how my hand trembles? The painting moved again! And this time I find there's no other way to interpret the signs. Somehow this painting wants *me*, wants something of me. It is, in fact, calling to me.

Perhaps by writing down the events, I can achieve some sense of things.

Father and I were shown immediately to Mrs. Northe's sitting room, where she stood to greet us, looking as charming as ever, if not a bit tired. Her vibrant eyes were ringed by faint dark tinges, as if the event had aged her slightly. It was the first time I'd seen her without Maggie present.

"I'm terribly sorry that you should have had to deal with such a matter as an intrusion. It rattles the soul," my father said quietly.

"Indeed, Mr. Stewart. But what good cheer to have friends on hand to banish the terrible thoughts from one's mind."

We sat and busied ourselves with tea. Father paced a bit before sitting down, his verbal awkwardness as much a handicap as my inability to speak.

I finally signed to Mrs. Northe, asking how she was faring and if there was any word from the police about the wounded intruder.

"Not a thing. It's as if he vanished into thin air. If you want my opinion, it's someone Bentrop hired. He's very angry we've made such a public and strong claim on the piece and will resort to trickery to come by it."

"Is it really so valuable?" my father asked, an eyebrow raised.

I made a face just as Mrs. Northe scoffed.

"Really, Mr. Stewart, you surprise me. You don't believe its composition, brushstrokes, and essence of life are unparalleled?"

My father nodded and sipped his tea. Clearly he was not

as enraptured by the portrait as we were. But that was just as well. He didn't know it was alive.

"Then why didn't he simply outbid you if he feels it's that valuable? Why go to all this trouble and risk a potentially damaging criminal record?" he asked.

"Certain objects, Mr. Stewart, will attract darkness. Something terrible happened around this painting and has imprinted the very fabric of the canvas. Not that the painting itself is to blame, but perhaps what happened to Denbury. Some people love to collect such objects and will use dark means to get them."

My father couldn't have looked more skeptical. "I fail to see an imprint, Mrs. Northe."

"Then, indeed, its dark clouds will hardly be noticed in the grand company of other works at the Metropolitan. Let's talk numbers, shall we? Natalie, darling, while I realize your new work is in acquisitions, I'll not trouble you with monetary trivialities. Give us a moment to ourselves, would you?" And she nodded toward the hall. In the direction of the painting.

I nodded, rising slowly and setting down my tea. The truth was that I longed to run from the room and to Denbury. Having him to myself again for a moment was a thrilling prospect.

I moved toward the grandiose staircase where a great purple curtain was hung on the landing with the portrait behind it.

Climbing the stairs seemed to take forever. The gas lamps were trimmed low, and I kept glancing around, afraid the house staff would disturb my moment alone with Denbury, afraid I'd be told to keep back, afraid some sort of trap had been set on the velvet drape.

I tossed caution aside as I slid back the curtain. Seeing him again was every bit as breathtaking as the first time. Would it always be so? The hairs on my neck stood, I blushed, and my breath was short. He was so exquisitely rendered that his presence was truly *felt*. His luminous eyes set a claim on those who looked at him. The painting had a seductive quality that made the rest of the world drain away. When one looked at Lord Denbury, nothing else existed.

And then I noticed that much like with Mrs. Northe, Denbury's eyes looked a bit darker, a bit older, and weary. Though he was still devilishly handsome, something had changed about him.

I studied the particulars of the scene. The book *The Girl* remained jutting out from the shelf.

And then I noticed a new shift. Something else out of place. Different.

On his desk, the pristine blotter bore droplets of ink, and the quill was lying on its side rather than upright in the shaft of the inkwell. Two words seemed to scream up at me from a note that faced my direction on his desk.

*Yes, you!*

I nearly fainted.

I scrambled backward, my small bustle grazing a potted fern that would have toppled to the floor if the corner of the balustrade had not caught its fall. I tore off my gloves and hastily gathered up the bits of soil that had spilled onto the floor. Perhaps, I thought, when I turn back to the painting, that note will not be there and this whole ordeal will prove to have been a welcome hallucination.

But no.

I looked again at the note and then up at Denbury. I *swear* to you that he stared back at me. I could just hear his ghost, who had indeed said the portrait was watching me.

My shaking hands closed his curtain again, and I had to hold the railing as I descended the stairs.

Standing outside the sitting-room door, I wanted to slip inside and continue on as if nothing had happened. But intruding would be improper when I had been excused, not to mention that I'd surely appear as though I'd seen a ghost. Because I had, in a way. One of them, at least, was reaching out to me in an unexpected, impossible way. I kept looking around for Denbury's corporeal ghost, he of the stifling presence and disturbing intent. Thankfully, the darker Denbury did not show himself.

My trembling stride took me into the first lit room I came across a gilt-bedecked room filled with books, the gas-lamp sconces of beveled glass glittering and inviting. It was a room full of heaven. I'd have killed for such a library. Some cases were enclosed in glass and had locks. I was tempted to pull on the knobs to see if Mrs. Northe had indeed locked them. Were precious volumes of all manner of occult things within?

Snatching up a paper closest to me, I found it was a spiritualist tract.

I was fascinated to read about the idea of one's essence being *more*, that life was more than simply our mortal coil. I was disappointed that the tract was about the cleanliness of the soul and maintaining a positive presence in the world for the benefit of one's self and others. There was not a word about communicating with the beyond. Ashamed, I realized that I, like Maggie, was more taken with the sensational aspects of spiritualism. The dead. Séances. Haunted objects.

But if life was more than just a body, something of Lord Denbury's essence lived on in a canvas and another part was walking somewhere around Manhattan. I liked his painting part a deal better than the other. Like a séance luring out the dead, was there somehow a way to bring his canvas to life?

# June 9

The plot has thickened, and how. Lives, sanities, and the very fabric of reality remain on the line.

The day began simply enough. Would that it had ended so!

Mrs. Northe came to call under the pretense of mere friendship and a sense of newfound "familial" duty. I heard her declare herself my new aunt to Bessie, our housekeeper of several years. Bessie simply nodded, happy that at least someone female was entering the house.

She had lectured Father countless times about the dangers of too many male scholars around a pretty girl my age. The damage had already been done with Edgar. Bastard heartbreaker. If only he'd ruined me, it would have been truly tragic. But I think Bessie would've killed him if he'd even tried. If Bessie had been around when I was a child, I wonder if I would have talked. If for no other reason than out of exasperation.

Seeing that I was alone in the house, Mrs. Northe promptly told Bessie that I would be in her capable company for the rest of the afternoon and escorted me outside. When I inquired after Maggie in sign language, Mrs. Northe replied, "While I do appreciate that my niece so admires and enjoys my company, I have to now and then return her to her own mother."

When the driver helped us into Mrs. Northe's fine carriage, I realized this wasn't just a friendly call. Mrs. Northe had a certain look on her lovely face, with something urgent signaling in the way her lips were pursed and her hazel eyes flashed.

"There's something I'd like you to see," she said quietly.

I didn't move to sign or act like I knew what she meant. Perhaps I hadn't left the spiritualist tract exactly where I'd found it, and she'd scold me for snooping. Maybe she meant the painting…

The staff in the Northe residence was curiously out of the way when we arrived. Actually, when I thought about it, I realized they were usually out of sight. Perhaps that's how Mrs. Northe liked it. But she was so friendly to them that I couldn't imagine their not appreciating her company. I'd even wondered if I should offer myself to her in employment if my father had another crisis about what to do with me. But no one greeted us at the front door once the driver hurried up the stoop and opened it for her, bobbing his hat and clearing our path.

Perhaps they felt the chill in the air that I felt as I walked through. Perhaps they'd noticed how the light curiously seemed to hover, hang, and direct one's eye immediately to the grand staircase and the purple velvet curtain, as if nothing else in the entire house was of importance.

Mrs. Northe watched my gaze.

"It's like he's magnetic, isn't it? He compels us, doesn't he?" she murmured. I nodded. It would do no good to pretend I wasn't fascinated; it was far too late to hide that.

"Did you notice anything different about the canvas? I highly doubt you passed by last time without peeking."

I wondered if besides being a spiritualist, she was a mind reader. I blushed, and that was enough for her to smirk.

"I'd be disappointed in you if you hadn't," she continued, and we were silent as we ascended the stairs to his level, as if ascending a dais to the throne of a king. He would have made a good king, I thought, wistfully imagining myself as one of his loyal subjects, falling upon my knee to kiss his smooth, white hand. My blush persisted. This painting had done wonders for my already overactive imagination.

We stood on the landing, and she drew the curtain back. Were I in the habit of making noise, I would have gasped aloud. But I did so inwardly with a small contraction of my rib cage and a skip of my heartbeat. Even though his face was emblazoned upon my memory, every time was like seeing him for the first.

This, I determined, was what it must feel like...

I was in love.

With a two-dimensional object. A mute in love with a painting. Lovely. Just *lovely*. I could do nothing but stand there and accept my absurd fate.

A healthy, rosy color was high on Lord Denbury's cheeks, as if he too were blushing, those blue eyes so bright and so alive.

Mrs. Northe was watching me curiously, and remembering myself, I turned to her, ready for her commentary. She pointed to the book and then to the paper. She saw the clues that I had glimpsed. They were there still. I hadn't dreamed them.

"I am not a girl," Mrs. Northe said pointedly. "And so I can only think that he means you. Ever since you and Lord Denbury were introduced, this painting has taken on a whole new life. Truly. And it can't have been Maggie. She'd seen him plenty of times before we met you. He's never *reacted* to anyone but you. You are the one he's chosen."

I looked at Mrs. Northe helplessly, my heart pounding in my chest. "What…does he *want?*" I signed.

"Why, I've no idea," Mrs. Northe replied. "Have you asked him?"

I looked at Mrs. Northe as if she were daft. She pursed her lips, refusing to let me think she had insulted me and added, "He spoke to you via note. Why don't you do the same?"

I again stared at her blankly. She was speaking to me as

if this were commonplace. I wondered if she was as mad as I was. Perhaps we both ought to throw ourselves into the nearest histrionic ward. She stared at me for a long moment, then up at Denbury, and then back at me.

"Our world is new, Natalie," she mused, staring at the painting. "Magic truly does exist. Though I've never seen any like this. Have you?"

I shook my head. "But I saw his ghost," I signed. I bit my lip.

Mrs. Northe cocked her head. "His ghost?" she breathed. I nodded.

"In the Art Association," I signed, my hands shaking. "He passed and spoke to me. Different. Not…a gentleman. He was frightening. His eyes were…off."

"Why didn't you tell me?" she asked sharply. I stared at her, helpless. Her gaze softened. "I'm very sorry, Natalie. I expect too much of you. I forget you are entirely new to such matters, though I believe you're suited for them. Of course you didn't dare say a word. You thought you'd be declared mad. But you've not lost your mind. Thank you for telling me about his other form. It helps me to know what we might be dealing with."

I raised my eyebrows in hopes she'd educate me.

"Oh, any number of unpleasant things," she replied. "But you'll have to ask Denbury himself to narrow it down."

When I turned back to Lord Denbury, my hand slowly

rose to my mouth. He had changed again. His hands were no longer behind him. Now his right arm was extended, his long fingertips outstretched, reaching for me.

What could he possibly want from me? Something wicked? Something courtly? Something sweet? I found each possibility titillating and terrifying. I'd heard his voice. And I *did* want it to call my name.

"He calls you, Natalie Stewart," Mrs. Northe said, again as if this were entirely ordinary. I was grateful that she was able to speak of such odd things with nonchalance. It kept panic from overwhelming me. "Just like in the old stories when a cursed prince needed to ask a favor of a young lady…well, here you are. Had you ever dreamed you'd be such a princess?"

I gaped at her. This was mad. She held out paper and fountain pen, insisting I take them. "See if a note will do."

I shook my head, trying to get my bearings. "How…?" I signed, feeling as though someone might be playing a horrible joke on me. But Mrs. Northe simply shrugged while pressing the pen and paper into my hand.

"I have seen things in this world, my dear, that defy explanation. While I have never seen anything like this, I am not inclined to think myself mad, nor should either of us be overcome by a female fit. Dark powers are afoot, and we must take them seriously. But not hysterically. You two have business. I ought to leave you to it."

She descended without another word and disappeared into her study, moving with ethereal grace. Perhaps her time with spiritualists had made her somewhat of a spirit herself.

I was left alone with my dark, odd fairy tale, and no idea what to do.

I moved to the small console table that bore a lovely vase of flowers. I edged the china vase aside and tried not to think about how purely ridiculous the scenario was before I scribbled:

*What do you want from me?*

I held up the note, lifting it to eye level as he stared out above my head. I'd never felt more absurd in my life. I looked away, my breath escaping in a bit of a scoffing snort. Looking up again, I froze. His fingers were curled. The eyes I'd first seen as cloudless sky-blue were now stormy as they gazed down at me. Pleading. He was beckoning me.

I wished he would just step down off that canvas and explain *what* the devil he *was*. Goodness, I thought, I hope he's not the Devil—but this is certainly not the stuff of angels. This is the stuff of magic and weird—of fairies and sorcery! Perhaps there is the Devil in sorcery. I've not much experience in these matters, but things *are not right…*

Alas, my thoughts run faster than my pen, as I seek to comprehend these recent events. I'd never wished for the faculty of speech more than in those aching moments when reality was as strangely woven as the spectacular threads of the canvas before me. So very real, and yet so very unreal.

Perhaps my query was too broad. I moved to the console again to scribble another phrase.

*Can I help you? How?*

I held up the paper again, trying to brace my arms to hide how much they were trembling.

But the paper fluttered to the floor, dropping from my slack fingertips as I noticed the latest change in Denbury's portrait.

His figure now pointed at the desk, to the blotter and the hasty, speckled pools of ink left there. Two words written there struck me to the core.

*Touch me...*

I stopped at this command, which seemed straight out of Wonderland. Alice, I recalled, had been subjected to as much terror as she was to wonder. The only sound and sensation in that moment was my heart, a roaring creature that had surpassed pounding in my chest and migrated its furious thump into my ears.

I shivered as if he'd read my mind. Could he sense me wondering if his flesh would be warm? Surely I'd feel only cold, flat paint. Perhaps I should have thought before I moved, but I was too intrigued to have paused. After all, what harm could there be in touching a canvas? Forgive me, fellows at the Metropolitan, artists, and historians who would chastise me for touching the oils of my skin to the oils of a painting. I do realize that, in time, such action would cause damage to the piece. But this was no ordinary canvas at my fingertips.

I moved closer, and the masterful brushstrokes became more evident, order descending into abstraction as I searched deeper. The strokes were now dimensional, piled artfully upon one another. My trembling fingers rose.

His hand had moved again, as if during the time I'd blinked my eyes he had returned, leaving his pointing gesture behind to again reach for my hand. I was unaware of time passing, only that I was alone on the landing with this mystery. My breath hitched in tiny, anxious gasps.

I removed my gloves, undoing their buttons, easing them slowly off, and then cast them aside.

My fingertips hovered before his, yearning to take his hand. My body was responding, almost without my own comprehension or consent. I was in his thrall. I touched the most protruding strokes of oil, where tiny peaks and valleys had been created by the thick layers of paint, but the reality of the sensation was nothing like what I expected.

I felt as though I were dipping my fingertips into water, as if the paint were not dry. It was as if I were reaching inside. Not into canvas or into wall, but *inside the room where he stood…*

And then I tumbled through.

The sensation was the most peculiar thing a body could experience. Perhaps if one had the memory to recall being born it might be something like this, a great, heaving pull and a tingling as the air and light became all antithetical: cool and warm, blinding and dark, somehow all at the same time.

I felt a roaring explosion of sensory input, a dazzling burst of stars, and then I heard nothing but my pounding heart and then gasping sounds coming from deep in my throat. I was too disoriented to be properly frightened. I was off balance, and I pitched forward. There was a blur of dark movement and then I was swiftly caught.

His hands gently cradled my head as he pulled me toward his chest. I suddenly felt as though I was the most precious thing in his world.

"Thank Heaven," he murmured against my hair. "There is yet hope."

His accent had a delicious, lilting British cadence. His voice was not the unsettling one of his ghost but the firm voice of a man in trouble. I took a moment to soak in his warmth and relish the feel of his arms around me. No matter that this was pure madness; it seemed as if some sort of fates had aligned.

Timidly, I pulled away from his chest and looked into his face. His luminous blue eyes were warm and inviting. This Denbury was far more striking and alive than the shell I'd seen walk down the Art Association hall. *This* was the true Denbury: vibrant, tall, broad shouldered, and, as I could tell from his hold, strong.

At the encouraging look he gave me, I could not keep myself from gently pushing back one of his errant black curls. My fingertips grazed his cheek, down to his chin, brushing his lips. Exquisite sensation. This was *not* how two persons introduced themselves…

And yet he smiled, a heartwarming sight. Only a faint darkening below his eyes signaled that he was anything but the strapping picture of health. His eyes gained a sparkle as a slight grin tipped his mouth. "I assure you, I am real."

His speech brought me to myself again, and I nearly jumped back. How horribly forward I'd been. I could feel the blush that set my cheeks afire.

"I beg your pardon! I don't know what came over me," I said.

I *said*.

I was too shocked to even consider my next words. "I…I…am…*speaking?*"

The sound of my voice was faint, far away, and a bit higher in pitch than I could have imagined—but it was not like any of the ungainly sounds I'd once made in the asylum. It was not the troubled noise I'd occasionally attempted in the privacy of my room. This was a sound I could live with. A sound I'd longed to hear.

I'm sure I should have been more terrified that I was alone in the study of a finely appointed English manor house with a beautiful man who, until a moment earlier, had existed only flat against a wall—and *that I'd just gone through a painting*. Yet tears of joy coursed down my cheeks at this turn.

"What…is…happening?" I asked, touching my mouth to see if I was indeed moving my lips, if I could feel the breath upon my hand, if this was honestly the miracle it seemed. It was. What I'd known would take years of brave, unrelenting practice, now, with odd assurance, was somehow my own, by the grace of a strange and magical God whose wonders never ceased and whose bidding was not yet clear…

"It seems we both defy propriety," Denbury said. He slanted me a slightly wicked smile once again. "But we find ourselves in circumstances that polite society hasn't yet come up with rules for." His smile became strained. "Magical curses that imprison a man inside a frame defy convention. I'm Jonathon Whitby, Lord Denbury. Until this recent madness, I was resident of a fine estate in Greenwich, England. Do tell me your name, fair one, now that you can."

"My name is…Natalie Stewart, resident of less fine apartments in New York City, and yes, until this moment… I…have not spoken since I was very little…I…did not think I could. This…this is the stuff of my dreams and fairy tales. It's a…miracle."

Denbury's broad shoulders eased. The intensity of his gaze positively cut my breath from me. "My God, getting a miracle out of this nightmare heartens me greatly."

"What…happened? To you?" My words were slow, taking a moment to travel from thought to my lips, but that was to be expected of something so unpracticed.

"I can't exactly say. I'd lived all my life in England, and life was grand." His bright gaze darkened. "Then my parents died, a devil was commissioned as solicitor, and I was taken for a bloody fool," Denbury spat. "All in one day…" He whirled on me. "Miss Stewart, could you tell me what year it is?"

"It is 1880, sir, and you are in New York City."

"I don't suppose you might know if I'm…"

"Dead?" I finished and then hesitated. "Or presumed so?"

"You may speak freely to me," Denbury pressed. But he added gently, "Now that you *can* speak, I hope you will do so freely and joyfully."

I smiled at him and then returned to the sobering matter at hand, wishing we had something else to discuss. Like flirtation. Alas.

"Yes, Lord Denbury, you are presumed dead," I fumbled. "Suicide, the newspapers say. What little I knew of you came in conjunction with the arrival of your portrait." I blushed, still having to speak slowly, still wondering at the sound of it, the feel of it, such a thrill amid so much trepidation. "But…I saw you, your ghost. It was you, but not like you. He was…different."

"Yes. Something overtook me and imprisoned me here. Something's out there…"

I shuddered. "My father works for the Metropolitan Museum of Art. I insisted they put you in the permanent collection. I…did not expect to be a part of it myself," I said, wringing my hands. A sudden stab of fear pierced me. Now that I was here, would I be able to get out?

When I could take my eyes off him, which was admittedly difficult, I looked more closely at our surroundings. The study was exactly as it had appeared in two dimensions, only now it was in three. But everything looked odd, foreshortened—like a stage set. The fine Persian rugs and gold fountain pens spoke of the grandeur of Lord Denbury's estate, and yet everything was slightly blurred around the edges. It was a dream state where things were beautiful at first glance but a bit off upon the second…

How then had he, and I, come to this unbelievable pass? Everything I thought I knew about the world had just been proven infinitely more complicated.

"You were never in England?" he asked suddenly.

I shook my head. "Why?"

"There's…something about you. Familiar. That sounds mad. Well, you're *in* a painting, which tops madness, but—"

He'd touched upon the same troubling notion I'd had when I'd first read the newspaper article about him. An inexplicable familiarity. We stared at each other. "What do you last remember?"

"Him. The demon. Unwittingly, I invited something terrible into my home. After my parents died, it all became a blur," Denbury murmured ruefully.

Of course he still grieved. He took to pacing. His movement didn't help my nerves, but it seemed to keep his energy more focused.

"The demon commanded me with terrible power." Denbury rubbed his head, disheveling a lock of that lustrous black hair, as if by touching his skull he might gain a clearer sense of his own predicament. "And I hardly can remember the face of the one who overtook me. But Crenfall I remember. He was the one who took me to—" Denbury halted, his face suddenly red, shamed. "Well, I…woke bound. There was some sort of terrible ritual. Then this prison."

He wasn't, obviously, being entirely forthcoming. But I didn't press him. He placed a hand on his chest as if testing his own solidity, saying, "I feel my body here. And yet…"

"And yet I saw you out in the world," I blurted. "Did

the…demon, as you say, have strange eyes, dark eyes, almost like—"

"An animal's," Denbury finished. "Reflecting strangely, like a dog's."

I nodded. "Then that's what I saw. *Who* I saw. He's taken on your face as his own."

Denbury pounded his fist on his desk in fury. "The bloody bastard!" He turned away, clenching his fists as if looking to strike something. He sighed. "My apologies for such language in the presence of a lady, Miss Stewart," he said as he came back to himself and turned to stare out at the world beyond.

"That's all right. I imagine I'd curse anyone who put me in such straits."

The frame of the painting looked like a doorway as I turned to follow Denbury's gaze. I vaguely recognized the area beyond the frame as Mrs. Northe's landing, but as if it were seen through a faraway lens, a pool of water between these two distinct places, shimmering and obscured.

And that was when I saw myself.

As if through a darkened glass, I stood with fingertips outstretched, my face blank. My goodness, I was in two. Part of me was here; part of me was there. "Oh my…" I breathed.

I was still so taken by being in Denbury's presence, by how it felt to be clutched in his arms, by the sound of his voice, and still reeling from the overwhelming shock of hearing my own voice that I couldn't be troubled that there were two of me. But it was yet another blow atop the many I'd already received. I'd never been so assaulted.

"Yes." Denbury gestured to my body outside. "Just as you see yourself, I also seem to be two, mind split from body. I shudder to think what the devil's making of me. Where am I, then? I've seen a tall woman. There's a light about her—"

"Surely that's Mrs. Evelyn Northe, Lord Denbury. You're in her home. She's a magnificent woman and an excellent hostess. She owns your portrait but plans to move it to the Metropolitan. Your canvas is truly an unparalleled work of art, but as it stands—"

"Oh, there's nothing else like it, I'm quite sure," Denbury muttered.

"And she knows it," I assured eagerly. "She's kept it out of evil hands. You have a friend in Mrs. Northe. She knew there was something about you from the very first. I wish you were truly *with us* in New York to appreciate her hospitality under better circumstances."

"I like New Yorkers," he offered.

"I like the English," I blurted. Then blushed. That was a stupid thing to say. Surely Maggie would have said something more clever. Or perhaps she'd have simply gaped at him. I couldn't be sure. I had to give myself credit for forming words at all, considering that speaking was *entirely* foreign.

But Denbury smiled and my blush persisted.

I debated whether to tell him of the robbery attempt, but if his curtain had been closed, he'd likely have no idea. For his sake, I hoped he was ignorant of what was happening around him. Being trapped while a fate befalls you that you cannot control would be most maddening. But the question remained, was I trapped here too? I looked through the glassy, waterlike barrier to where the rest of me stood.

"I'm sorry, Miss Stewart," he murmured, "to have quite truly dragged you into all this. Such things as I've been through should not be spoken to a lady, yet I'm so grateful to see you—I…" He turned away, clenching his fists. If he had further fears, he did not share them.

"I cannot fault your manners, Lord Denbury, as the situation is far from normal—"

"I'd just begun to live!" He pounded his fist against the desk again, the small room boxing his energy. He was a beautiful animal confined in a most unusual cage. "I had a calling. I was about to do great things. I would've been someone whom my parents could have been proud of, if we had all just been given the chance." He stared darkly out at that murky beyond, the true world, and said through clenched teeth, "Perhaps the Devil knows when a man could do great things and stops him from them. Wreaking havoc in his path instead."

"Perhaps."

He looked around him, pacing the perimeter he'd no doubt paced thousands of times before. "So now I've only this room and no sense of time. Surely you didn't hear me calling for you—"

"No, but I dreamed of it," I replied and immediately turned away, blushing, a hand flying to my mouth. No matter what the circumstances, a girl does not admit to a boy she has just met that she dreamed of him. "Pardon me," I said, my back to him. "Spending a lifetime *thinking* things rather than *saying* them has not prepared me for an actual, proper conversation with a gentleman."

Denbury laughed. A wonderful sound. He took a step toward me and put a hand on my shoulder, turning me back to face him. "The lovely Miss Stewart dreamed of me? I'm honored."

He thought me lovely? I was going to swoon, particularly if he kept that hand on my shoulder. Maggie would kill me out of jealousy. I didn't know what to say, but I was fairly sure I wore my heart on my sleeve. How could anything escape his piercing gaze? Surely he could read my soul and see that I was utterly compelled by him. And the more delicious fact was that the knowledge didn't seem to deter him in the least.

"But gaining your voice, Miss Stewart, it heartens me. You see, I hope to establish my own physician's practice, in order to help people. A friend and I started a volunteer clinic in London, but I want to do more, so much more. If this harrowing chamber made a mute girl find her voice…" Another delicious smile played upon his lips. "Such a gift makes it worth the prison."

Touched by his sentiment as I was, I couldn't help but wonder aloud: "Thank you for saying so, Lord Denbury— you are kind. But am I imprisoned here now too?"

Horror crossed his face. "Oh! I hadn't thought—I didn't think you could join me. I just wanted you to know someone was inside. You…I had to reach out to you—"

"Why me?" I pressed.

"Because of your colors."

I blinked at him.

He tried to explain. "When I first saw you out there—" He gestured out past the frame's edge to the world as I knew it. "Blurry as you were, you were still surrounded by green and violet—a halo, if you will. I've noticed light around only a few. You, Mrs. Northe, and another girl."

"That's Maggie. She's your friend too," I blurted.

I looked down at myself and saw no such green and violet halo.

"Yours was the strongest light of all," he murmured in a quiet, concerned tone as he took a step closer to me. "The devil who imprisoned me performed a terrible rite. As he cast me backward into this prison—like being pushed into deep water—colors crackled around him like a sorcerer's spell, all red and gold, the veritable fires of Hell with a hint of sulfur scent. His halo was in colors exactly opposite yours. When I saw you, your light made me…forget everything else."

Denbury raked his hand through his hair, gauging my reaction. Evidently it wasn't what he hoped, for he sighed in sorrowful exasperation. "It's madness. I had to try to tell you something *lived* beneath the illusion. I couldn't have known you'd come in. It isn't you the demon requires, it's me. You must trust me that I'd never intend you harm."

I nodded, believing his intentions, but still my mind reeled and I could not trust my sense or sensibility. There was potent magic about him, yes, but not all of it was good. Not what had brought him here. Colors, curses, halos…I fumbled for something practical. Like how to get, for God's sake, *out*.

"What happens when you try to escape?" I asked. He held up the back of his left hand. It was scarred and red. Burned. I winced. "I wonder if that holds true for me."

"Careful," he blurted.

But I'd already reached toward the pool that was the other side. I had to understand the particulars of this world. The thought of being trapped in one room for the rest of my days, even if it was alongside such stirring company, choked my breath. My incessant nightmares often included being trapped in rooms, knowing my voice couldn't shout for someone to let me out. My body seized with panic at the thought. My fingertips again touched cool, thick water...

The reverse of my entrance happened, and a great force had me in that same strange, suctioning pull. I felt myself falling forward. I was thankfully in no pain and felt no burning, but I was off balance. I turned to Lord Denbury, who was reaching for me.

He grabbed my arm at the last minute. And even though I pulled as hard as I could, trying to bring him with me, I saw a flash of red and golden fire and heard a hiss of pain and a most ungentlemanly curse. Then his grip was gone, and I was tumbling freely through a dizzying kaleidoscope of colors.

I regained my body, snapping up rigidly against the bones of my corset and fighting nausea, and looked back at the portrait. There was a flash of furious helplessness in his gorgeous eyes. But beyond that, nothing of the moments we had shared was evident. He was still. He was a painting. He was subject to the rules of this outside reality again.

I wanted to reassure him, but when I tried to speak, all that came out were faltering sounds. I, too, was subject to this reality. A place where I could not—did not—speak.

Tears welled in my eyes at the injustice of it all, and I kicked at my white gloves lying limp upon the floor at my feet. To so easily gain the effortless, blessed gift of speech and then to have it taken away again? I tried to convey everything I was thinking in a single look. *I will come back for you. I will help you.*

But am I brave enough to make good on my promise?

# June 10

I took my leave from Mrs. Northe's quickly after those
events inside the painting, too overwhelmed to have
gone into details with her.

She didn't press me beyond saying, "You look as though
you've just seen a ghost."

I stared at her and nodded. "I met *two*," I signed.

At that moment, Father came into the foyer and I brightened my expression. "Natalie, darling," he exclaimed, "we
mustn't wear out our welcome here. Come along."

"I'll see you soon, Natalie," Mrs. Northe murmured as
she helped me affix my favorite hat—the one with a small
tulle veil and a satin rose—atop my head and sent me out
the door. "You've a story for me, I can tell."

And so the next day there I was again in Mrs. Northe's
study. She'd come to fetch me at my home while Father
was at the Metropolitan. Bessie was again all too happy to
send me on my way, and while I was seriously questioning
my sanity, I felt I had no choice but to tell Mrs. Northe
about having fallen into another world.

I sat in a sumptuous chair with a cup of tea in hand while Mrs. Northe simply stared at me patiently. Amid the terror of the situation, her calm strength was a most gracious balm. I rejoiced in this motherlike figure who was not stricken in the face of what I feared was madness.

I debated for a moment about inventing some lie or feigning that my corset had been laced too tightly the day before. But she herself had said that fate had brought us together. This sort of thing could not go on without comment—not to a woman like her, invested as she was in this situation. She'd see through a lie. If we two had light and colors that Denbury could see, that made us both players in this strange drama.

The first thing I signed was to plead for Mrs. Northe's discretion. I wished for Father to hear none of this.

"Go on then," she said. "I promise not to say a word. To *anyone*. You mustn't hide what magic has been wrought here."

I signed to her how the painting had changed, how it lured me and then dragged me under like a tide, how Denbury had caught me against him, how the event had created such a shock that it drove me to speak. I felt my cheeks redden in frustration that the miracle had not held true of my voice upon my return to this world.

Mrs. Northe's eyes widened, and she stiffened in her chair as I relayed the events. I felt I had a warrior in the room with me, as well as a confidante. She was as amazed as I, and yet, to my great relief, undeterred. I described the incredible and otherworldly aspects: the particulars of that oddly exquisite little room with a hazy window onto the world beyond, the wild desperation of Denbury's imprisoned soul in contrast to his stoic painted appearance, and the strange sensation of tumbling in and out of another reality.

I accepted another cup of tea, wondering if I'd ever stop shaking from the madness of it all and signed something to the effect of: "Does spiritualism have a precedent for this?"

Mrs. Northe shook her head. "Hardly. I fear I'm out of my depth in this matter. While I've no experience, I do have some ideas. But remember, Natalie, this is the blackest of magic. I deal in spirits, human forms transcendent to energy. I embrace and use positive things, beautiful but generally simple things along the veil between life and death. This matter is entirely different. We are dealing with demons and vile, complex magic. I'd take a mere haunting any day over this."

And then something that had been nagging me from the first inkling of the supernatural reared its head. There was something I was ignoring, avoiding. Something that made my eyes well up with tears as it bit the back of my mind.

If what had happened today was real, then so was the Whisper. The movement at my eye was real. Perhaps messages came from the beyond after all. From Mother. This event cracked open everything I'd ever wondered, hoped, or believed. My heart burned with all of it trapped inside.

"Do you speak to the dead?" I signed.

She stared at me, deeply and for a long time, as if measuring my worthiness to the weight of her answer. "I have," she replied quietly, "but I'm not sure Denbury is dead."

I stared at my lap. My present concern had nothing to do with Denbury. "No, not him." Shaking hands did not make for good sign language. "Would you…" I couldn't look at her.

"Speak with your mother? Or at least try?" Mrs. Northe finished simply.

Tears fell again from my eyes, and I batted at them. I did not want to get the reputation of being a weepy, weak, or sniveling girl. I was no orphan, no cripple, and I was not fond of tears. But I wanted to speak to my mother. It seemed a reasonable request.

"In due time, if you feel it is right, we can try," Mrs. Northe replied gently before cautioning me, "But with forces like these afoot, we don't dare draw anything so meaningful to you. We can't summon anything as tied to your heart as her. Your desires could be used against you. We must keep careful guard around sacred and loving connections, and use them in the proper time and place. They are our greatest vulnerability and greatest weapon."

I glanced at her, and I know the disappointment I felt was evidenced on my face.

She patted my hand. "I'm sorry to deny you," she murmured. "But you must steel your heart, Natalie. Lock it tight against those who would pry it apart. Keep your energy close, your spirit sound. Else unsavory forces may suck the very life out of you." My eyes widened, and my hand went to cover my throat.

Mrs. Northe set her jaw. "No, I don't mean one of those vampires in those dreadful penny theatricals. Though such a creature may indeed exist, there are worse things than such carnivores. Denbury *chose you*. If you're found out, you will also be a target of such magic as was used against him."

I stared at her, eyes wide. Panic surged in my veins.

"Denbury was cursed," Mrs. Northe clarified. "We simply have to find the counter-curse. And as I doubt the magic will let me in, it's likely up to you to find it." She smiled softly.

"What I learn, I'll tell you," I signed. "In *words*, I hope."

My fear turned into a little thrill. It was true: I had *spoken*. My teachers had told me that I was capable of the act if I only trusted myself. Apparently, when faced with the impossible, an act I'd written off as impossible refused to be ignored and showed itself to be possible. It was just like I'd dreamed; I had slipped into a fantastical world only Collins or Poe would believe, and there indeed I had my voice.

"What was he like, really, in that moment?" Mrs. Northe asked.

A glimmer in her eye reminded me that Mrs. Northe had surely once been young and in love. Once she'd cavorted and danced with men like Denbury in fine society. Once she too had been rendered breathless by beauty. Her expression said all this, and her simple question held wistful echoes. I began to sign, attempting to keep my flattery—and my blushes—within reason.

"He's so…compelling. And a true gentleman. He wants to continue his studies in medicine and open his own practice. Despite his youth he's already opened a clinic in London he seems quite passionate about. Why would anyone want to harm him? But then again, I hardly know the truth of his character." How could I judge someone's character when I wasn't sure whom I had met, a man or a phantom? "Regardless, he's magnificent," I added, my blush rising to the tips of my ears. Mrs. Northe's eyes continued to sparkle. "But the strangest thing of all is that there's a familiarity—as if we know each other. And yet, of course, we don't…"

She shrugged and again spoke as if the oddest things were obvious. "Remember when I told you that you'd know when people were meant to enter your life? When they do, those persons seem oddly familiar at first glance." I bit my lip. He and I were *meant* to meet.

Mrs. Northe rose to her feet. "You must come to call again, Natalie, and soon. We cannot leave that poor boy trapped, and I pledge to assist in every way I am able."

I stared at her. My hands flew in signing a blunt question: "Why are you so kind to me?"

Mrs. Northe stared directly back at me. "Because I was told to be."

"By whom?"

She smiled enigmatically, dodging the question. "Running from fate will be of no use. Magic will follow."

I let the matter alone, rose, and embraced her. We were suddenly sisters in a supernatural bond, too overwhelmed to do anything but agree to the compact. Neither of us could deny the impossible. We had crossed a point of no return.

And as I write these words, I keep trying to reassure myself that the man I met inside a magical world isn't evil. He's panicked, maddened, desperate...but not evil. Surely not?

Sitting here on my sill, looking out into the dark New York night, with its roving spots of light and life down the avenue, it is all I can do to behave normally until I am able to see Lord Denbury again, no matter if it's dangerous. Until I can *speak* again. Until life is magical again. Yes, I partly fear the unknown, the magical, the supernatural. But when pitted against excited resolve, fear is outmatched.

# June 11

If one could gain royalty through nightmares, then I would be crowned queen.

Though I have suffered from nightmares as long as I can remember, none have been so vivid. I don't usually note every detail, yet those atrocious visions will remain emblazoned upon my mind.

The first thing I remember is walking through a door. Suddenly I was in Denbury's study, his prison. He looked as dashing as ever, if a bit tired. He turned to me in shock as the door through which I'd entered closed behind me.

"Miss Stewart!"

"Hello, Lord Denbury," I murmured, the sound of my voice still strange in my ears. I've often been able to speak in my dreams, so this was no additional shock, yet Denbury stared at me and then at the door.

"How did you do that?" he exclaimed.

"What do you mean?"

"Come through the door. I've tried, but…" He strode to the door, extended his hand, and tried the knob. But red and gold sparks crackled around the edges of the door. Denbury's portrait frame crackled too, fire racing around the edges in warning and leaving glowing traces of something strange. Wincing, he pulled away, his hand clearly scalded.

The picture frame had faintly glowing marks all over it: strange hatch marks, crosses, and triangles. Symbols of a kind I'd never seen appeared in faint traces all around the back of the frame, which would have been hidden against Mrs. Northe's wall but was visible to us on the inside.

"What on earth is all that?" I asked.

"No idea. But they're familiar," Denbury said ruefully, unbuttoning his cuff to reveal angry red marks, as if those same symbols had been carved into his flesh. I shuddered. "Part of the devil's magic, surely. When the spell was cast, my arm burned with this brand."

"I'll have to ask Mrs. Northe about it. She might know something that could help."

Madness after madness. I stared at the closed curtain. Something was missing. My body. "I must be dreaming then, am I? I don't see myself."

Denbury set his injuries aside and instead offered an unexpected but dazzling smile. "So the rumors are true indeed! Miss Stewart dreams of me." He took a step toward me, his blue eyes warming. "I maintain that I'm flattered."

I blushed and stammered, "But…are you dreaming? Oh! Could we be sharing a dream?"

Denbury shrugged his broad shoulders. "I wish I knew. I never know whether I'm dreaming or not. I seem to reside here in a perpetual state of consciousness."

"It's not healthy not to sleep."

He set his jaw and spoke bitterly, "I daresay it isn't healthy to be cursed, severed from your body, and trapped in canvas. Please add sleeplessness to my long list of maladies."

I bit my lip, looking at him helplessly. "Perhaps I can help you through," I offered, going to the door. The ornate brass knob turned in my hand. It opened wide onto a long and darkened corridor. I heard a whisper. *That* Whisper.

Something shifted in the dark corridor beyond. A flicker of something ephemeral and gauzy white. I felt Denbury behind me, peering over my shoulders.

"That's...not my home," he said tentatively.

"No..." I said with difficulty. "If I came from there, then what's out *there* came from *me*."

"Oh."

There was a long, uncomfortable pause as we stared into the darkness. A figure was visible deep in the darkness, a tiny bit of glowing white. My blood was ice cold. I managed to choke out a question: "Did...did you hear a whisper?"

"No. Did you?"

"I always have," I said, turning from the uninviting corridor. "You see, I lost a parent too, Denbury, when

I was four years old. I don't remember my mother, but I've always wondered if she's whispered to me in the years hence. If it's indeed her, I wish she'd speak more clearly."

"I'm sorry for your loss," he said.

"As am I for yours."

He nodded, turning away. His grief was fresher than mine but I knew he did not wish to show it.

"I suppose that's what accounts for my nightmares," I added.

"Your mother?"

"I've always heard a Whisper and glimpsed a bit of white lace out of the corner of my eye. I don't think the worst of the world, but…I feel as if shadows follow me. Perhaps I suffer from paranoia. But I swear there's something in that hallway."

"It's *your* mind. What do you think it could be?"

Oh, God.

If Denbury owned the grief of the moment, then I brought the horror.

The doorway was empty one moment but not the next. I was greeted by a sight of unequaled terror. An ugly sound came from somewhere deep in my throat, and I clapped my hands to my mouth.

A dark-haired corpse in a white dress stood at the threshold, her head bent, mussed hair shrouding her face from view. I knew it was a corpse from the pallor of her arms. That and the congealing blood that was dripping from her fingertips and tapping onto the threshold…

Here my voice left me again. I wanted to scream but couldn't. Instead, out of panic, I turned and buried my face in Denbury's shoulder to avoid the ghastly sight.

"Good God!" Denbury cried, seeing it too. He wrapped a protective arm around me and shifted me behind him so that he stood between the horror and me.

Even in that moment of fear I recall breathing him in as I pressed close against his shoulder, catching a whiff of bergamot, as if he'd just drunk a cup of Earl Grey tea. He took a challenging step toward the door, keeping hold of me behind him.

"Leave her in peace!" Denbury cried. As he did, a bit of light rippled up from him, pale and silvery, like a halo. Perhaps like the light he'd described around Mrs. Northe. A light like one might expect of an angel. A guardian angel.

While I'd always wondered if the Whisper was my mother, I couldn't bear staring at a corpse to see if there was any resemblance to the daguerreotype on our mantel at home. And indeed, I couldn't think that if it were Mother she would wish to frighten me. But my own mind, my own nightmares, oh, they were most certainly cruel.

After a long moment, Denbury gently urged me, "Look, Miss Stewart. Darkness only."

I turned as he bid. Darkness only. I looked up at his

beautiful face, reluctant to move from his side, where I felt so comfortable and safe.

I glanced at the frame. The markings had faded. All was as I'd found it. But still, it was a prison.

"We are so haunted, you and I," Denbury murmured, and bent to kiss my forehead in a wonderful gesture that seemed perfectly natural, even though it was bold.

I had to physically force myself not to melt against him. It would have been so easy to forget the madness of our reality and just let him hold me. But he was in even direr straits than I. I straightened and clasped his hands. I wanted to thank him for his bravery, to reassure him of my commitment to help him. Yet all thought fled when he leaned closer, his eyes darkening as he tilted his head for access to my lips. Bold *indeed*…Before I could think how to respond, my senses went to black. I had a hazy sense of my body in my bed, my head on my pillow, comfortable and safe.

Though I would've liked to have felt that kiss…

At least something good came out of the nightmare, for indeed, I slept more soundly than I had in recent memory. Even with the deep sleep that followed, I still awoke remembering the dream, when it would usually have faded entirely. But apparently with all things Denbury, the experiences will not be forgotten, be they dreamed or lived.

Ah, it's time to transfer the painting to the Metropolitan. I must go!

## LATER...

Father insisted that Mrs. Northe not ride with us, saying, "Such a fine woman as she is not to be seen in a cargo vehicle!" But I demanded that Father take me along to transfer the painting.

Mrs. Northe greeted me warmly and said she'd meet us at the Metropolitan.

It was good of Lord Denbury to have put everything back in order. Nothing was out of place, neither book nor note. As his portrait was being taken from the wall on Mrs. Northe's landing and wrapped in fabric, he looked exactly as I'd first seen him.

Once on our way, jostling along Fifth Avenue, I sat on an uncomfortable bench of the rig specifically built for cargo and gently kept hold of the sides of the frame.

Father eyed me. "I do hope you'll be as gentle and fastidious with a Rembrandt," he stated. I nodded. My grip upon my charge tightened.

Partway through the ride, the folds of burlap slipped at one corner and an exposed part of the frame came into view, golden in the dim light of the large cab.

And that's when I noticed the markings on the frame. Just like in my dream.

Subtly carved into the wood on the back of the frame were small symbols, triangles, crosses, and hatch marks in strange arrangements. It was not an alphabet that I recognized. I'd seen a bit of Greek and Hebrew, and this looked nothing like either. It couldn't be merely décor or detailing, for why would such care be taken with the part of the frame against the wall?

I dearly hoped Mrs. Northe could tell me what the marks might be.

As we arrived, Father took the painting in hand and we ascended the stairs to the grand redbrick, arched edifice.

Mrs. Northe stood beneath one of the foyer's great archways, Maggie at her side. Maggie waved at me once before turning to evaluate staff and patrons, whoever was best dressed or most attractive. Mrs. Northe seemed as glad to see me as I was to see her, and Father's cheeks were heightened in color when he laid eyes on her. I'd say we're all getting to be a regular little family.

Upon catching my eye, Mrs. Northe cocked her head, seeming to understand that there was a new development. It was uncanny how, in such a short time, she could read me, my face, my eyes, my expression, and my body movements as language in and of themselves, her knowledge of sign language notwithstanding.

"There are markings on the frame," I signed to Mrs. Northe, keeping my face expressionless so the matter would stay between us rather than being public. She nodded and smiled, as if we'd just exchanged a small pleasantry instead of the clue to a mystery.

Museum workers took the burlap-covered canvas. Maggie moved to my side so we could eye them with the fastidiousness of jealous girls, but they proved careful with the piece. Mrs. Northe suggested a downstairs exhibition room as Lord Denbury's temporary home, a room not yet for public use, and the workers set to securing him. Father seemed in no hurry to rush Mrs. Northe off, so we lingered to watch.

"You cannot put a man like this in the basement!" Maggie exclaimed, once she saw the workers preparing to mount the piece.

"It's only for the time being," Mrs. Northe stated in that tone that went without question. "Just think how much more exciting the unveiling will be when I put together a proper reception. A few of my dearest friends are abroad, and I simply cannot host an event without them."

"The space is flexible, and we can move him at your leisure," Father replied. "There is talk already, you know, of an expansion to the museum."

"I do know." She smiled. "My friends and I shall be most interested in helping with the funding."

At this, Father beamed.

"More parties!" Maggie clapped, and we shared a girlish grin.

Once a drape was mounted and hung, the workers left it open. I couldn't keep from staring at Denbury. I had to make fists in my skirts to keep from reaching out, to keep from touching him and inadvertently falling against him. What a potent lure he was. I wanted to tell him of the dream. But what if he hadn't shared it? To me, it had felt so real. But to confess I'd continued dreaming of (and nearly kissing) Denbury wasn't necessarily something I wanted to share directly with the subject. The potential for mortification was too high. Perhaps I could tell Maggie.

I turned to her, but she too seemed far away. Without my having the faculty of speech, we were still strangers. I thought of how easy talking to Denbury had been, how my speech had flowed aloud the way it always did in my mind, full of long, rich sentences that never quite translated into the efficiency of sign. But that had been another world.

"Natalie, as you are our new acquisitions apprentice, we'll have to discuss and schedule your hours here," my father said with a smile.

I plucked my small notebook from my drawstring purse and scribbled immediately: "As many hours as you'll let me."

I turned to Maggie and scribbled for her to see: "As often as I can steal into this room."

She giggled and we shared a smile that made my heart warm, the distance between us bridged just a little. Amazing what just a few common words, and the sight of an attractive man, could do. A terrified anxiety may have kept me from speaking, but it did not mean that I did not want friends. And if I spoke in Denbury's world, perhaps this was my turning point, with my new friends here in this room. I could feel Mrs. Northe watching me.

Could Denbury sense that his circumstances had changed from what little he could discern beyond the murky water that separated his reality from ours? Likely he wondered if I was ever going to step in to him again. I wondered if I even could. I feared for my access to him.

Eventually it seemed odd that we had been standing so long in one room with one painting (though I could've spent a lifetime under those blue eyes), so Mrs. Northe invited us back for dinner and Father graciously accepted. I found it a great blessing that Mrs. Northe's company was one thing that he and I so immediately and thoroughly agreed upon.

"I wish I could come," Maggie pouted. "But Mama's insisted I dine with *Gran*. Ugh. I'd much rather be with you, Auntie. I can't bear dining with *old* people."

"Take care with your remarks, Margaret. One day you'll no longer be young," Mrs. Northe retorted.

"Yes, but Gran's constant commentary about how New York is going to hell in a handbasket and the misery of the weather grows terribly tedious. Every day she exclaims that she's sure she'll get killed by some Lower East Side gang and we have to remind her she's never *been* to the

Lower East Side, not to mention she's not a particularly interesting target."

Mrs. Northe and Father chuckled despite themselves. Maggie turned to me. "I've invited Fanny and Elise over for high tea at my house tomorrow. You must come, Natalie. Can she, Mr. Stewart?"

I turned to my father hopefully. He nodded, and I hugged him, which made him smile wider than I'd seen in some time.

"Mr. Stewart, could you drop Maggie at home in your carriage? I'd like to speak to the foundation about an estate grant. Go on to my home, and have Marie bring some tea or coffee to you in the parlor. I'll be after you in a moment."

Father nodded, collecting Maggie and me and ushering us up the stairs. As we ascended, I glanced back to see Mrs. Northe shut the door to Denbury's room. I kept a smile to myself. She wasn't going to be talking money; she would be investigating those markings.

Maggie kissed my cheek as she hopped out of our carriage at the grand mansion before us. "Tomorrow, then. Wear your best dress, Natalie. That's important. Do you hear me?"

I nodded, annoyed that she should think otherwise. Of course I'd want to look my best. I was terrified they'd make fun of me, but I wasn't about to turn down Maggie's invitation.

Once we were finally settled at Mrs. Northe's home, she invited me to help with some light pastries. We left Father in the former Mr. Northe's den with a fine cigar, a snifter of brandy, and innumerable books. We could have left him there indefinitely. Mrs. Northe was immediately all business.

"Firstly, runes. Secondly, it is most certainly you, my dear," Mrs. Northe said quietly once we were alone. I stared at her, not understanding. "The markings are runes, and good of you to notice them. And only you can go through that portal into Denbury's realm. I tried several tricks after you left us and before I packed him up for transit. The canvas is a door only to you."

My chin tilted higher. (Upon recollection as I write, I think my reaction was, in fact, stirrings of jealousy. I've been jealous before, of course, of Edgar's damnable bride and the stable boy's preference for Mary O'Donnell at school, but I digress…) I do believe I was jealous at the thought of *anyone* else going into that painting with *my* Denbury. *I* was the girl destined to save him. The glass slipper fit only one girl, remember…

Mrs. Northe brushed a fond finger over my cheek. "Is that a twinkle of pride I see in your eyes? Does Denbury have his princess in you indeed?"

I shrugged and blushed. I wasn't sure. Did he? Mrs. Northe chuckled.

"It would take a very wise young woman to know that she shouldn't always trust a fairy tale." She grinned. "Especially not where blue eyes like his are concerned."

I shook my head. "The *other* ghost's eyes are the problem," I signed. "At the Art Association. That wasn't the same man I met *inside* the painting. The man inside is wonderful, a gentleman." I shuddered. "But which one is truly him?"

Was it possible to separate the essence of a self from a body, to trap it elsewhere, and then leave the empty body behind? Perhaps to be filled with something terrible instead? I grappled with how to sign this concept, but Mrs. Northe understood.

Her brow furrowed. "We speak of such concepts in spiritualism—the body and soul as separate entities. And so on a theoretical level, I do believe such separation is possible. But I'd never dream it could be so horribly *used*. Death cleaves energy from its mortal shell. And I can say for certain that energies can live on past that original composition. The difference here is that something unwelcome ripped him apart and then took residence inside his body. And the question remains: If the poor man's soul is in the painting, where is that body keeping itself?"

She rummaged in the beaded reticule that hung from her wrist and pulled out two keys on a tassel fob.

"I told your father I wanted access to Denbury. So I made duplicate keys for you—a museum key and then a skeleton key for the downstairs rooms. After all, he's still mine." Her eyes sparkled. "The portrait, at least. If you free him from his prison, you may be lucky enough to get the man himself."

At this, my heart skipped a beat and I busied myself with my teacup.

"You'll need time away from watchful eyes," Mrs. Northe continued. "This will give you the freedom to seize your opportunities when they come. The dear lad may not have much time." She pressed the keys into my hands. I tucked them immediately into my bodice, the cool metal a thrill against my warm flesh. "Now, about what's on his frame. Runes."

I looked at her eagerly, awaiting explanation.

"An early form of alphabet often used in creating talismans. They've regained popularity within the past few decades. Some Scandinavian scholars think runes are full of magic. While that may be, they're also simply a method of writing. But whoever put Denbury into his situation clearly has lent them importance, imbuing them with a particular power."

She jumped up and went to a library shelf, one locked behind glass. She shook loose something hidden high on her wrist under the buttoned lace cuffs of her silk dress. A delicate silver chain decked with small silver keys glimmered into view against her palm, one key for each of her locked bookcases. She knew without looking which was the proper fit and opened the lock with deft grace. Just as expertly, she plucked out a spine, closed and locked the case, opened the book to a ribbon-marked page, and then handed it to me.

The page showed many styles of a similar alphabet, including characters I recognized. But the explanatory text was incomprehensible. I gave Mrs. Northe a questioning look.

"It will take a little time to translate the text from Swedish, but I jotted down some of the markings on the frame to study further, and I'm hoping we can get some answers here."

Lest Father think we were conspiring, we soon rejoined him for some pleasant conversation, me scribbling things down on paper so that I could include him. Eventually we made our good-byes, and here I sit writing after mending a few pulled stitches on my very best dress in hopes for a pleasant tomorrow. Good night!

## 3 A.M.

Another nightmare, and this time no pleasant rest afterward. Worse.

I dreamed of the study again. Of coming through the door again and surprising Denbury, who was attempting to distract himself with one of his books. The curtain was open to the world, the scene displaying the empty

Metropolitan exhibition room, bare and lonely. Denbury jumped up and greeted me, and I closed the door behind me swiftly, wishing not to see whatever my mind would have placed there.

"You're dreaming again," Denbury murmured, glancing at the door I would not have come through otherwise. "How long has it been since you were here? I've no sense of time."

"A day since my last dream, but reality is odd here, let alone in dream worlds. You've been transferred. Look, you're in the Metropolitan Museum of Art now! In a room all to yourself…Would that we could stroll the exhibits—"

"Rather than *being* one," Denbury retorted.

Then I heard the Whisper. I must have shown distress because Denbury drew close, putting a hand on my shoulder to steady me. "You hear something again? Your nightmares come to call?"

Before I could answer, movement in the room outside caught our attention. A shadow. A tall, dapper-looking silhouette with hazy sparks of red and gold crackling around his person. The possessing devil.

"Natalie, you must go." Denbury's voice was urgent. He began pushing me toward the door from which I had come.

"I can't go back, not there!" I protested. "That horrid phantom in the dark—"

"But you can't stay *here*. What if he sees you?"

The fiend outside drew closer, and the runes around the back of the frame glowed bright as if lit by infernal fires. Denbury moved to the window, trying its latch only to be singed again by the confining magic of the room. He cursed and turned to stare for a long moment at the bookshelf. He grabbed me by the arms and nearly shoved me against the wall, so that I might be hidden from view by the wide and prominent bookcase. His eyes flashed me a warning, and he returned to stand at his center mark as if nothing were different.

I pressed my back against the wall, which trembled as if it wasn't sure whether to be a wall or canvas. I pressed my shoulder to the bookcase, which felt sturdier. Red and golden light crackled around the room as a small liquid sound filtered into the room, like pressing a face into a basin of water. Then came a voice. It was Denbury's voice reverberating through the room, but a sick, mocking interpretation that jeered and chortled.

"Greetings! I prophesy a *harvest*. Names. Souls. All for the greater society. By gathering terror from the saddest New York ward and taking their fear unto me, I further the greater cause. You'll see much of me and bear all my weight. As it should be. The strong shall use the good of heart. I am strong. And you *were* good. I am the turning of the world. You'll see…"

Denbury lunged forward with a vengeful cry, his hands

outstretched to choke the beast, but he was met by a wall of fire that, because he threw his arms up to shield himself, only managed to blacken the cuff of his fine suit coat and consume a few loose hairs.

With a sick chuckle and more crackling fire, the demon in Denbury's form withdrew from the frame.

Denbury was singed and furious, his gorgeous blue eyes hot with hatred.

The Whisper sounded again. A warning.

Unbidden, the study door flew open. There on the threshold stood the same white-clad corpse I had seen previously.

But horror of horrors, she was now beheaded. Her dark-haired head was at her feet, facing backward into the corridor.

This time the dripping sound of blood, thick down her body and falling from her fingertips, came with an omen. Her forearms were turned out to reveal careful knife wounds. The name "Barbara" was carved into her dead, gray-white right forearm.

My hands flew to my mouth, as I made that same ugly cry as in the dream before.

"Demons, *be gone!*" Denbury bellowed, the air around him flashing like lightning. He rushed to throw the door closed on the phantom's face, no matter that his hand smarted with the touch.

Finally overcoming a stupor of fear, I ran to him and threw my arms around his neck. "I'm so sorry," I declared. "I'll not bring this trauma upon you any more. I'll try not to dream of you—"

Denbury grabbed my chin and forced me to look into his crystalline eyes. "You're the only good thing that has come into this world. Don't you dare take yourself away. These terrible things aren't your fault," he said, and folded me in a tender embrace.

"But they are," I murmured, breathing him in. "It's coming from me."

"I'd rather face all the specters of your mind than be left alone," he stated.

From there I felt myself fade away, slipping from his grasp into my bed, my heart hammering with the manifold shock of the demon's appearance, the beheaded corpse, and being held by the man who captivated my very soul, awake or asleep.

I shiver and shudder as I write this with moonlight streaming into my room. I can feel the terror fade away, leaving instead the lingering sensation that was so rich and pleasurable in the dream—being well and truly tightly *held* by Denbury. But it was only a dream after all, and in dreams, one may fancy her hero as she pleases, her hero who slams and locks the door against her nightmares.

# June 12

Today began with high hopes, descended into bitter awkwardness, and has ended in what's become commonplace, it seems—terror. I cannot trust my mind. I cannot trust my dreams, save that they are portents of disaster and death.

But first, *tea*.

I arrived at Maggie's beautiful home, knocked on the carved wooden door with beveled glass, and was greeted by a harried maid who took one look at me and said: "You must be Natalie, the quiet one. How I wish they all were like you."

I hardly had time to wonder at this or to enjoy the lavish appointments of the home before I was ushered into the parlor, where Maggie and her friends jumped to their feet, all chattering at once. Having grown up in a home that was preternaturally quiet, I wondered if the maid didn't have a point.

"Natalie, my dear, you're here. Good. We're driving Mama batty so she's sent us out to have our high tea in the park. Isn't that a lovely idea? Natalie, this is Fanny. She lives just a few blocks south, and her father runs a very successful mill." Maggie gestured to a dark-haired girl with plump cheeks and a pinched nose, who waved at me but then continued staring at my dress as if she was a bit confused. Perhaps I'd worn the wrong thing? I bounced a bit of a nodding curtsey back.

"And Elsie, who lives just north and whose mother was an actress but married into *old* New York money, so she redeemed herself." Maggie giggled, gesturing to a blond with wide bright eyes and a small mouth, who also nodded to me. "All our lives the three of us have sneaked away at dinners and other functions to gossip," Maggie explained. "Girls, Natalie doesn't speak, but don't you mind that. She's very nice. Her father works for the Metropolitan and has been wrapped up in the business of that haunted painting!"

The girls all cooed at once. Heavy with the burdens of nightmares and wondering if I'd ever have another magical turn inside Lord Denbury's room, I could feel my heart sink. Could I ever begin to share such things with these young women who I hoped could accept me into their circle?

"You've seen it then. What do you think?" Elsie cried.

"Ells, she can't respond to you, so don't ask," Maggie said.

I waved at them not to worry and fumbled with my notebook.

*Exquisite*, I wrote and showed it to each of them, drawing closer to sit on a poufy chair nearby.

"Is that how you…communicate with the world?" Fanny asked.

I signed: "Yes, or by sign language." And then wrote what I'd signed for them to see.

"Ah." Elsie nodded. "Your voice doesn't…*work*, then?"

Rather than attempt to explain, I simply shook my head.

"Girls," called a matronly voice, I assumed a housekeeper's. "The carriage is ready."

Everyone jumped up and rushed out to the portico. Maggie hung back a moment and drew close to murmur in my ear.

"Natalie, dear, it isn't that you don't look nice, but that's more of an evening dress than a day dress. I'm sure you've not many dresses, but it's best if you know the difference. The one you wore out with Auntie and me would've been better."

My cheeks burned bright red. That's why the girls had looked at me so curiously. Surely they thought me an unfortunate in more ways than one. I'd thought about wearing the dress Maggie had suggested, but I didn't want her to see that I only had a few. I scribbled in my notebook: "I could go change."

Maggie batted her hand at me. "Don't worry, we're not out to prove anything or catch any particular eyes today."

She rummaged in a closet by the door and pulled out a thin, summery shawl and a parasol. "Here." I took the items and followed, feeling shamed.

A sour-faced housekeeper trundled us into the carriage, the folds of our skirts all touching, which gave the others more time to evaluate my green taffeta and wonder how much mending had had to be done. Their dresses were all laces and muslins, satin ribbons and light embroidery. Lovely summer flowers, each of the girls. And all I could do was stare out the window as the open spaces, clumps of trees, and sculpted knolls of the park came into view, hoping that my silence would, as it usually did, return me to simply not being noticed. It would seem that I'd fare better that way in this crowd.

The chatter was nonstop, high pitched, and in a language I hardly knew. Some of the names they tossed about I knew well from the papers, but as for the turnings of the societal wheels down to the movement of each and every cog, such details were lost on me. It was as if they were spies, these girls, knowing details I'd thought only a butler would or should know. And the plotting! Which eligible bachelor would be where and how one might catch his eye and ensnare him by trickery, wit, or, shockingly, pregnancy. Nothing seemed off limits in the making of a name, a fortune, and a housewife. I had been sheltered indeed.

We were trundled just as awkwardly, amid doubled skirts

and crinolines, back out of the carriage by the housekeeper, whose name I overheard was Mrs. Ford—not that she'd been introduced. Elsie was quick to pick an open spot near both the avenue and a confluence of walking paths, an area shaded but widely visible. Clearly the girls wanted to see and be seen, as they kept glancing over their shoulders at any well-dressed passerby or particularly fine carriage, instinctively smoothing their skirts like preening birds.

The ceaseless flow of plotting continued without pause or even a breath as we spread the blankets, dove into the confections brought from a basket, and poured tea from a latched decanter into small teacups. The three of them were perfect princesses, and I found myself glancing at Mrs. Ford, the designated chaperone, who was watching from afar by the parked carriage. Her hard gaze softened after watching me for a while.

Perhaps I looked like I belonged better with the help. Not, clearly, one of the princesses. I wasn't in the right costume, and I could not talk, let alone speak their language, so how could I ever have held court? They all spoke so swiftly that even if I did have something to add, they wouldn't have waited for me to write it.

I do have to give Maggie credit for attempting to include me. At one point, the unending tide of gossip turned to what possibly could have happened to the real Lord Denbury: if he'd had any lady friends, what would happen to his fortune, and if he was really and truly dead or if it was all a ruse.

Despite my flare of jealousy and my keen desire to offer up this diary as an account of what had *really* happened to Denbury and to scandalize the living daylights out of each of them, I smiled at Maggie when she turned to me and said: "Natalie sees it too. It's truly like the painting is alive, isn't it, Natalie?"

I nodded in agreement. Oh, if only they knew.

And just as soon as I'd been included, I was forgotten again. I couldn't blame them, really. It was hard to know how to include me. People were often awkward about it. Even Father, and he loved me. But all that awkwardness? That's one of the reasons it felt impossible for me to open my mouth. I didn't want a strained conversation made worse by my fumbling attempts. Silence was simply a less stressful existence. But oh, such a lonely one.

And at that, speak of the devil, I saw the very demon impostor walking along the park path. We were not far from the Metropolitan; thus, this area might be one of his haunts if he indeed strove to check in on his "other half." It was good the girls weren't paying attention to me, so they didn't notice how my teacup suddenly began rattling on my saucer and how the color surely fled from my face as I felt my blood ice over and my heart lodge in my throat.

I couldn't look away from him. Inside the portrait,

Denbury was utterly magnetic. Here in the real world, he remained all-consuming. And while he was still handsome in these dimensions, my shortness of breath upon seeing *this* Denbury was far less pleasant.

In a suit so fine it was nearly gaudy, pinstriped and sveltely tailored, Denbury strolled with a crystal-topped walking stick, a fine hat, and a sprig of something on his lapel. He was every ounce a tall, broad-shouldered, clean-shaven, neatly trimmed, and perfect dandy. And ungodly beautiful. Save for the shimmering of his eyes when he looked from one way to another with an odd swiveling of his head and a strange reflection in his gaze that reminded me he'd become inhuman.

And because it seems I've been crowned the queen of all things uncomfortable, of course the devil turned to stare right at me.

He waved. Jauntily swinging his walking stick, he looked me up and down, just as he'd done at the Art Association. A glimmer of recognition flickered over his face, and he put his finger to his lips and winked at me, very amused with himself. The lascivious look made me want to retch.

Unfortunately, his dashing figure would not go unnoticed. But while the *real* Denbury was engaging, charming, and indeed a bit of a flirt, this creature was a pale and paltry imitation. Even if he looked the same outwardly, he was a disquieting mockery of the man who'd held me in his arms. My strange entwined reality with Denbury felt more real to me in that moment than did the sun warming my cheek through the leaves.

"Why, doesn't that look like Denbury? Just like!" Maggie breathed, catching where I'd fixed my stare.

"Oh, Mags, you see him *everywhere* we go, silly," Elsie scoffed.

"I don't care who he is, just that he's gorgeous," Fanny breathed with a bit of a purr. She lifted a hand to wave, causing Elsie to giggle and bat her friend's hand down. "And wealthy. Look at that suit!"

"No, truly—" Maggie insisted.

"Well, whoever he is, he seems to have eyes only for Natalie." Fanny scowled, staring not at me but still at Denbury's body. None of the girls could take her eyes off him, and certainly neither could I. And that oddly reflective gaze would not release me.

"Honestly, he's drinking her in like she's some *catch*," Elsie gasped in shock, still not looking at me. Gazing at me to the last, Denbury's devil half turned down another path and disappeared behind a flowering shrub before Maggie could determine his identity for certain.

"To some, a deaf and dumb girl has her advantages," Fanny offered. "I bet my father would give his eyeteeth to strike me mute." Maggie's face colored, and she admonished Fanny softly.

I could no longer bear it. I clutched my notebook, the charcoal snapping into a stub in my hand with the furious pressure I exerted in writing: "I am *not* deaf and most certainly not *dumb!*"

I stood up, leaving the shawl and the parasol with Maggie, and strode away, nodding curtly to Mrs. Ford as I passed her. She nodded back with a bit of concerned confusion. Clearly I did not belong with these girls. I was perfectly capable of removing myself to somewhere where I would be more wanted.

I longed to run to the Metropolitan and throw myself into the painting and into Denbury's arms, but I had to remember what had been real and what had been a dream and maintain some sense of propriety. All of it was made of madness, though, so what could I believe? I had known Denbury for only a few days—and part of that only in dreams. But even those brief moments had been enough for me to recognize that he was the one person who made me feel alive, beautiful, whole, and good for something. Funny how extraordinary circumstances breed close kinship.

But rather than darting up to the Metropolitan, I continued downtown, ignoring the glances of those who wondered what a girl in a relatively nice evening dress was doing walking unaccompanied down Fifth Avenue. Surely they thought I was either a dress lodger looking for a gentleman to pay for my services or a neighborhood eccentric. I hoped that the burning frustration knitting my brow and narrowing my eyes betrayed the latter.

I didn't realize where I was going until I was at the door and facing its hefty bronze knocker. I lifted it and let it fall, anxiously hoping I wouldn't regret my intrusion. I waited for a servant to appear, but instead I was greeted by the very woman I'd come to see, dressed smartly neck to toe in charcoal gray, hardly a summer day dress. Mrs. Northe didn't seem influenced by what was or wasn't proper fashion. She was always elegant, ever beautiful. She was everything I wanted to be someday.

"Hello, Natalie, I'm so glad to see you!" Mrs. Northe exclaimed, bringing me in the door and directly to her parlor. I almost sagged with relief at her warm welcome. But before I could get too comfortable, she surprised me with a wary question: "I don't suppose you saw the papers today, did you? The *Herald*?"

I shook my head and signed: "I was preoccupied. The girls…"

"Ah, yes," Mrs. Northe said brightly. "Margaret had you over for tea. Did you have a nice time?"

I hoped to convey everything in a look. Explaining was too difficult. Mrs. Northe's elegant, stoic face curved into an amused expression, her hazel eyes sparkling. "Oh, Natalie, I'm sorry to seem amused. It's just that girls can be so *terrible*."

Rallying a faint smile, I accepted the tea Marie offered, even though I'd had plenty already that morning.

"I have it on high authority that you're not like other girls, my dear, so don't worry about being like *anyone* else. Do you understand?" Mrs. Northe said.

"I think so," I signed. She smiled in return, but then the smile faded, and with its departure, a chill crept into the room.

"And I'm sure we'll have plenty of cause for tea and company. But I wish it were under better circumstances. There's something in this morning's paper that you must see. Unpleasant, I'm afraid."

"Unpleasant" wasn't the half of it. I've included the article here so you will understand my distress.

The *Herald*, June 12, 1880

YOUNG ARISTOCRAT SLAYS WOMAN IN BROTHEL NIGHTMARE

Late last night just off Cross Street in the hellish zone of the Five Points, nineteen-year-old Barbara Call was found beheaded in the back room of a house of ill repute and with bizarre markings carved into her forearm.

Witnesses described Miss Call's "suitor" as shockingly handsome, with a fine suit of worsted wool, black curls, and bright eyes. The British-accented man called himself "Barry." A composite sketch is rendered here from accounts of witnesses who saw the man take Miss Call into a private room after he'd taken care to ascertain her name. No sounds were heard from within the room, and no one saw Barry exit. Nor did they see Miss Call alive again.

The New York City Police Department requests any information the public might have about this man or his further whereabouts.

On the opposite page was a newspaper artist's sketch, and there I saw my Denbury!

"How similar and yet frighteningly different a face can be, can't it?" Mrs. Northe murmured. "Barry, the fine clothing, the accent…it's as if his every feature is heightened, a caricature of itself, not," she scoffed, "that newspaper artists are known for their verisimilitude. I daresay the novelty is a handsome killer and so grisly a deed. Is this what you saw at the Art Association?"

The dark circles below his eyes were like paint, his curls twisted into near horns on either side of his head, and the high cheekbones were set even higher as if to hollow his cheeks—but even then, there was a haunting beauty to him. My blood ran cold. I nodded. The devil that held Denbury's body hostage was a killer…And my dream had foretold it. Barbara. A beheaded woman in the Five Points.

"I dreamed…" I signed, not bothering to hide how much I shook. Mrs. Northe was patient as I struggled to relay my thoughts. "I visited Denbury through the study door he cannot access. I brought nightmares. The demon Denbury came. I hid against the wall. Then, in the corridor, I saw…a corpse. Headless. 'Barbara' was carved into her arm."

I gestured to the paper and shook harder as I wrote on the margin of the paper: "My nightmare *foresaw* this! Why am I tied to this? Worse, I just saw the fiend strolling in Central Park! What can I do?"

I fought back the tears welling in my eyes. Mrs. Northe remained ever calm.

"You must ask Denbury to tell you every detail about his imprisonment. We cannot solve a mystery, supernatural or no, without clues."

"The Denbury I know in the painting…Tell me he's not the one responsible—"

Mrs. Northe shook her head. "From everything you have said, your Denbury appears just as much the victim as Miss Call. At least, part of him is. And we must do everything in our power to make sure that the side of good prevails. Trust in his good, and it will not fail you."

I gulped and nodded. It was dizzying to think about such impossibilities. What a contrast from the chatter of society ladies and upper-echelon intrigues! "Did Maggie see the article?" I signed.

"I doubt it. She only reads the society pages."

I asked about what the murder could mean. Why beheading? What about the symbols carved on her arm? Would logic have any bearing in such circumstances?

"I can't say," Mrs. Northe replied. "Perhaps those were more runes. I've made progress on the verses carved around the painting, but the translation isn't yet complete. What's clear is that this is the work of devils, not spiritualists. But come to the museum. You must meet with your father, and we must keep up appearances. I'll see you in the exhibition room when you're done."

We rode to the museum in silence, sitting overwhelmed with the shock of the murder.

I am reminded that I've lived a sheltered, protected life. Were my circumstances different, I could have easily been Barbara Call. If my father had less respectable work, less stability, I could have been forced to such a house of ill repute as poor Barbara. My heart goes out to all the women whom society has cast onto the streets and put at the mercy of devils. Perhaps women like Mrs. Northe and me are the sort to do something about it.

But none of this to my father. Such things as this troubled him greatly; his heart was a delicate one, an artist's heart, and I hoped he would hear nothing of this brutality. In Father's estimation, I hadn't a care in the world, and I appeared unusually compliant as we discussed my schedule and duties. I might not speak, but I'm a decent actress. We agreed I could spend several days a week at the museum, and he suggested several pleasant activities such as cataloguing and sketching. He did not need to know how much of the time I would spend sneaking in to see Denbury.

I do believe this apprenticeship will lead to very little work and a deal of watching, giving a restless female something to do and giving Father the sense that he's doing right by his daughter. When he introduced me to his fellows, it was clear no real responsibility would be offered to my hands. All those stoic male tones confirmed as much. But I cannot take issue. It's best that my duties remain vague, that my tasks are set on observation and time for sketching, that time is not always entirely accounted for…so that I may slip into the other world of Denbury's quarters to unfold magic and mystery.

I've taken these few free moments, as I sit amid the glorious Greco-Roman sculptures, to write down every mad detail thus far. The pieces *between* important events may provide a truer sense of the whole.

Mrs. Northe will meet me here in a few minutes, and then we're off to see my lord. My Lord Denbury. Forgive me, God, if that sounded disrespectful. My compulsion to see Denbury is total. Unseen hands push me toward him, terror be damned. Everything has been shaken inside me, and I've begun to pray more heartily than ever before.

How odd that when one is faced with the expanding petals of a blooming, supernatural rose, one must cling to faith to keep one's head. I'll report anon.

## LATER, JUNE 12TH INTO THE 13TH
*(I write late at night and into the next day, burning the gas lamp low but steady.)*

My poor Denbury has been terribly scarred!

When Mrs. Northe and I arrived in his room, his canvas portrayed him in his usual stoic position, tall, broad, striking, and bold. But today he had a bright red gash upon his cheek, and his mouth was taut with pain. The curators would think that someone with an errant brush has offered a foul addition, but I knew better. Something has been inflicted on his soul from the inside out, made manifest upon the artwork.

I turned to Mrs. Northe in alarm. She clearly saw the wound too. "Should I go to him?" I asked.

"Yes," she replied. "We must find out what he knows. And by the time you're out again, I'll have finished the runic translations of the frame."

I nodded. One weird task after another. My heart pounded. I braced myself for that most peculiar sensation. Dipping my forehead and my shoulders and then swiftly launching my weight, I was in. Denbury was at my side in an instant, catching me again. My body thrilled, flooding with heat in that delicious moment. I could feel the press of his firm hand at my back as it lingered there.

"Oh, Natalie," he murmured, flushed. His breath, hot on my cheek, smelled of bergamot, of Earl Grey tea. Another detail my dream had foretold…

I used tending to his wound as an excuse to remain close. I plucked a kerchief from my bodice and pressed it to his bleeding cheek. "Are you well? What happened?"

"I'm so glad you're here," he said, wincing in pain. "You *are* here, aren't you? This isn't one of your dreams, is it? I can no longer trust my senses. I don't know what's real…" He trailed off, as I stepped away, the bloody kerchief in my shaking hand.

"My dreams? You…*remember?*" I gestured to the door that in my dreams was a portal. I ran to it and tried the knob. It was locked and would not open. Not in *this* reality. I turned back to him, blushing and confused.

"Of course," he replied. "You shared your dream with me."

"Oh…" I blushed, remembering how easily I'd fallen into his arms, how instinctively I'd run to him for protection, how we had nearly kissed…

Reaching out, I pressed the kerchief to his cheek and lifted his hand so that he could hold it himself. A shivering energy passed through our hands as he took the linen from me.

"But today you're really here, not just your mind, but

your spirit," he clarified, looking past the frame where my body stood, his hand upraised. "I can touch you." And as if to demonstrate, he smoothed my hair and then brought his thumb down my cheek, just as I had done on first meeting him face-to-face. It was true; this place did make one question all reality, and tactile sensation seemed to be the only grounding force. I could not tell him not to test me.

He took a deep breath as if registering my scent, and I was glad I'd rubbed some of my lavender oil behind my ears. Seeking further sensation and confirmation, he brushed my mouth with his fingertips, and my lips parted involuntarily in a little sigh.

"I am real to you now, here," I told him. "I feel you as you feel me. And I *am* here to help you. You must tell me what happened. Did the demon hurt you?"

"You were there to hear his threat, but then you were gone so quickly. It almost felt as if you were a ghost. I was afraid I'd imagined you all along."

I shook my head.

"Within an hour after you both were gone, the museum room shifted as if the devil wished me to see through his eyes. The images were clouded, as if viewed through some fortune-teller's globe, but I saw dim, distant flashes and the form of a woman struggling. The room crackled with red fire. I felt pain and smelled blood."

He gestured to his scarred cheek. "Then everything went black. I heard screaming. I've no sense of time, but when I collected my senses again, there was stillness and my museum view had returned. I can only imagine the scene that devil left behind him—"

He turned to me, cheeks pale and those unearthly blue eyes now heartbreaking. "Please. Please tell me *that* was a dream."

I bit my lip. Ignorance would do him no good. "I wish it were otherwise." The more I spoke in this world, the more my voice became a foundation with less faltering. I had to be strong for the both of us. "There's been a murder in the Five Points. Downtown. A difficult place, a poor place."

I described the particulars of the situation, fumbling over the word "beheaded"—truly the most horrifying word I could imagine speaking—and we both glanced at the doorway where the same terror had stood, a terrible omen down to the victim's very name.

"There was a picture in the paper, an artist's sketch, of the last man seen with Miss Call. It…looked like you," I murmured.

"Natalie, it wasn't me. It was that wretch *outside* me. You must believe me—"

"I believe you!"

He raked a hand through his hair and tried to remain calm. "He preys on the weak, the unfortunate. As if to spite me. There has to be a way to stop him, a way to get *me* back," he insisted.

I took his hands in mine. It was a bold act, an improper act since we were not in courtship, yet in our moments, broaching custom had *become* custom. "Listen to me. Strength and noble virtue draw evil like a magnet, like a moth to a flame. The light of your will is attractive." I blushed and tried to mitigate what sounded flirtatious. "To both the noble and the ignoble."

He stared at me with such sudden gentleness that butterflies took flight in the pit of my stomach. His moods, with their shifting directions, were enough to make anyone reel. I became dizzy again, because in the next moment he darkened.

"But it *is* my fault. Perhaps in part. Can I confess something, and will you promise not to hate me?"

My throat went dry. "Please tell me you're not somehow a killer—"

"No." He spoke with such quiet conviction that I could not doubt him.

"All right then, I'll not hate you…"

Restless, Denbury moved to the bookshelf and slid out a book. It was Dickens's *Hard Times*. Oddly fitting. It shook a bit in his hand, its image flickering like a candle, caught between mist and mass. Things weren't entirely solid here. Only he was.

Denbury shook his head, weighing the book in his hand. It was not real, and yet he was requesting it to be so. Staring at Dickens's sullen work, he pondered: "This room responds to what you expect of it, but here I am testing its limits, forcing this volume to become what it represents. This dread room is full of phantom objects. If only that were the case with the way *out*. The longer I'm here, the more these objects strain against existence. Will I be the same?"

I placed my hand on his shoulder. "No. You are firm. Strong. Remember how your light bid my nightmares fade? Like a guardian angel? Hardly a phantom."

He smiled, and the dark circles of weariness below his eyes seemed to lessen a bit. Bolstered, he had an idea.

"So help me demand these to be real. Until I find a way out, I'll have to keep living, keep hold of something tangible, else I'll go mad. Come, let's alphabetize the books while you talk to me."

I nodded, accepting a few books he thrust in my hands. "But I believe you had something you were about to confess to *me*."

"So I do," he sighed.

We moved methodically. The task kept him from having to look at me, which is always best with a confession.

"I returned to the Greenwich estate upon my parents' death. The servants were hysterical, driving me mad. A solicitor awaited me there, Crenfall. I didn't like him. He was eerie and odd. Yet he was the only one not screaming, crying, or demanding something of me as a new *lord*." Denbury ground out the words as we hovered back and forth along the shelves. "Over properties and ledgers, he promised he'd take me to a place to cure me of all pain and frustration. I didn't realize he would take me to an opium den."

I shouldn't have gasped, but I did. It was a bit shocking. Denbury was blushing and ardently avoiding my eyes. But he continued.

"There were beautiful women strewn about, all dazed and blissful. Everything was dark and filled with sweet scents. I took a pipe into my mouth and I was lost. I don't remember a thing past the drug overtaking me. I awoke bound to a truss and trapped in the Greenwich study with a mad artist painting my doom."

He moved closer, shifting a book over my head, and I could feel the heat from his cheeks, which were burning with shame. My heart broke further for him and his plight. "So you see, Natalie," he murmured, "I was Adam. I bit the apple. I tasted. I fell. This is my punishment."

"No. That wasn't fair." I shook my head, looking up at him. "You were vulnerable. Tempted, tricked—"

"So was Adam. He paid the price. We all did."

"You can't think that way. People make mistakes. You were targeted. Crenfall counted on you being inexperienced, vulnerable—"

"Still, I should have been smarter—"

"I don't think less of you for one mistake in the throes of grief. And regrets won't fix your present situation."

His tortured grimace eased as he reached out as if to touch me and then suddenly dropped his hand, thinking better of it. I bit my lip. I *craved* that touch again. We touched in moments of emergency and fear. Touching for the pleasure of it was new. Still, it felt so natural, right, comfortable. If it were reality—Oh, who was I fooling? *Reality* meant I couldn't talk and I would never be the sort of girl to attract a man like Lord Denbury. I don't turn in all those godforsaken societal circles I'd been hearing about all morning.

I changed the subject, handing him more books to sort. "Tell me more of your hopes for the future, about your work as a doctor."

He nodded and brightened. "Ah yes, a doctor's noble work…A horrible cholera outbreak during my childhood made me wish to understand its causes. Ever since then, I've felt my purpose in life is to tend to those afflicted and have studied whenever and wherever I could. A lot of English wealth was built upon the backs of the poor. It's my duty to make a return on that investment of blood."

As he moved to place a book on the same shelf as I did, he gestured toward my mouth and we were close enough that his fingertips inadvertently brushed my throat. I couldn't hide my delighted shudder. "That this strange affair granted you a voice is my only comfort. You are my only comfort. My only friend."

The brush of contact had me thinking of our near-kiss in my dream, and I had to steady my hand upon the shelf. Denbury's next words were sobering enough.

"I wonder if I'll survive another day if the demon strikes again. If consequences of death fall on me, I wonder how long I have." He threw a few books onto a cleared shelf.

"I don't know," I replied.

As he glanced at me, the wild light of his startling blue eyes stilled me. It wasn't the foreign, reflective darkness of his other half, yet it was still frightening; his natural gallantry had been supplanted by slow-building desperation. And yet with us standing only a few feet apart, the heat between us was palpable and the effect of his fingertips a wonder. I didn't know what to do around this man: how to act or what to say. Every moment was charged, meaningful, and unexpected.

My mind spun with the crime and its results, but Denbury's magnetism overpowered all. I didn't just wish to take his hands again; I wanted to bring them to my lips, confessions and all. My own impulses were dangerous. The mad shifts of emotion that this world evinced affected me too. My eyes closed and opened slowly. I had known from the first that I was under his spell, so why deny it?

"We...shall meet each day as it comes," I stammered, trying to regain some sense of myself, only to find that he'd drawn closer. "You're not alone. Mrs. Northe is your friend too." I turned to face the frame, having entirely forgotten about her and my mission for information.

The room was empty except for my stilled body on the other side of reality, alone in the exhibition room.

"No one else comes through," Denbury stated, gesturing to my stationary self. "Not that I called to anyone but you, and only then when I saw your light. None who've handled the piece can travel through its portal, save you and the demon."

"But Mrs. Northe is versed in magical things. Why me?" I asked.

Denbury looked at me curiously and suddenly chuckled, wincing from the pain of his wounded cheek but unwilling to let it keep him from smiling. His ability to maintain some humor did him credit. "Haven't you read fairy tales? I'd have thought a girl like you would know all about the manner in which they work magic."

I bristled and held my head high. "I'm nearly eighteen years old, I'll have you know, a *woman*, not a girl. While I read fairy tales in my *youth*, they are foggy in my memory as an adult."

This was an outright lie. I read my book of fairy tales cover to cover at least once a month. Still, I wasn't about to have a man near my age thinking I was a child. I wasn't exactly sure what he was getting at. He just kept smiling at me.

"You must be special. The moment I saw you, my world shimmered, like bright light through dark water. Like an angel."

"Does that mean you're a frog? Or a sleeping princess?" I asked, unable to hold back a giggle. "You need a kiss and you'll be free from this painting?"

Wincing as his expression caused a drop of blood to weep from his wound, Denbury pressed the kerchief to his cheek again but valiantly maintained his smile. "I'd be lying if I said I wouldn't be honored by a kiss from such a fair maiden. If you'd like to try, I daresay it would make for a most pleasing experiment."

My cheeks were on fire. He kept that delicious grin on his lips, the lips of a prince in need of kissing.

"I am a gentleman, Miss Stewart. I promise," he assured me. "But in a circumstance like this, it's easy for one's fantasy to get away with them, for I exist in a fantastical premise. You must think I'm a cad."

"What, for wanting to kiss me?" I breathed. I thought it was a fabulous idea. "Would you think me not a lady if I wanted to kiss you too?"

"I think in this particular case, being a lady is overrated." He stepped closer and took my hands in his.

I wasn't adept at flirting. I'd only cast longing glances at

Edgar Fourte, and look how far that had gotten me. I'd have to write Maggie for advice. Surely she was a genius. Though I wasn't about to tell her I wanted to sharpen my wiles upon her professed *beau*.

But as his mouth lowered toward mine, I had a moment of panic. "What if by kissing you, I become trapped here too? A girl doesn't simply press her lips to a man, however attractive or titled, unless she's *quite* sure a curse won't similarly imprison her."

He released my hands. "You are too sensible by half, Miss Stewart."

"You know, you're the only person who's ever told me so!" I said, pleased with the idea of being sensible, even if he perhaps hadn't meant it as a compliment. I shook my head, clearing its fog. "This place bewitches me. We *must* talk business. If I'm to help you, I need to know every particular of your predicament. Mrs. Northe awaits me, and I need to tell her we spoke of something other than kissing."

His humor was gone and the wildness in his eyes returned, making me shudder. I liked the flirting Denbury so much better. But flirting would not solve his imprisonment. We eagerly took up the books again.

"What of the curse itself?" I prompted. "Were there words? Powders and explosions? Magic wands—"

"Words. But not ones I recognized. The artist had a French

accent. There was an odd phrase in Latin, but…something was off. Do you know Latin, Miss Stewart?"

"I can read a bit of it. Never quite saw the sense in learning a dead language. Considering my inability to speak, I thought it would be doubly pointless to learn it."

Denbury laughed. "Again, how very sensible of you."

"It's a shame, really. Speaking here, I realize I'd like to know every language on this planet, living or dead, to feel them all on my tongue and taste each syllable on my lips." I paused as I noticed him leaning toward me and focusing on my mouth. This peculiar place had its witchcraft!

"Business, Miss Stewart, yes." Denbury rallied, stepping back.

It seems mad to assume a man as exquisite as Lord Denbury would be "under the spell" of a girl like me. While I maintain that I've been told I'm pretty, I've nothing to offer a titled man of his station. However, I tell you that this odd place brings out the honesty in two souls. When we look into each other's eyes, it's as if we already know one another intimately, our strengths and our weaknesses plain to see. But we finally recovered ourselves from fawning reverie. This world wasn't real, as much as we could lose ourselves in it. The wound on his face was a garish reminder of unfriendly territory.

"Mrs. Northe needs details," I stated. "If anyone can help, surely it is she."

Denbury went to his desk. "I wrote an account. Please, take it. I've had time to reflect on every detail of the horror—if nothing else, to try to keep my sanity."

He pulled papers from the top drawer and handed them to me. His penmanship was hasty and strained, the script reflecting the fear I'd seen in his eyes.

"Thank you. I shall study these with great care."

"Mrs. Northe knows what has come to pass here?"

"Yes, she alone. Thank God, she doesn't think we're lunatics. She awaits my report." I brandished his account. "This will be vital evidence." I had no other place to tuck it but into my bodice, directly against my skin, which prolonged my blush. But he had not handed me a love letter. I held a damning account of supernatural terror against my bosom. That was enough to cool my cheeks.

"Oh, and there's this," he said grimly, lifting back the cuff of his sleeve to showcase freshly scabbing red marks on his arm, just as he'd revealed in one of my dreams. The same sort of marks that coursed around his portrait frame. Runes.

"Last night, after the fiend came to declare his evil, this sizzled fresh onto my skin as if I were again branded, perhaps at the time of the murder," he said bitterly. "It was part of the screaming and everything going dark…"

I snatched a pen from Denbury's desk. The implement shook in my hand—as it took on the reality I demanded of it. I began to copy the marks upon my own flesh.

"Careful," he cautioned. "Take those symbols lightly. Don't curse yourself in effigy."

"Mine's hardly in blood," I retorted. "Still, there's sense in your warning. These are runes. Mrs. Northe is working on the translation of what's around the frame."

I altered the characters from what was written on his arm by omitting crossing lines. I'd present the whole of it to Mrs. Northe and let her guide me. I glanced out at the museum beyond. Mrs. Northe stood as a hazy shadow, watching. What was time like for her? I moved about the room, wondering what she'd see from the other side. I went to the window at the side of Denbury's bookshelf and tried to peek out, but my head and hands hit resistance, as if a wall was there, though dimensions appeared to carry on beyond it. The room remained terribly deceptive.

"I've thrown myself against every wall," Denbury said. "The only way out seems to be through the front, and even then, not for me." He glanced then at the door that would have led, if this were truly his study, to the rest of the house. It was the way to him via my dreams. But it was no way out.

"I'll...I'll keep trying to find a way," I promised. "Awake or asleep."

I glanced out the "window." The sky was beautiful beyond, and the rolling hills of the Denbury estate were stirring. This was England at her most lovely, but it was all a flat pretense. Eerie and unwelcoming, the forced cheer was painted with perfect reality, more clear and realized than any photograph, and yet so false.

I heard Mrs. Northe calling as if from a great distance, an echo beyond the murky expanse between us. She drew close. And then she touched my body's arm. I felt split in two. I felt both sides of me—the me outside and the me at Denbury's side, both of them in excruciating pain. This was the pain he must have felt when he was banished here, and it was awful.

As with two magnets that at first repel but once turned slam against one another, I felt a violent push and pull between my spirit and my corporeal self. I was nearly sent to the ground. Denbury moved to steady me, but I was roughly tossed into my own body again and I gasped as I fell against Mrs. Northe in the exhibition room beyond.

"Oh, dear! I'm sorry!" she cried. "Did I startle you? I didn't know my touch would affect you. Are you hurt?"

Nauseated, I had to keep my arm steady upon her. I opened my mouth to attempt to speak but was hardly capable or brave enough to try out the sound. I pressed my shaking hand to my bosom to reach for Denbury's account…

It was not there. Something itched against my skin within my clothing. I heard a sifting noise onto the floor. Glancing down, I saw that the pages of Denbury's account had turned to dust and sand upon my bosom. The paper could not withstand the cross between worlds. How on earth, then, did I? A small sound of defeat gurgled in my throat. I was far from answers and farther from a solution.

Mrs. Northe helped me onto the bench outside Denbury's exhibition room. "Your father came looking for you. I could hear him calling so I made up some excuse. But as we can't have you simply disappearing, we'll have to keep your forays within reason of your 'apprenticeship.'"

"Denbury wrote an account," I signed to her and then gestured helplessly at the mess made along the collar of my dress and the sand on the floor.

She looked at the remains of the papers and frowned. "His portal is the stuff of spirits, not objects," she said. I furrowed my brow. That didn't make sense. I gestured to my skirts and brushed my sleeves. She caught my meaning.

"Why, then, would your clothes go through?" she clarified. I nodded. She shrugged. "Have you ever seen a naked ghost? They usually appear in the clothes in which they died. I'd hope your spirit would travel with a sense of itself. And of propriety."

Somehow she made the most ridiculous ideas almost make sense. I smiled.

She touched the flaked paper remains in the folds of my skirt and ran them through her fingers. Her mouth contorted with the same frustration I felt. "I will need that information or we're all helpless."

"Let me go back in," I insisted, my hands shaking as I signed a viable excuse. "Tell Father that I've gone to the ladies' room and to meet us at your home, that you'll take care of me. Tell him…how fond of you I am. That I can't ration our time together. You're trying not to hurt my feelings by humoring me."

Mrs. Northe eyed me with admiration. "Why, Natalie, you're quite good at fabricating plausible, emotionally substantive lies."

I grinned and signed, "It comes from my literary heroes. I'm a born storyteller." I gestured to my throat. "The greatest irony."

Mrs. Northe laughed and touched my cheek with a mother's fondness. "You are so much cleverer than Maggie. Bless her heart how she tries."

My face fell. I wanted to like Maggie, obnoxious friends and all. She'd tried to be as nice to me as she knew how, and who could help swooning over Denbury? And yet I was Evelyn's favorite. That she trusted me with things she would not entrust to her niece gave me a rush of pride. I felt a keen desire to keep the place I'd unexpectedly earned intact and without competition. Any good society lady would do as much, as I'd heard firsthand from Maggie and her friends; one should jealously guard the place of privilege one has gained. I wanted friends my age, but I needed Evelyn Northe more.

Always attentive, she watched my face, and I doubted this would be the last time I'd wonder if she could read minds. "Oh, I care for Maggie, Natalie, don't worry. But you are meant for things she is not. She has been given every advantage in this world, while you have not. You need me. She does not. That's the simple truth."

I nodded and turned my thoughts back to Denbury, signing, "I fear for him. He's hurt. When the demon strikes, Denbury suffers."

Mrs. Northe nodded. "Yes. We can't let this continue. I don't know how many blows he can take. Go on then, all the more urgent to get the details," she encouraged. "I'll await you and fend off your father as you've suggested. Then I'd like to tell you what the runes say."

I rushed back into the room, stepped into my position, reached out my hand, and fell forward into Lord Denbury's world. He was eager to see me again, his altered sense of time not realizing it was a mere moment since we'd last met.

Oh, goodness, and I'll have to tell you all about it in the morrow. It's late. Even madness such as this cannot entirely win over the need for sleep. It won't do if both Denbury and I look so wearied around the eyes. I wonder if I'll dream of him again. I wonder if I can help myself.

# June 14

I f I did dream of him last night, I do not remember it. And I would be hard pressed to forget anything about him. So one quiet night among my many troubled ones. Perhaps there is hope for my subconscious and its travels. Though one could hardly blame me for wishing to travel to Denbury. The problem is all the other things I seem to bring along.

I've a day at home, blessedly, a day I shall fill with words of yesterday's happenings again, from where I left off…Pardon the crumbs in the spine, dear diary. Bessie brought me scones since I've been spending most of my free moments bent over my desk writing. She made some sort of comment that Jane Austen didn't die of starvation so I'd best not either.

I did go back to Denbury immediately to hear from his lips what he'd written in the account that had been destroyed in my transition between the painting and reality. He caught me again, per custom (clearly my favorite part of this odd routine), and brought me up to meet his gaze.

"Hello again, fair lady. Do you come with news?"

I shook my head. "Sadly, no. Your papers turned to dust," I said, closing my eyes and allowing myself a moment to relish the sound of my speech in my ears and the feeling of it in my mouth. I opened my eyes again and added, "It seems my spirit is the only thing that can pass through this portal. Nothing more."

He shrugged. "I'd rather have access to your spirit than to all the papers in the world."

If left to its own devices, this world would encourage me only to stare into his eyes, to reach for his hands, and to lose all sense of urgency to the desire that was increasingly difficult for us to ignore. I blushed at his kind words but sobered at a thought I didn't bother to hide.

"Here, I'm your only tie to reality. But in the outside world, I doubt we'd be so bold. I'm a middle-class mute. Hardly the sort of girl you'd notice, let alone be allowed to notice."

He looked as if I'd slapped him. "That isn't true," he protested. "And you're not mute any longer," he said proudly, as if he could claim some personal triumph.

"Out there, I am still," I said sadly.

"I'm sorry about that," he said, looking at the floor, kicking the edge of the rug, and adding defiantly, "But I'd still notice you."

My heart leaped. But I had to stay on task. Attempting

to ignore the seductive charms of this world, I spoke as crisply as I could: "I need to know everything about what happened. I'm told that this doorway is the stuff of spirits, not objects. I'm sorry the papers were destroyed. You'll have to tell me."

"You couldn't have known. Though I did hope to spare telling you of these horrors personally. Somehow reading them lessens their effect."

"I don't know," I replied with a little laugh. "I've been keeping a diary, and writing about these mad events seems as vivid as living them."

A partial smile tugged at his mouth. "Perhaps you're a better writer than I."

"There's no withholding now," I replied plainly, bracing myself. "Tell me."

He breathed deeply. This time, to preoccupy himself, he began to sort his desk, which I noticed had become rather cluttered with papers, doodles, pen scratches, and random measurement devices. I wondered if some were medical equipment that he happened to have kept lying about.

"As I said, it was something of ritual and witchcraft," he began. "I can scarcely remember the face he wore before taking mine, though his presence was potent, his accent was French, and his manner was odd. As, of course, were his eyes. While I was trapped with my hands bound behind me, he painted, working furiously. Sometimes he would pause to ask questions. The questions were too personal: about my family, about whether or not I planned to take a wife—"

"Do you?" I blurted.

He eyed me, a smile playing at one corner of his mouth before he returned to an open drawer. "For your information, I do not have a girl at the ready." Any amusement faded. "The fiend asked why not and then began to rhapsodize on the beauty that is woman, but he talked too much of servitude, dominion, and pleasure for my taste. I got the distinct impression that I was in the company of a hedonist."

"But surely you're promised?" I asked, curiosity besting tact. "Aren't all landed young men eagerly positioned for politics and money?"

"You, too, with such personal questions?"

I blushed. "I am asking merely for investigative reasons, not personal ones." (That was an outright lie.) "I assure you I am no hedonist," I added. (That's not a lie.)

"I hadn't yet found a girl I fancied," he replied, his British accent never more charming. "And I had determined that I would marry for love, not for wealth or convenience. My class has done the latter for generations, and it's an abominable practice."

I had to bite my lip to force myself not to ask what type of girl he fancied. He dropped a pen, which fell from the side of the desk and rolled on the wooden floor until it hit the edge of the rug. I moved to pick it up and hand it to him, bending as gracefully as my corset would allow.

Our fingers brushed together, and the surge that flooded through me rattled up and down my spine. For propriety's sake, I should always have been wearing gloves while visiting him. Yet I'd taken off my gloves upon first entering the painting and doing so had become habit. I couldn't imagine touching the painting—or him—differently.

He continued his grim account. "The fiend said humanity is a vessel for great and terrible things. He spoke of the body he inhabited as a marvelous vessel for art. There was business about my name. He kept calling me John. When I asked him about this, he sneered. 'What's in a name?' he quoted Shakespeare with an odd laugh, while mixing powders and liquid like a mad chemist. His body moved like a marionette's, as if his body and the mind that controlled it were not agreeing."

"Perhaps the devil possessed that artist before overtaking you?" I asked.

"At the time I thought he was merely a mad French artist. Nothing against artists, but they do perceive the world in such peculiar ways. Wonderful ways, but perhaps terrible ways too. He put this around my neck," Denbury said, then fished beneath the layers of his cravat to pluck out a curious talisman inscribed with yet more markings, entirely different from the runes. "I've tried to remove it, but, as you've seen, things tend to burn me when I fight back."

If I guessed correctly, thinking back to travelogues I'd read in the school library, the markings were hieroglyphs. From Egypt. "Any idea what it means?" I asked.

Denbury shook his head, hid the pendant beneath his cravat with a grimace, and went to a drawer, where he resumed fiddling. I thought of asking if I could help, but the business seemed to calm him. Helping would just have been an excuse to stand closer to him.

"More talk of vessels when he placed it around my neck," he continued. "He painted swiftly, pausing only to feed me soup and water, saying I'd do him no good if my vessel was dead. Once the painting was complete, I was struck by the likeness despite myself. Granted, it didn't reflect my bound hands or horrified face. Once the final strokes were in place, the true terror began.

"He gagged me so I would stop cursing him. Babbling nonsensical things and citing gods, the forty martyrs of England, and ancient prophecies, he made my head spin. He traced a circle of powder on the floor, inside it a five-pointed star, and dribbled what I thought at first was scarlet paint. But from its copper scent, it was blood. Wax and other powders were involved, some that he rubbed against the painting frame, some that he rubbed against my skin."

"Perhaps that's where the smell of sulfur came from. Some compound?" I suggested.

"Perhaps. He chanted in languages I strained to hear, some unintelligible, some phrases in Latin. I understood 'door,' 'soul,' 'through,' 'blood,' and 'sever' or 'split.' He placed the painting directly behind me and removed the truss to which I'd been lashed. My body had no will to overcome him, to move. I must have been drugged with a paralytic. He came close enough for me to truly gauge his features, which were gaunt. He was an average man but for his eyes. His eyes were inhuman. Blood moistened the corners as he blinked."

We both shuddered, both having seen those canine eyes.

"His foul breath said a phrase in Latin that I dare not repeat, but it translates to something like 'I send the *soulren* through the door...' The middle word I couldn't recognize. I knew the Latin 'soul' as *animus* but it was conjugated incorrectly. I felt as if these words had struck me and saw myself parting from my own body. It was agonizing, as if I was literally being torn in two. Light crackled around me. The artist crumpled and fell. At this, I roused with hope of victory, but it was not to be."

Denbury had stopped fussing. He was sitting in his chair, leaning in to me, and I had drawn close enough to perch on the side of the desk. Despite the heat of each other, only the chill of the account remained.

"Out of that man's body came a dreadful shadow, black like a silhouette, and I fell onto the Persian rugs painted into this reality. I looked at where my shell still stood, separated across this frame, and saw it overtaken by a dark cloud. I heard a wet and terrible sound. Everything felt on fire, with red and orange light erupting across my eyes. Then silence. A drape was cast over the canvas, and I became as you see before you."

Denbury sighed, exhausted by reliving the memories. He eased forward, his broad shoulders falling. "And that's the lot of it. I've no sense of time. I've read as many of these books as will open, and those I'd already read ten times before." He stared at me, rallying. "A man's library should always be well used, don't you think, Miss Stewart?"

I nodded, trying to smile after such a dread tale.

"So!" He pounded his fist on his desk with a flash in his bright eyes. "What do you think of my tale? Terrified?" he asked with a resigned, cold tone I didn't like at all. I suppressed a shudder. This man was still a stranger. His events had perhaps changed him from the noble man with good intentions, and his soul might be as threatened as his body. All the more reason to get him out before nothing noble was left to save.

"Terrifying indeed," I replied quietly, rising and putting a few paces between us. "But full of clues." I had information to relay and work that then had to be done. But he was a doctor. Surely he knew this was no reasonable disease. "I must go and relay the information to Mrs. Northe."

"I'll see you again," he said, part plea, part demand. In that moment I saw him as the lonely young man whose family had all been lost. My heart ached.

"You shall," I replied quietly. Before I could promise anything more, I slipped out again and back into the exhibition room, woozy as I came into myself, pressing my hand to the boning of my corset to test my solidity and keep myself upright.

Mrs. Northe was at my arm. I nodded to her that I was all right. "Welcome back, my dear," she said. "Did he tell you the terrible narrative?"

"The stuff of nightmares," I signed. "And I should know. If I were you, I'd have a stiff drink on hand when I tell it."

She nodded gravely and cupped my cheek. "You're a very brave girl, Natalie Stewart."

I wasn't sure about bravery, but if Mrs. Northe said so, I'd believe her.


## LATER...

*(I hardly even know the hours or the dates anymore. My life is one odd waking, walking dream.)*

Mrs. Northe, Father, and I ate together that night as planned. Maggie too. I braced myself and tried my best to smile and act as if nothing remotely uncomfortable had passed between the two of us. To my delight, we embraced like sisters and she seemed just as happy to ignore that I'd stormed off the last time we met. She kept up her usual chatter about beautiful dresses and beautiful people, and I smiled and nodded.

But she watched my every interaction with Mrs. Northe like a hawk. While Maggie remained ever cordial, I wondered if she felt supplanted and didn't like it. But Mrs. Northe had said I was meant for things that Maggie was not. Who was I to argue? It wasn't as if I understood why.

Still, I wanted to remain Maggie's friend. I liked her better with just the two of us together, not with the others. So, when she pulled me into the parlor before she was demanded again at home, I was eager for whatever she wished to share.

"I dreamed of him," Maggie confessed, splaying herself on the settee and running her hands over the fine plum taffeta of her dinner dress. She looked up at me, and her eyes were wide with excitement. "Of Denbury, I mean." She bit her lip, as if waiting for a response. I raised my eyebrows, gesturing for her to continue.

"The other girls have absolutely forbidden me to talk about him anymore because they think me…well, *mad*, to be so fixated on a man who doesn't exist. But they've no imagination! I'm sure he's alive somewhere and his suicide is just some sort of mystery that needs solving. Do you think I'm mad, Natalie?"

I shook my head vigorously. Maggie smiled, relieved.

She was right. It was exactly as she assumed, and so much worse. But could I tell her that? Who would seem more mad, her and her dreaming of him, or me with what I'd experienced?

Instead I plucked out my notebook, sharing her smile and partly confessing the truth. "I've dreamed of him too," I wrote.

"Have you? I bet it was wonderful," she breathed, and launched into her recitation. As she first spoke, the thought occurred to me: Could Maggie also share a dream with Denbury's mind? If he was in that peculiar state, couldn't more than one mind have access to him? That familiar flash of jealousy flooded my body, and I forced it down. It soon became clear that we had not dreamed of the same Denbury.

"He was…shadowy," she described. "I was taken by the hand and led down a dim corridor somewhere, I don't know, perhaps a New York alley. It was like he was stealing me away somewhere illicit. Oh, Natalie, promise you won't say a word. Dreamy *scandal* is what it is!"

I gestured to my mouth and gave her a look.

Maggie screwed up her face, apologetic. "Oh. I'm so sorry, Natalie. Of course you can't say a word. I just…forget."

"I promise not to sign or write a word of it either," I wrote, smiling to absolve her of her momentary guilt. She grinned, and all was well again. (Of course, the only reason anyone could forget that I don't talk is if the person never paused for a moment to allow actual *conversation*. But that's beside the point.)

Maggie continued: "He had his…hands on me, and he was murmuring in my ear. I'm not sure what language it was, but it was…seductive. He drew back enough under the gaslight for me to see his eyes shining and his face hungry. Hungry for me. He clutched my arms tightly, and I could feel his nails on my skin as he pulled me close. I faded then, a swoon into darkness, and that was all I could recall." She shuddered in delight.

I shuddered too, but for another reason. That sounded like the demon, not Denbury.

"What do you think, Natalie?"

My pencil was on the paper immediately. "Wouldn't he be more of a gentleman about it?" I wrote. And then regretted it. Maggie's face fell, and the color on her cheeks heightened as if I'd shamed her.

"He didn't take *too* much advantage, Natalie. Goodness. Can't a girl dream of touches?"

I nodded. Of course a girl could. I'd be quite the hypocrite otherwise. I scribbled an apology. Maggie stiffed.

"Well then, what did *you* dream?"

"I was having a nightmare," I wrote. "And he was there. He banished the horror like a guardian angel."

I decided to leave out the part about our near-kiss, which, in my opinion, had been infinitely more pleasant than the exchange Maggie had described. There was no need to turn this into a rivalry. But perhaps I had somehow already failed at this.

"Maggie? Natalie?" Mrs. Northe called.

Maggie didn't look at me again as we rose and wandered out of the parlor, an uneasiness having settled about us again. I suppose I'm not very good at the friendship process. I hadn't made lasting connections at school. It is hard when all manners of issues and disabilities have brought a group of people together.

Considering the blind, the deaf, and the truly mute, rather than my selective condition, we were in separate sensory worlds. You'd think our disabilities would have made us closer. But not if, at heart, some of us are just lone wolves. Lone wolves who are very particular about things and have strong opinions, who are passionate and perhaps unconventional. While we may want a bosom friend, we don't always know how best to relate to one.

And yet, how could things with Denbury then feel so easy?

Perhaps because, on some level, I wasn't registering him as real. Anything can happen in a dream world. I could be my best self, nightmares aside. I could talk. I could be pretty, smart, and witty. The idea of interacting with Denbury in this quiet, "real" world of mine was suddenly as awkward a prospect as the picnic with the girls had turned out to be. But at the end of it all, I didn't live in that world. I lived in *this* one. And I had to help him make his way home to it.

Father again was all too happy to relax with reading, fine liquor, and tobacco, and he took to the den as if it were his own. It was then that Mrs. Northe ushered Maggie toward the door. Maggie was quick to protest.

"But why do I have to go home if Natalie gets to stay?" she whined.

"Because her father is, thank God, hard at work finishing my late husband's stash of horrid cigars. They were too damn expensive for me to throw out in good conscience. Not to mention that your mother scolds me if you're here past nine. She thinks I'm experimenting on you as a medium."

"But I'd *love* that!" Maggie cried.

"And that's why your mother hates you coming here, except for the fact that she'd like to make sure I remember your family when I die!" Mrs. Northe retorted. "Bill will see you home. The carriage awaits." She gestured toward her footman standing down the stoop and kissed Maggie on the head. Maggie looked at me, forlorn, and I offered her a genuine look of sadness. I did want to be her friend. But there would always be secrets between us. Nothing could change that now.

"Now, then!" Mrs. Northe stated brightly once Maggie was gone. She took me by the arm and led me into her library, where she filled a small glass of cordial for us both and lifted her glass. I did the same.

"To the mysteries of the universe." She lifted her glass, and we clinked the fine crystal.

"I've been thinking about the murder in the Five Points," she began. "I believe it's the beginning of some ritual. The intruder to my home might not have been trying to steal Denbury at all, perhaps merely to haunt him, as you yourself saw at the Art Association. The demon will likely haunt his likeness again, provided he's not interrupted. I believe these...*things* are creatures of habit. That is the way with many psychopaths and followers of the foul and vicious. If we could spy upon Denbury's possessor, we could follow him, having heard his plan, and learn of him. The trick would be how to spy on the creature without it suspecting it may be followed."

And that was when I began to entertain a whole new brave and foolish notion. But first: "Tell me of the runes, and then I'll tell you his 'spell,'" I prompted, using a mixture of signing and writing out words.

"I've done the translating already." Mrs. Northe plucked two books and a piece of paper from her table. "Very modern, this demon. Likes to think he's an intellectual, playing at culture. It's not a spell. It translates roughly to a poem. I recognized it as Baudelaire. I've the first edition here. But the carvings on the painting have one word missing, in the last line. Here's the poem in its entirety. It's from his *Flowers of Evil*. A troublesome work. Some critics adore it, but many think it as silly as it seems. The poem is aptly titled 'The Possessed.'"

I shivered as she set the books and paper in my lap. I looked first at the runic alphabet as translated into our common alphabet and then at a manuscript in French. An odd combination, I thought, but then again, it wasn't as though this all made a great deal of sense.

## LE POSSÉDÉ

Le soleil s'est couvert d'un crêpe. Comme lui,
Ô Lune de ma vie! Emmitoufle-toi d'ombre
Dors ou fume à ton gré; sois muette, sois sombre,
Et plonge tout entière au gouffre de l'Ennui;
Je t'aime ainsi! Pourtant, si tu veux aujourd'hui,
Comme un astre éclipsé qui sort de la pénombre,
Te pavaner aux lieux que la Folie encombre.
C'est bien! Charmant poignard, jaillis de ton étui!
Allume ta prunelle à la flamme des lustres!
Allume le désir dans les regards des rustres!
Tout de toi m'est plaisir, morbide ou pétulant;
Sois ce que tu voudras, nuit noire, rouge aurore;

Il n'est pas une fibre en tout mon corps tremblant
Qui ne crie: *Ô mon cher Belzébuth, je t'adore!*

—Charles Baudelaire

Mrs. Northe presented me with another paper. "I've done my own translation, with a few liberties, perhaps, but the gist remains."

## THE POSSESSED

The sun in crepe has shrouded his fire.
Moon of my life! Partly shade yourself as he.
Sleep or smoke. Be quiet and be dark,
In the abyss of dullness drown whole;
I love you this way! However, should you care,
Like a brilliant star from eclipse emerging,
To flirt with folly where crowds yet surge—
Gleam, pretty blade, from sheath and stab!
Light your eyes from glass chandeliers!
Illuminate lust-filled looks of louts who pass!
Morbid or petulant, I thrill before you;
Be what you will, black night or red dawn;
No thread of my body drawn tight,
But cries: "Beloved——I adore you!"

Mrs. Northe continued: "There's a blank space where the word in question should be in the English translation. That was the word missing. As you see in the original French poem, that word is *Belzébuth*—translated, it is Beelzebub…a name for the Devil."

I stared up at Mrs. Northe, gulping. She concentrated on the poems.

Her subsequent scoffing response amused me. "Really, I'd thought love poems to the Devil would be too low and messy for high magic like this, too dramatic and silly. I'm surprised."

That made me think of something Denbury had said, and I wrote out his exact phrasing for her: "Artists perceive the world in such peculiar ways. Wonderful ways, but perhaps terrible ways too." Mrs. Northe nodded, squinting in thought.

"Why do this?" I signed, gesturing at all the runes. Copying out the poem seemed a lot of trouble to go to only to omit the most important part, the dedication.

Mrs. Northe paced the room shaking her head. "Tell me everything else." We paused as tea was brought in for us, and I took it gratefully, the hot liquid such a comfort. Perhaps my body would get used to shaking; this grim business would likely chill me to the bone for some time to come. "Natalie, tell me everything," Mrs. Northe demanded gently. "Everything he told you."

I stared at her, allowing the fear that I felt to register on my face and in my eyes.

She placed her hand on mine, and her expression calmed any doubts. "No matter how mad you fear it sounds." She was, as I had to be, a true believer in the impossible.

I signed and wrote Denbury's story as best I could: Crenfall, the den, the French painter, the odd tangents as he worked. We had plenty of shudders between us in the retelling.

Mrs. Northe asked about the mechanics of Denbury's world, and I attempted to sign explanation: that time passed differently and that his basic human needs were suspended. Outside, my body stood frozen while lifetimes could have passed for us within that dream state, and while in his company, there was neither hunger nor thirst.

"Your spirits exist together there, your minds and souls. Your identities, then, are tactile to each other."

I thrilled at the idea that our spirits coexisted on some otherworldly plane, but I dared add, "We *share* my dreams. When I visited him today, he knew I'd been there. He was with me in my terrible nightmare all along."

"Oh? Why, that's magnificent!" she exclaimed, ignoring my shudder. "It simply goes to prove that minds and spirits have ways to move about the world and that movement is not limited only to the body. It's a theory I rarely see in practice, but something that proves useful in dealings

like these. There is being awake, being asleep, and then…
sometimes there's another type of existence entirely."

I moved to ask her more about that, but she demanded
the particulars of the ritual itself.

I tried to describe the vile act of possession that had
cast Denbury's better self into a painted prison. Mrs.
Northe was astute about every detail: the business about
the name "John," the powders, the liquid, the blood, and
the symbols.

She took a deep breath. "All spell components," Mrs.
Northe declared. "Oh, Natalie, this is magic *most* foul. I
daresay even Shakespeare's witches couldn't have dreamed
this up."

Tapping a pen to a notebook, she suddenly drew a symbol.
"That circle around the room that Denbury described, with
the star inside, I wonder if it was this…" Her drawing was
of a five-pointed star with two of the points facing upward.

I raised my eyebrows in query.

"A pentagram," she explained. "A symbol of protection
and goodwill when it's drawn or worn with a single point
upward." She turned the paper to make it just so. "But
inverted…" She turned the symbol on its end again with
the two points upraised like horns. "It's often taken to
mean homage to the Devil."

I shuddered and yet I couldn't hold back an admiring
smile. "You're not a spiritualist. You're a scholar," I signed.

She looked at me. "A woman should be as educated as humanly possible about anything that interests her. And while I'm *not* interested in black forms of magic, I am interested in dispelling, discrediting, and fighting them at all costs." Mrs. Northe did not linger on this thought. "What else?"

I described how Denbury was bound and trapped and told her about the final Latin words, with the word within that didn't quite match up.

"That's the crux of the spell," Mrs. Northe murmured. "That's the *sending* part of it."

Oh, and I'd nearly forgotten. There were so many overwhelming aspects to retain. His arm. I lifted my sleeve, showing her what I had copied of it onto my arm with his pen, and then I replicated it on paper, filling in the lines I'd left blank. "This was on his arm," I explained, "sizzled into his flesh during the original rite and refreshed during the murder."

Mrs. Northe considered the runes and checked them against her books. "John. The markings mean 'John.' I wonder if those markings on that poor beheaded girl's wrist mean, similarly, 'Barbara.'"

This struck me, and I stared at Mrs. Northe in terror. "It must. My dream." I fumbled to sign. "The corpse with 'Barbara' carved on the arm...remember, I foresaw it."

"Yes, Natalie. And how awful to receive such omens.

But it reinforces that you're entwined in Denbury's fate. What else?"

I signed about the sparks and light Denbury saw around the demon, as if particular colors were refracted from a prism and seen at times of struggle or when he tested his prison walls, and how he saw my halo colors as opposite.

Mrs. Northe sat back in her finely upholstered chair. "This is powerful stuff indeed," she said finally. Her brow furrowed. "Are you baptized, child?"

I stared at her. "Who wouldn't be?" I signed.

"One cannot and should not make assumptions. Otherwise I'd do a different blessing. But a blessing you need, child. I don't like this one bit." She gestured at the marks on my arm. "I don't want these dark things to linger on you any more than they have already." She eyed me. "Be sure to go to church on Sunday. We need all the blessings we can get. Ritual to combat ritual."

She took a small vial of clear liquid from a shelf, uncorked it, dabbed a bit on her finger, and marked my forehead with a cross in oil. She laid her hands on my head and murmured a familiar blessing. After noting the marks, she used the same oil and her handkerchief to rub the ink from my arm, while offering another blessing. The marks smeared black and ugly, the ink stubborn.

I went on to mention Denbury's necklace, the talisman the demon had put around his neck, describing and transferring the symbols onto paper for her perusal. I was correct that they were hieroglyphs.

"A cartouche of sorts," Mrs. Northe murmured. She went to another bookshelf and plucked another fine volume, musing as she flipped through pages. "Dear Lord, add Egyptian gods into the mix now too? What a mess. A cartouche is a set of hieroglyphs, similar to what we think of as a monogram. But this cartouche, I believe, means vessel."

She put the book down and returned to sit with our notes, saying, "The fiend spoke of vessels, so it would follow…" I could practically hear Mrs. Northe's mind reeling at great speed. She continued. "Remind me, I must check the nameplate of the painting attached to the frame." I nodded. "Baptized you may be, but do you consider yourself a Christian, Natalie?" she asked.

This was not a question I expected. Just as I had assumed everyone was baptized, I'd never considered myself otherwise. I nodded. "Lutheran," I clarified for her, writing in my little notebook.

"Indeed, as I am Episcopalian," she replied. "Therefore—" She stopped short as she noticed my expression. She set her jaw.

"As I have said, Natalie, spiritualism does not preclude my Christianity. Would you tell any of my Quaker colleagues that they do not believe the Bible? They'd give you a calm, thorough argument and they'd win. We must here abandon prejudices. The methods to solve these riddles may not be found in *our* faith at all, but in others or in dark things with which we have no business.

"That's what frightens me most, all this borrowing. 'I am a jealous God,' says scripture. Every religion has a jealous god, in some way. Poor Denbury is in a pit of jealous gods, each offended that their separate parts should be so oddly and disrespectfully thrown together. That's quite a mess of energies that I'd rather not be in the middle of."

I sat utterly overwhelmed. Mrs. Northe seemed worried but not defeated. Perhaps forces were at work to bring us good parties together, a ragtag battalion against the darkness. I liked to think so. I didn't think God would care about which denominations we were, as long as we were unified in rejecting any works of a devil.

Mrs. Northe was still musing aloud.

"We need to see what factors emerge consistently in the crimes. But letting more women die just for the sake of empirical evidence won't do. We don't have the luxury to wait and see. We are dealing with separation of body and soul. Then the imprisonment of the soul and the possession of a body. Identity and the transfer of it. We know who we are because of our soul and consciousness. Our soul is *who* we are, not *what* we are. *Who* Denbury is remains in the painting. The *what* of Denbury—the mortal stuffs, the shell of his body, and all the animal that remains—walks the streets of New York City freely. Now, how to bring those two parties back together?"

"The body isn't afraid to be near the soul," I signed. "It haunts the painting."

Mrs. Northe nodded. "So the trick will be in the reversal. To reverse the curse when the two are face-to-face. And for that, we need every word that was spoken. We'll put it together with the runes. Tell me again, those dread words…write down the spell."

I wrote out the words Denbury had spoken to me.

Mrs. Northe shook her head. "Maddening." She too stumbled over the word that Denbury himself couldn't make out. *Soulren* was not a word. "I imagine we must know *every* word of this spell for it to hold any power. The actor must understand every phrase of Shakespeare to make his soliloquy clear and the poet every word of her prose. The priest must understand the words of scripture to be able to give his blessing, and so must those who wield spells comprehend every word. Thus, any empty word would render a spell meaningless."

She ruminated on the details, pausing to write down key words. After pondering a long while, she looked up.

"Should we mention this to your father?" Mrs. Northe asked quietly. I shook my head. "Why, because he will not believe?"

"He would not *want* to," I countered. Having never

fully recovered from Mother's death, he was more sensitive than he would ever let on. This would do his heart no good. "What about Maggie?"

"Not a word of it. She's too flighty for such grave things. She wouldn't understand."

I thought about it a moment and nodded. Truly, jealousy aside, if I'd been the one drawn into Lord Denbury's danger, then his company was to be my reward and mine alone.

Mrs. Northe reached forward and squeezed my hand. The warmth of her touch made me realize my own chilled extremities. "Good work in gathering evidence, Natalie, very good. But I fear you'll have to do far more."

I nodded, feeling like I'd aged a year in a few days.

And as I've been in this room for more hours than I dare count, I'm off to kneel before the altar at Immanuel. I prefer the space when it's quiet and I'm left alone to my prayers without the kind but pitying looks of the congregants.

Afterward I'll make a pilgrimage to my beloved Central Park. I'll clear my mind and bolster my heart with natural beauty by sitting at the feet of my sacred Angel of the Waters as she rises above the Bethesda Terrace. Hers is my favorite visage of those the city has to offer. It can't hurt to be near angels in times like this.

# June 15

**3:30 A.M.**

*(Awakened by a mixture of determination and fear)*

I will attempt to re-create my latest nightmare as best I can, turning the key of my bedside gas lamp high. In the light, the shadows of my mind lessen into a creature whose teeth recede. But goodness, my mind does have its fangs.

A street corner at dusk. I stood with the city moving around me. Before I even knew where I was, I was struck by the quality of the lamplight. It cast shadows long and deep. But, as with many things in my life of late, the shadows were a bit off. Surreal. Full of a life one would not expect of shadows.

Cast by carriages and their horses, by persons young and old, men in top hats and women with too many ruffles on their skirts to be practical, the shadows swirled like mist or a drop of ink into water. But when I looked at the shadows directly, they were only that, a shape that blocked light. The moment I focused on a passerby or an architectural detail, the shadows were off, moving into the corners of my eyes again.

Glancing about, I realized I stood in the middle of Manhattan, at the southern foot of Central Park where the city begins again with those grand blocks where the Vanderbilt mansion is lord, with its pomp and impressive circumstance. The grandeur of wealth attracts passersby at such a twilight time. It's an hour to be seen, that particular moment of dusk when there's a bit of magic in the air, when women don fine clothing and lovers might steal a moment in the shadows before they are expected beneath the glittering chandeliers of polite company.

The others on the street reflected my own fascination. It is hard to live in New York and not be compelled by the city's grandeur. Each passing face was full of hopeful possibility, persons en route to a fine dinner in some nearby mansion, out to the symphony or the opera, or off to an exclusive society club.

New York, the great city of bustling desire.

It moved around me, as if I were a stone in a babbling brook.

Out of the sea of faces I then saw *him*, there before the estate of one of the most powerful New Yorkers. His silhouette—I would know it anywhere. Perhaps I was dreaming of the sort of life Denbury would lead were he an English lord in New York City, free from his curse, and

I was looking in on his life and the places where it might lead him.

But then he turned to stare me down. This was not the face of the compelling soul of the Denbury who entranced me, but the odd, primal gaze of the one who repulsed me. His lip curled before he lunged at me. I was seized by the specific sort of panic that, from an early age, has made speech impossible.

Instinct made me run. I picked up my skirts and fled, thankful to be wearing sensible boots on the treacherous cobbles. The fiend was after me like a predatory animal, the blue eyes now replaced entirely by that eerie reflective gleam. Even a form as beautiful as Denbury's could not entirely hide the ugliness that had overtaken it.

I was pressing downtown, or so I thought, but I abruptly found myself caught up in a tangled mess of alleys and lots instead of that magnificent stretch of Fifth Avenue. Suddenly I was in what I imagined the worst parts of the city were like, barely lit, a maze of brick and cast-iron facades with industry and horse manure and huddled hordes tucked in shadows, hardly the promenading parade. From grandeur to struggle, so too was this the heart of New York. Perhaps these were those infamous parts where the killer had struck.

A door beckoned at the end of the alley. Safety? Or greater danger?

The closer I came, the brighter the light from beneath it grew.

I reached for the glass knob, threw myself against the door, and tumbled into Denbury's painted study.

The dear man must be commended for being so quick on his feet during urgent times, no matter the strange ties of our conscious and unconscious states. He seized me and whirled me to the side, pressing me firmly behind him as he stepped boldly forward to place himself between me and the demon who hesitated at the door, snarling.

There at the threshold, the true Denbury and his horrid doppelganger were face-to-face. And in that brief moment, the true Denbury was just as ferocious as his dark twin. What a beautiful sight that was as his righteous fury lit up the air around him.

"Demon, you've taken everything from me. You'll *not* take this girl!" Denbury cried, and even though it hurt him to do so, he shoved his demon self back and slammed the door, crackling with fire, upon the demon's face.

But the demon pounded at the door, taunting and calling.

I was shrinking away from the demon's hissing of "pretty thing" and mad with fear, but Denbury grabbed me by the elbows and swung me around to look him in the eye. His confidence and conviction broke through my terror. While in his territory, clearly he would not allow anything to get the better of us.

"Natalie, you can make it go away. This is your dream. You can change what's on the other side of that door. You are not at its mercy. If I can keep what little mind I have left, then you can face your nightmares and tell them to bugger off."

I half smiled despite myself. He took a brief, measured breath.

"Excuse my language. But do it, please."

I tried to form a command on my lips. I thought of the renunciations of evil used during baptisms of the young and old, a call and response between pastor and congregation, a core principle of the faith I adhered to out of respect and a bit of awe—something that had never seemed as imperative as now. My voice was faint and trembling, not what I hoped it could be: "I renounce thee…"

Denbury repeated the phrase with me, and in doing so I was strengthened.

"I renounce thee!" we chorused.

I turned around, and the demon was gone from the doorstep. But in its place was that same woman's corpse, still in her white shift. This time it retained its head, but the body was bent slightly at the waist, creating a curtain of dark hair that made the face still unrecognizable. The arm was carved bloody, inscribed again, but with a new name: *Cecilia*.

Trembling and shocked, I fumbled for the words to banish the hideous specter.

"Go on," Denbury urged. "Be rid of it. You have the power."

I opened my mouth. An aspirated, ungainly sound came out. A few tears fell down my cheeks. Denbury cupped my chin in his hand and forced me to look into his heart-stopping eyes.

"You are stronger than this, Natalie. Now, turn around and tell the nightmares you're no longer ruled by them." A product of a mostly Protestant country that would have had somewhat similar liturgies to mine, Denbury then supplied the question: "Do you renounce sin, the Devil, and all his empty promises?"

And because liturgy was like muscle memory, I was able to answer: "I renounce them."

With a bit of the Whisper, that tickling, maddening murmur at my ear, the phantasm faded. I took a deep breath.

That the Whisper was connected to such sights was a bit too much to bear, considering the association with Mother. But if she was somewhere present, I hoped the disembodied noise was in fact information or a clue. I just wished she'd be clearer about it after all this time.

I stared at the open door and the dark corridor beyond that was no longer a New York alley or a threshold for the dead but a dim hollow place of uncertainty that awaited something to light it up. Denbury gazed out into that murky fog, and his hand reached out to cup my elbow in a gentle press.

"You're a very nice girl. A very pretty girl, Miss Stewart. Why in the world is your mind so haunted?"

I looked at him for a moment, wanting to tell him something meaningful. When he and I were alone in this place where time stood still, I spoke with such ease that it broke my heart to think that my ability to speak would be gone upon waking.

"Because my nightmares are clues. Perhaps they always have been. I am meant to see what I see." I took a step toward him. "And those who have stared into the darkness can empathize with those who have it thrust upon them, can't they?"

"Yes, indeed. I am grateful to have you as my only friend in the darkness." He smiled. "I realize I've often called you by your first name. This place does breed familiarity. Do you mind?"

"Not a bit."

"Then please call me Jonathon. The world calls me Denbury: friends, colleagues, acquaintances. But you… you're something different from a colleague. You're…"

I held my breath. What was I?

"Very special," he declared. "You are…closer to me. I'd rather you call me something more…personal."

I smiled, thrilled at this, at our special, *personal* relationship. "Of course, *Jonathon*…" I thrilled at saying his name. "You're the angel to guide me through my nightmares."

Our warm closeness was tempered by the urgency of omens. "But if my previous dream was anything like this one, we need to do something, or some poor girl named Cecilia will die."

He shuddered. "I'll try to demand information from the demon, should he come here again. I'll try to fight him, Natalie, however I can."

"As will I," I said, and that pledge shot me straight into consciousness, as if it were rousing me to action. I had no pleasant embrace or near-kiss to slip me into waking hours, only dread urgency and the name "Jonathon" upon my lips.

## LATER...

The first thing I did after waking, going to breakfast, and kissing my father on the head as he read the paper was to snatch it out of his hands for a moment, scanning the headlines anxiously. He patiently waited for me to be done with it.

"Looking for something exciting?" he asked with a touch of affectionate amusement, as he always did when I was passionately focused on something.

I plucked a pencil from the breakfast table (we always have plenty lying around for communication purposes) and wrote "gossip" on the margin and smiled at him. He chuckled and thankfully left it at that.

After darting down to the newsstand on a nearby street corner, I continued to scan the papers with shaking hands, waiting with a leaden heart to see news of a dead "Cecilia" somewhere off a dim and dirty alley in some dim and dirty room.

But such a demise was nowhere to be seen. I hoped that my mind had played only a cruel coincidence in having named Barbara before her death and that my dreams were not portents but nightmares alone. Still, I couldn't sit idly by.

The last time the demon went on a rampage, he'd inflicted a terrible scar on Denbury. And a woman named Barbara had indeed been beheaded downtown. Might another murderous rampage do Lord Denbury's soul irreparable damage? My dear Jonathon.

Mrs. Northe had said that more women should not die for the sake of evidence, and I agree with her. Today I've begun making preparations. I will indeed turn and face my nightmares and go from the pursued to the pursuing.

We need information to reverse the curse. The police can't be trusted to understand supernatural subtleties. If anything happens to the body in question—Jonathon's double—all is lost. His body can't be caught, not yet.

So I will follow the beast myself.

If it happens like last time, the devil will likely visit the portrait before his crime. But since the demon quite liked the look—and the vulnerability—of me, I'll have to not be *me* to observe him.

I'll become a night watchman. Using Father's seal, I'll forge an assignment on the lower level of the Metropolitan and wait for the fiend to appear. Then I'll follow the abomination…into the mouth of Hell, if that's what it takes.

The plan laid out in my mind as if it was divinely inspired. Perhaps it was. Because the moment I thought it up, I knew it was right and I knew there was no turning back. And I hoped, for my sake, that I'd have a host of guardian angels on my side. I'll need them among the dark places the demon's kind has created, where poor creatures lose their moral compass and where others fall victim to their own poverty and weakness. Dark places where some women are set upon because they were unfortunate enough to have been born girls.

Father has been talking of cleaning his closet for some time. In the guise of good housekeeping, I today alleviated him of an old suit. Our local tailor down the street thankfully knows my condition and is always prepared to greet my note and instructions without so much as a second glance.

Mr. Tabb thankfully did not raise an eyebrow when my note said to alter the suit for a "smaller-sized cousin." (That "cousin" being *me*.) There's no going into the belly of a

# SCHOLASTIC BOOK FAIRS

SEED SCHOOL OF MARYLAND

FAIR:   3626647

TERM: 410-105-400              TRANS: 0000668

06/06/2016                          09:00 AM

**SALE**

```
* UNFRIENDED......................  8.99
GOSSIP FILE (MC)..................  6.99
ALLIE FIRST AT LAST...............  5.99
```

```
               Sub Total:        21.97
               ----------
               Net Sale:         21.97
            Non-Taxable:         21.97
               Taxable:           0.00
            6.00% Tax:            0.00
               ----------
              Total Due:         21.97
     PURCHASE ORDER 147:         21.97
               ----------
             Total Paid:         21.97
```

TOTAL ITEMS                              3

* Item Contains Mature Themes
Thank you for shopping at our
school's Scholastic Book Fair
Visit www.scholastic.com
for great information on books
and reading!

beast as a woman. As a mute man, I was still at a disadvantage, but in men's clothing the world is more accessible. Remaining unrecognizable to my target was imperative.

I've learned a thing or two from Shakespeare's roles where women dress as men for protection and information. There's plenty of artifice and espionage in great literature, so this adventure of mine will merely carry on a familiar legacy. At least, that's what I tell myself. Truth be told, I'm terrified.

Yet the truth remains that the moment I stepped through that canvas, my life changed irrevocably. I will never be the same because of Denbury. Fantastical, difficult, and dangerous possibilities follow in his wake. And I'm helplessly wrapped up in them. In him.

Before I undertake what may be life-threatening, I need to spend more time with Denbury, to truly befriend him and get to know him, because what I'll attempt is too much to risk for a mere stranger—though I feel I know him closely...*intimately* (an unsettling notion in and of itself). I need to truly know what sort of man I may be risking my life for. Madness, portents, runes, and spells aside, we need a moment to be *friends*. Mrs. Northe also insists that I "tend his soul."

I'm off to the museum and I'll write anon.

## LATER...

I wore my prettiest dress, feminine and appealing, a light green the color of my eyes, to the museum in the afternoon. I found Father, indicated I'd be sketching somewhere downstairs, and went promptly to the exhibition room. Staring up at Jonathon, I could see that his striking face looked exhausted. Truly, we did not have much time.

I dipped my hand into the canvas and tumbled, per usual, into the arms of the prince of this dark tale. I let him hold me and did not ease away. He took in my appearance, and from his expression, he was pleased.

"Your real self is brighter than your dream self," he said. "More solid and sure."

"Would that that were the case out there as well." I indicated my body on the other side.

"Your beauty would remain the same."

I smiled widely, and the whole room seemed somehow charged with hope, possibility, and passion.

"I do not want you to be some trapped secret," I breathed, twirling about his space as if it were an open field. "I want to stroll proudly arm in arm with you along the East and Hudson Rivers and show you the wonders of my great city. I want to use my newfound voice to laugh, to giggle, to make blessed, normal *noise*, for us to enjoy the fruits of the world as a normal boy and girl might do.

No dread silence, no souls split from bodies, curses, or demons to spoil it…"

"All of that sounds wonderful. We must cling to that hope."

"Yes. I'll need it for what I'm about to do."

His brow furrowed. "What do you mean?"

"I have an idea," I said nonchalantly, not wishing to arouse his worry. "About how to help you. But not until nightfall. In the meantime, I was hoping we could talk—a normal conversation having nothing to do with demons, black magic, or curses. If I wouldn't be bothering you."

He shifted my weight against himself, reaching down for my hand. He brought it to his mouth and kissed it. I shivered with delight. "Nothing about you could ever be a bother. But don't you dare risk anything for me—"

I placed a finger to his lips, and we both shuddered at the touch. "I'm not sure I have any choice."

My voice had grown soft. Danger was replaced with a different kind of tension as we drifted closer, inexorably pulled together.

But despite all the custom that we'd abandoned, I was nervous. And in this reality, nerves meant I was chatty. An opposite of the outside world, where nerves made me silent.

"Mrs. Northe told Father that she is coming for me. Which means she has ideas to share," I said quietly, wanting nothing more than to give in to the spell of this peculiar world and to Jonathon's magnetism, but awkwardness overtook me. "So we'd best…take care. At any moment our unlikely chaperone might arrive." I glanced out past the frame into the museum room, staring at that odd statue of myself on the other side.

He reluctantly slid away from me, but not far.

"Tell me tales of tending the ill," I said, flouncing my skirts around me in a dainty circle on the Persian rug, preening as I'd seen Maggie do and wanting to pose for him as if I were his artist model. "Bide the time with me until Mrs. Northe comes."

His eyes lit, the sunken circles lessening, as if his life was rekindled. A soul without purpose withers. Recalled to his purpose, Jonathon was magnificent.

He began by telling me how he had watched many friends and extended family die of disease. Ours were both hearts that had been steeled by loss. Frightened that death was somehow a curse, he had sought refuge in science and medicine. From the age of twelve, he had studied anatomy books to learn whatever he could. He was told by professionals that he was gifted, and this encouraged him to think what he might be able to do in the world. The passion and zeal with which he spoke of medicine nearly took the weariness out of him and almost healed the scar on his face.

I could have listened to him for hours.

But I noticed Mrs. Northe, a hazy figure, standing

patiently beside my body. I could not keep her waiting, as much as I wanted Denbury to keep sharing his passions and interests with me. His enthusiasm reminded me that I was helping a noble soul. He was indeed an angel in my dreams, and he embodied that in my waking hours. I needed to believe in him. It was good to be reminded why I should pin my heart on him before I undertook risk on his behalf.

"I'll come again. I promise—"

He bent down and lifted me to my feet. "You, Natalie, I want more of you. I want to know everything about you, my partner in magic and madness, absolutely everything."

No one had taken such an interest in me, and whether it was only because he hoped I was his savior I couldn't know, but I didn't care. I was important to him. I was his link to the world. I was all he had. And as for me, I'd never had something to fight for. As odd as my life had become with him, it was impossible to imagine life—waking or sleeping—without him.

He snatched my hand again and kissed it. "I want to know *everything*…"

I wasn't sure what he meant by those words, but the look in his eyes had my body on fire. My experience within the painting went beyond fancy, intrigue, or schoolgirl obsession. This was undoubtedly much deeper. I couldn't understand all the magic. But I did understand desire. If

I wasn't careful, it would distract me from my purpose. Once a girl had been kissed, everything changed. It was a matter of time...

But this wasn't the right moment.

"Indeed," I replied, wondering what sorts of promises my eyes were giving him. "And so you shall."

I sank back with that uneasy drop into myself, not sure I would ever get used to such an odd feeling. Mrs. Northe steadied me, now accustomed to the dizzy wave that followed.

She didn't ask about our chat but likely made assumptions about my blush. Instead she had turned to stare intently at Denbury's nameplate, which read:

JONATHON WHITBY III, LORD DENBURY, 1880

"What's odd about this, Natalie?" Mrs. Northe asked.

After staring at the nameplate for a while, I gestured to how the plate did not match the frame, and I ran my finger below Lord Denbury's name, searching for another plate where I would expect the artist's name to be engraved.

"Exactly," Mrs. Northe said, undoing her cameo brooch from around her throat. "The artist's name is missing, and the plate doesn't quite go, does it? I'd be willing to bet that the body that crumpled in the Denbury estate was that of the artist used for this work, discarded when it was no longer useful. I'll corral my contacts in England, and perhaps I can find out the painter's identity."

"Without a manhunt?" I countered in sign. Surely none of this could be left to the average police operation, not the New York police, nor Scotland Yard; no average detective's methods were suited for this.

"My contacts are always discreet," Mrs. Northe replied. "In no way do I want to jeopardize this painting or the sanctity of the body that's been overtaken."

She suddenly knelt, brooch in hand. Using the dainty edge to unwind the screws holding in the nameplate, she had it off in a moment. As she removed the thin brass strip, I saw that something was painted below. Another set of runes. No, not runes. Hieroglyphs.

Mrs. Northe flipped open a small pad of paper and copied down the markings. Outlined by an oval on its side, the set of markings resembled another cartouche of sorts. Mrs. Northe just as efficiently returned the shining gold nameplate to its position on the edge of the frame. "I'll look this up tonight," she said. "These are disparate pieces. But together they'll make a whole."

And she returned me home.

I'm left to contemplate what questionable bravery is ahead of me.

From the Desk of Mrs. Evelyn Northe

June 16, 7 a.m.

Dear Natalie,

I do not know if I'll be able to meet with you today, and in the interest of your father (and Maggie—dear Lord, the girl asks me too many questions) not thinking we're up to something suspicious, I shouldn't see you daily. But I must tell you this:

The frame truly is a door, Natalie. The hieroglyphs found below the nameplate mean "ba." It signifies a doorway through which the spirit may enter. The Egyptians believed that the soul had seven parts: the *aakhu*, the *ab*, the *ba*, the *ka*, the *khaibut*, the *khat*, and the *ren*. One of these, the "ba" part of the soul, passes through a false door set into the stone of their tombs. Ancient Egyptians were preoccupied with death almost more than life. This furthers my idea that the fiend has created and perfected the ability to split the soul (including, it would seem, the reasoned consciousness) from the body and cast it across a "ba" threshold and into a prison: a box, a painting, perhaps anything.

The frame as a doorway explains the duality of Denbury's body both outside and inside the frame. It also confirms that the fiend has created a veritable portal that has a certain flexibility, and it is my hope that where you have been granted the ability to travel between, so may the devil that created the threshold. The trick will be switching them out, one for the other.

"Vessel" is writ on the cartouche around his neck, and "ba," the spirit door, writ upon the frame. The building blocks of the spell are clearly labeled. I hope to determine yet further ingredients. Tell me if you glean anything more from Denbury.

And I'd like to take you shopping next Sunday. A seamstress, then a milliner. What think you? You don't seem to own any mauve, and I think you'd look charming in mauve.

Yours, Evelyn

I received that letter first thing in the morning, and thankfully Father had left for work. I had feigned disinterest in going to the museum. (It would not do to seem predictable. Father knew me as a woman of many moods. I needed to remain consistently unpredictable so he wouldn't question what had become of the daughter he knew.) But the daughter he knew was changed. Different. Haunted.

In love.

And scared.

But there's much to do! I'm thankful for having the day to do it unhindered. If I'd spent time with Mrs. Northe, I most likely would have confessed my plan and she'd surely have stopped me.

This spying in disguise is not the only possible plan hatching in my feverish brain. Something else is burning at the edge of my mind, thoughts of a confrontation yet to come. The thought of it hangs like that billowing bit of white lace and the maddening Whisper of my childhood, truth just on the edge of my sight, a sound too faint to be heard.

But first…espionage.

I'm not sure where my bravery has come from, save for the simple knowledge of what must be done. This course is as clear to me as a mathematical equation with only one solution, an adventure plot with a single way forward. For as impossible as things have become, the choices I face are startlingly clear. My instincts feel guided by some higher force. Still, I'm stewing with nerves.

Considering what I am about to undertake, I wonder if I've gone a bit mad, at last cracking under all this strain.

## 10 P.M.

*(The house is asleep.)*

Staring into the mirror, I don't look half bad.

A pretty youth.

Beauty, no matter its gender, has opportunities and advantages—an English lord surely knows that.

But my inability to speak worries me most. My vocal

success, thanks to the world of the painting, has not translated into my reality. All I can emit are strangled sounds unable to be connected into words. I know I need to practice, but I can't bear the sound or the idea that my household might discover me healed and rush to entirely readjust my world as I know it. No, one upheaval at a time. And on my terms.

As for how to justify my silence, being simply mute as I dare to enter a den of iniquity would be begging for trouble. How could I lend my silence a threatening quality? The answer made me grin despite myself.

I went to a small box I cherished from school. A makeup kit.

When the Connecticut Asylum attempted a theatrical production, it was a pitiful event, but I admired the teachers for their optimism and their efforts. I was the resident wizard of the brush; my artistic skills with grease-paint and prosthetic were legendary. Our presentation of *A Midsummer Night's Dream* was the height of irony, for our Titania was blind and could not see when Bottom had gained the head of an ass, and so the entire comedy of her infatuation was moot. However, the effects I offered the fairies and mechanicals were highly praised.

This evening, in under an hour I created such an ugly, off-putting gash around my throat that no one dared question why I was silent or, hopefully, the type of company someone with such a token would keep. It would be my most identifying mark, one that would disappear at the end of my night.

And where was I headed? Well, wherever the demon would lead. If his first strike was any indication, and if, like ghosts, he was a creature of habit, he would go again to the Five Points.

The infamous, legendary Five Points. A few miles south from my home but a whole world away. While the crime in the area was severe, I wondered if legend had made it larger than life. I recall some of my father's friends championing the area as having been one of the most culturally interesting places in the city—a place where boundaries hardly existed and cultures mixed freely. That was the area's virtue and its bane.

But the horrific Draft Riots had changed all that when I was a toddler. Negro men, women, and children were chased, mobbed, and beaten, a man even torn to pieces by angry Irish mobs who resented being drafted into the Civil War when the rich could buy their way out. So the ward certainly had its historical demons, let alone any who wished to terrorize it today.

As for the logistics of getting to this infamous neighborhood, I'd follow the demon's lead and take a carriage—I would have one waiting for me. Handing a large enough bill to the driver would ensure service. I dearly hoped my poor father didn't count his bills each day, lest he miss these few grand ones that would hopefully gain me entrances and keep me alive. I'd beg fresh ones from Mrs. Northe and claim dire necessity. Surely she'd understand the urgency.

I have tucked my small yet trusted knife into my pocket. One may wonder how a young lady might come to be in the possession of a knife. I'm not ashamed to tell you that I'd gained it by disarming a boy at school. Having threatened me, this boy justly deserved to lose the ivory-handled piece. If I've learned one thing about boys, it's that they dearly need to understand the notion of consequences for their actions.

Here I pause to recall the moment of glory. I disarmed the cretin myself (I grow prouder of this moment the more I recall it), and while he was far larger than I, I was a quick study.

I'd been watching a fighting class from my window, looking down onto the green where the deaf and the mute boys (not the blind ones, of course) practiced fencing, sword fighting, and basic moves with a staff. I stole any moment I could to practice thrusts and parries, a stick in hand, while watching from two flights above.

I was, at least in perfect imitation, quite good. And so when the heathen (certainly no gentleman) brandished the knife in front of me, I disarmed him. He was appropriately shocked and too embarrassed to ask for it back, and

I wouldn't have given it to him anyway, as I had earned it. But I digress.

This is the story of my trip to the Five Points, not about my personal armory. However, the knife story is one that should go down in my annals, and so it has, to bolster me. But enough of proud memory. I tucked the knife in my trousers, in a place of close reach, and there it remains. A small comfort against the enormity of my nerves. Say prayers for me, dear diary. I'll need them.

## LATER...

Here I sit in my hiding place at the museum, waiting for the fiend's visit.

I could have easily walked the distance from home to the museum, but when I saw an available carriage, I hailed him by stepping in front of his lanterns.

Holding out a previously written note for the driver, I stared at him with hard eyes that didn't wait for him to ask why I didn't speak instructions to him. He nodded, and I jumped in. In moments I was out again and starting up the museum stairs, wondering how long I'd have to wait before a familiar, beautiful face with the shade of a devil might tread these same stairs.

The moonlight was bright and illuminated the redbrick and gray granite details of the museum, making it look like a Gothic palace in a haunted tale. I'd heard talk of renovations and expansions to create a building that would loom large and luminously white over Fifth Avenue. How much more grand and ghostly would the museum look in the future?

I had no guarantee that the beast would come here. But instinct—and my dreams—told me that his visit was likely enough for me to try.

As I ascended to the arched doors, I held the keys Mrs. Northe had made for me tightly, feeling guilty for having lied to her. I had promised her I would do nothing rash and nothing alone. Denbury exists in the painting, a friend in this odd quest, though trapped and unable to lend a hand. But I couldn't put Mrs. Northe in jeopardy in what's clearly my task. I have been chosen for this. Forces beyond me have stated this implicitly. Perhaps I was born for this. I am just as capable as the young men I'd read about in adventure books (save that I'm mute and a girl). Then again, adventure often favors the improbable.

At the door, I flashed the guard a note saying I had been hired as a rear post. The note was stamped with a Metropolitan seal that I'd gained from Father's desk. The guard could have cared less and opened the front doors for me. I'd hoped the guard would be lax, but his indifference did make me fear for the safety of the art.

As I descended to the exhibition room, I straightened

masculine coat sleeves that felt oddly at angles on my body and wondered what Jonathon would think. There was no turning back, I thought, as I drew back the curtain. I did not hesitate to slip my fingers onto the canvas and into the cool pool, and to step through.

I fell, as usual, against him. But instead of the embrace I'd grown unashamedly accustomed to, I was greeted with: "Who the devil are you?"

"It's Natalie," I replied.

Jonathon gaped. "What on earth are you doing dressed as a boy?"

"When your double comes to call, I plan to follow him," I replied.

His eyes widened. "You cannot be serious."

I shrugged. "I cannot involve the police. They'd arrest your body, and then what would you do? We need information! We need to know about the runes and the poetry, the carving on your arm, the cartouche, and the ritual. We need to discover our lynchpin, to find out how it all comes together. I won't interact with the beast, merely observe."

Shaking his head, he stated, "I cannot allow you to undertake such risk on my account, to descend into the very depths of Hell itself."

"It's not Hell, it's the Five Points. Though I have heard the two equated."

"I will keep you here by force." He grabbed my arm, his face flushed, defiant, and never more handsome.

"And what good will that do either of us? Let me take my hiding place in the alcove around the corner so that I may listen, slip out behind him, and see what occurs."

"You're mad!"

"Do you want out of this mess or not?"

Jonathon gaped at me. "You're not frightened?"

My subsequent laugh sounded a bit hysterical, my nerves now on display. "Oh, quite. But Mrs. Northe has assured me that our fates have become entwined whether we like it or not, so I might as well try to be useful."

"You're the bravest woman I know…" He approached me, taking my hands, lifting my cap to touch my curls, and seeking the me who was more familiar to him. "Don't do this—"

"Hush, don't be sentimental and don't act like I'm going to die, please," I grumbled, though I couldn't help leaning into his outstretched hand a bit. It was then he noticed the tip of the red gash I'd fashioned and he gasped.

"Good God—"

"Theatrical effect," I assured him. "To explain my lack of voice in a way that denotes the company I keep rather than my weakness."

His horror turned to admiration. "That's brilliant. You are absolutely *brilliant*."

"I've read too many books," I replied, and we shared a grin.

"Promise me you'll be careful. I couldn't bear anything happening to you," he said achingly.

"Of course you couldn't." I smiled. "Without me you'll be doomed."

"In more ways than one."

My heart fluttered.

As he caught my hand, I didn't want to look at him. I didn't want to second-guess this or have time to think of all the terrible possibilities. I needed momentum to propel me forward, but he grasped my hand and cupped my cheek, and I truly thought he was going to kiss me after all. My knees weakened at the thought of it, but he seemed to remember himself and kissed my forehead instead.

"You beautiful fool, be careful," he murmured. "I'll be with you. If your dreams are connected to me, then surely I can project myself to you."

"Like my guardian angel."

"Always."

I think that if I hadn't been dressed as a boy, we might have kissed, then and there. I resolved to come back very soon. In a dress.

"Why are you putting yourself at such risk for me?" he asked.

I paused and almost said it was because I loved him. But a nervous wash came over me and kept me from the words.

I wasn't sure how he'd take them. "It feels like destiny," I said instead, breaking from his gaze. "When the demon comes, press him for answers—where he's going, what he's doing. Mrs. Northe insists our best clues lie in *why*. Make him explain himself."

Jonathon smirked wearily. "You mean we can't rely on literary convention and wait for the beast to simply state his evil plot to his unwitting prey?"

I chuckled. "Oh, it's a better tale if you bait him. And if you're furious, I daresay he'll tell you more."

"Of course. I'll do whatever I can," he promised.

I smiled, turned, and stepped forward. He instinctively reached for me but drew away as I stared at his hand. "I'll see you soon, Jonathon," I said over my shoulder. "I'll return in a dress."

I tumbled back out and into my disguised self, and turned to the portrait, where his lordship stood as handsome as ever, if not a bit worried looking, at the center. I took my place behind the small, nondescript locked door opposite the open one that awaited the demon of the hour.

It's here that I've written down these most recent accounts while I wait. Since having fallen through worlds to meet Lord Denbury, time seems so differently fluid, even when I am outside the painting.

I feel the temperature around me chill.

There's a hissing crackle.

The beast has come!

## FIFTEEN MINUTES LATER

Back in the carriage, I've instructed we maintain pursuit. I must take down details!

It was a shock to see the devil of Denbury again in the flesh. From the keyhole I could see him framed in the doorway, standing in my reality, his beauty unmatched in this world or in any other.

My breath stilled. There stood the man who had changed my life. A strong impulse made me want to fling open the door and run to him, to shake him loose of the demon, to speak as I knew him, to save him by my very presence. He already knew me and was already intrigued by me. He *wanted* me. Meeting in our mutual world could set him free to be my prince after all.

But then the creature laughed, and I was jarred by the cruel illusion. I couldn't trust my senses. If the painted world of Jonathon's spirit had witchcraft that lured me, his bodily reality had the same magic outside the prison. But this stolen vessel was a murderer, made beautiful and cruel. The trouble was that both Denburys continued to have a profound effect on me.

Looking at this Denbury played tricks of the mind, so

I stayed against the wall, straining to hear through the keyhole. The villain spoke, pressing his face in through the barrier of the painting, as if it were a basin of water. His words careened around the room through a super-natural echo like wild birds flapping desperately with no way out. I shuddered. The demon owned Jonathon's voice but with something inhuman layered upon his fair British tone.

"Hello again, my vessel," it said. "My, you look well. We'll soon fix that right up, though."

There was a rustling sound, muffled but angry. I felt a surge of pride. Jonathon was doing what we had asked, baiting the demon with his fury. The more defiant he became, the more the demon would drive home his hopelessness. It was the way of evil. Just as Iago condemns Shakespeare's audiences into becoming accomplices to Desdemona's murder by the provoked Othello, so were we, Jonathon's soul and I, condemned to this eager confession.

"You can do nothing to stop me, boy. Barbara's blood is hardly dry, yet there is plenty of other tender, vulnerable meat directly nearby."

There must have been a further challenge. I could not hear it, but the creature made a chuckling reply: "It is human nature. Hypocrites will tear down one house of sin only to help build another next door. Sin moves easily, a vagabond, and we move fluidly within our own. I feed on the weak, and you suffer the consequences. It is as the Creator intended—"

I started at this blasphemy and so did Jonathon, evidently, for his response had the beast roaring with amusement.

"Yes, yes, blind fealty to your Creator, but where is He now? I walk among you, but *He* does not. Fitting to do my work in your form, you who are so fond of weaklings. Where are the holy namesakes of these women as their lifeblood runs through my fingers?" He cackled, a disgusting laugh. "The world is not prepared for our new dawn. These first sacrifices are but the birthing pains. We've an empire to build, my dear Englishman."

And then the beast withdrew from the painting. He walked away whistling, life and death his playthings.

Thankful for deep shadows, I followed, my heart in my throat and terror at the ready to overtake me in a swoon. But I thought of Robinson Crusoe and the Count of Monte Cristo, of the Musketeers and all the idols whom I've worshipped since I had first devoured their adventurous tales. I was doing them all proud.

The hired carriage awaited per my instructions, sheltered from moonlight by a copse of trees on the uptown side of the building and ready to follow surreptitiously down the avenue. Knowing the building intimately, I slipped out a shaded side entrance devoid of guards and hurried to the driver, pointing at the fine carriage already paces ahead. He nodded, and we were off.

The demon's words ring in my mind, my dread of him pounding in syncopation with my heartbeat. I had hoped for an insight into the beast's specific madness, not premonitions of some infernal revolution…Forgive my bobbing script. It was good that I hardly ate anything at supper; otherwise, I might lose it as the carriage tosses and turns.

We proceeded on a slanting course down Broadway, where the finer blocks are lit by gas lamps but many others are not. We passed the occasional theater, stable, and grand palace where ill repute supposedly reigns in back rooms. Farther down we passed the even grander shopping palaces lining Ladies' Mile, a place I've always yearned to promenade.

But promenading is the talk of fine ladies. Fine ladies don't journey to the Five Points to track a demonic murderer inhabiting the body of the man they love.

Well, if I'm indeed living an adventure novel, there must be a love story. There's *always* a love story. I'm so fond of literary tradition, and right now, its consistency remains my only comfort.

The carriage ahead of us slows. The puddles are thick—the street hasn't been cleared of horse manure or foul human waste. We must be nearing the Five Points area. The carriage appears to be slowing near Anthony Street. Searching for what, I don't know. Number 66. And there goes my quarry! Down from the carriage and gliding up the stoop. I shall wait a moment and then follow him. You, dear diary, will remain tucked into the bandages binding my chest, right over my heart. You may make a nice shield against a bullet or a blade.

I've been captured! I know not where I'm going. I'm in a carriage. Heading north, I think. I can write only a quick note:

Dear Father, if you find this diary, please know that I love you and that all of my actions have been to try to help a dear soul who deserved help. You'll never believe a word of it, but it's all true. I love you and thank you for everything you've done for me.


## LATER...

Obviously I'm not dead.

Thank the Lord, I live to write these words. I must recount what happened inside that frightening residence turned house of horrors.

I'll have to tell you of Cecilia and Midge and the whole of the events in the Five Points, but first let me say what happened in regards to my capture.

You see, I had relaxed too soon. All seemed well and my escape assured. I had gleaned important information while inside 66 Anthony Street. Upon leaving the premises and breathing a sigh of relief, I was grabbed roughly and tossed into a cab heading uptown. I tried the door—willing to fling myself into the street to escape—but it was locked from the outside.

Could Crenfall have trailed us or discovered that I was a spy? How could anyone have known? I was so unremarkable…Or maybe my disguise was absurd.

I did recall that a carriage had pulled in behind us, making a trio as we headed downtown. It was a cab that had sidled onto Fifth Avenue from the shadows. In my recollection, the traffic had been heavy around Longacre Square and Forty-Second Street, a place so filled with carriages that it was impossible to determine whether we still had a tail. I gazed out the window and couldn't stop shaking.

Surely it was Crenfall, I thought. My father wouldn't have the good sense to have me followed.

The team of horses came to a halt, and I couldn't help a sigh of relief at the familiar sight outside the window. Mrs. Northe's Fifth Avenue town house—

But then panic seized me again. If she'd called upon my father, I'd never be let out of my room. I'd lose any freedom my post at the Metropolitan had offered, and I'd be off to the convent for sure.

The man who had collared me outside 66 Anthony Street dragged me roughly out of the carriage and nearly pushed me up the walk to Mrs. Northe's home. He likely expected me to ask him who he was or make some claim of protestation. Maybe he knew I didn't speak. He didn't say a word either but gripped my arm as he pressed the bell. I shrugged him off to stand proudly. I had nothing to be ashamed of.

And yet, in the next moment, I stood ashamed and dressed as a boy in Mrs. Northe's foyer as she looked me up and down.

She examined me as if measuring my disguise, circling me and clucking her tongue. Despite my fear and embarrassment, I detected a bit of pride in Mrs. Northe's face.

"You," she said, her tone scolding, "have read too many books."

She waited. I assume she wanted me to agree. I shrugged.

She continued. "And you put yourself in grave danger and I shall not easily forgive you for it. And I may have to tell your father."

I furiously signed pleas, begging her not to doom me.

And then she smiled. "Unless you tell me everything that happened. I had my man follow you in case you did something unforgivably stupid. He was to bring you directly to me once you satisfied your…curiosity."

"Your man?" I signed. "He was hardly a gentleman," I added, rubbing the arm he had grabbed.

"I don't pay him to be a gentleman. I pay him to be quiet and brilliant."

"I was gathering evidence," I signed. "You said we couldn't sit back—"

"Indeed. Do tell. But only after you've made yourself back into a woman. And good God, wipe that terrible thing off your throat. That's hideous. But quite well done, I must say."

I loved this woman. Once dressed, I did tell her everything, and she escorted me home at a full three in the morning! I slipped in and up the stairs while everyone was asleep. I still wonder how she knew to have me followed. Her instincts were usually uncanny, yes, but that had been downright psychic.

But without further ado, here's the tale of 66 Anthony Street.

It was so dark in the place that one could easily get away with murder. And so likely the fiend assumed, rightly so, that he would not be recognized again—even with the newspaper descriptions. He did not bother to remove his hat or his cloak, which served to further obscure his face.

I did not immediately slip in behind the creature, of course. I have more sense than that. I waited until a few minutes had passed and then mounted the crumbling stairs and slipped into another world. It was as distinctly different a threshold as stepping through a painting...

I did not worry that the vile possessor of Denbury

would notice my entrance. The place was hazy with smoke and deep in shadow. Even after the darkness of night, my eyes needed a moment to adjust. I was shocked that the place was unlocked, though I had noticed silhouettes at windows, likely paid to watch the front door from up above and from across the street. This was an area the police were loath to visit. Vice had a reprieve here.

From the exterior, the building looked like an average town house, not terribly run down, but its drawn curtains and shuttered windows hid the hazy, acrid reality from outside view.

Once inside, I could see that the main parlor was strewn with bodies. The fiend walked among them, keeping his face to the shadows and tucking a wad of money into his pocket. I shuddered anew when I saw another familiar face already within the establishment. Standing against the wall and looking like an awkward statue as a shaft of light unpleasantly illuminated him was Crenfall.

It was good indeed that I was in disguise. A frisson of fear ran through me. Almost immediately, I felt a hand upon my shoulder. But no one was there. I saw a faint pulse of hazy white light. My angel. He was reaching out to me, aiding me in a way only his soul could.

And I suddenly felt invincible.

I thought I'd walked into a veritable morgue, but the bodies strewn about stirred listlessly, a swarm of nearly naked flesh with pipes hanging from their mouths. Permeating the room was the stench of body odor, perfume, sweat, and smoke. The smoke had a peculiar scent, and then I realized what it must be: opium. An opium den. As I reached that realization, a portly man towered over me. His eyes were slanted in suspicion—the proprietor, no doubt. His Irish accent was brash.

"I don't know ye, boy. And I know everyone who walks through that door," he said, and then his eyes flickered over to the fiend possessor with confused fear.

Likely, as Denbury's possessor had said, the familiar clientele had merely moved to a new address, and I was not a welcome member. I had prepared my written tablet and prayed to God that the proprietor could read.

*I want a girl,* my paper said.

The proprietor laughed. "And yer too scared to say so? How old are ye, thirteen?"

I shifted my cravat to reveal the scar. I turned the page of my notebook, the phrase having been written: *You do not want to know how I received that.*

The proprietor seemed delighted and intrigued, and his nervous glances toward Denbury eased with this new game. "Pick yer lass if ye got the money," he said.

I lifted up a promising bill. His watery eyes widened.

"How 'bout the quiet one? Ye'll make quite a pair." He reached into the shadows—with frightening nimbleness

LEANNA RENEE HIEBER

for such a round man—and pulled a scrawny young woman, likely my age, into the lamplight. She cringed and would not look me in the eye. My heart broke for her.

A larger, fierce-eyed woman launched herself from the wall upon which she'd been leaning and moved closer. Her gaze flickered from Denbury's body to me to the proprietor to the girl he had grabbed. The girl also regarded the form of Denbury with horror. The women strewn about the ground were too drowsy and in the haze of opium to notice him. That could be the last mistake of their lives.

I nodded to the girl and then turned to look at the other woman.

"You're a pretty lad. Why don't you take me and leave poor Cecilia alone? You need a woman to teach you a thing or two, boy, not another mute."

Cecilia.

My heart convulsed. I heard the Whisper. This is why I was here. I would yet save a life tonight.

I had to calm my racing heart and focus on the larger woman protecting this girl. I liked her for it, though I shuddered to think they actually believed I was a boy. I stared at Cecilia. *Another mute?* My heart broke further. I wished I could help any and every woman who had fallen into this trap. This entire situation was unbelievably upsetting.

The proprietor was hovering. "No, Midge, the boy takes Cecilia. We need to get her…"

208

He trailed off when I handed him another bill, hoping money would ensure his cooperation or at least keep him from being meddlesome. The wealthy had long made a habit of getting away with things relative to how much they could pay for silence. I made a motion for him to leave us in peace. He whistled and did so.

Cecilia stared at me blankly. She took my hand in her tiny one and began to lead me down the hall. I resisted and held up a hand, motioning for her to wait. I was on the lookout for the beast in Denbury's body. He had taken up the pipe of a hookah and was sitting with a woman splayed across him. My blood roared in my veins to see a man I cared for so sullied. It took everything in me not to draw my blade upon the beautiful creature, to call him out for everything he was and demand he be accountable. My own reaction was startling. My protectiveness toward Jonathon had made me brave. Or stupid.

There was another stilling hand upon my shoulder, a reminder sent to me upon the wings of our tied souls. The man I cared for was not physically here. I needed to stay on task for him.

The tall woman, Midge, leaned close. "You're interested in that dandy, aren't you? Your eyes keep flickering over to him and have since you walked in. Are you here for him, rather than for a good time?"

I shook my head, not wanting my business known. I

took Cecilia's hand with more authority and began to lead her into one of the open rooms lit by a tallow candle just a yard away. At the door I paused. Cecilia led me into the tiny room furnished only with a bed and reeking of smells I do not wish to recount.

She shut the door behind her and turned to me, trembling, in her moth-eaten chemise and thin skirt. These were her underthings, and the idea of having to sit in rooms only in one's undress was horrifying. She batted mousy brown hair out of her eyes and began to fumble at my cravat, noticing the scar with a frown.

Moving her hand aside, I backed away. She looked at me, confused, and gestured to herself as if her body was self-explanatory. I shook my head. I was with one of my kind, which was perfect—no one would know what we were talking about!

I signed: "I need help. Information."

She stared at me blankly. "There's a man out there." I gestured beyond the door and kept signing. "Handsome. But odd—"

She kept staring at me with a hollowed gaze. My heart sank. Of course she didn't know sign language. I scribbled the same sentences on my pad of paper. She stared at the paper, then up at me, and shook her head. Of course she couldn't read.

I was a privileged fool, and I made note to thank God

and my father more often for what I had been given that so many women of the age had not.

Her tired face with its sunken cheekbones softened, and it seemed almost as if she wanted to laugh. We were quite the pair.

I pulled out the newspaper. Perhaps the picture would help. I pointed to the police sketch resembling Denbury. Cecilia pointed out to the main parlor. Her eyes widened. I pointed at the picture and opened my hands, helpless. I hoped she would see that I needed information, and then I'd find a way to warn her of the danger I inexplicably knew she was in.

Cecilia held up a finger and left the room before I could reach for her. The proprietor was immediately barking at her, telling her he'd kill her if she abandoned a client. He then started barking at Midge. I opened the door and held out another bill into the hallway. I didn't want to attract the demon Denbury's attention.

Cecilia returned with Midge, who laughed and closed the door behind her. "I suppose Cecilia still doesn't know how to take off a man's clothes." She started in on me, and I had to bat her hands away. "Oh, don't be scared, little boy." The tall woman chuckled. I shook my head.

I again lifted the newspaper article. I wrote on my pad. I would try again with Midge.

"Did you know Barbara? What do you know about him?"

I wrote and gestured to the hall. The tall woman could read, at least passably. I was relieved. But her eyes widened.

"Jesus, the police are sending them young these days. How old are you, thirteen? You're too pretty to be much older. You some sort of spy? If you're here to arrest us, I'd like to see you try."

I vehemently shook my head.

"Or…perhaps you knew Barbara?" she asked. I made my gaze tortured. "Ah," she added. "I see. I'm sorry. Terrible way to go."

"Did you see 'Barry' that night?" I wrote.

"No," Midge replied, "but my friends, they did. He's been about the area for a week, I'd say, 'round the Points. Hadn't thought him the violent type, big with the smoking and taking a lot of women. He's a fine-looking one but weird, they say."

Poor Denbury, his gentlemanly body thrown to such depths.

"Weird, how?" I wrote.

"The other girls at Cross Street said he wanted to know all their names. Like he was obsessed with them, so the boss tries to make nice and Knox starts rattling off a list, you know, and when he got to Barbara, Mr. Fancy over there let out a strange noise. 'That one,' he said. 'I want that one. I want her head.' Right crazy, if you ask me," Midge muttered.

Something jarred me, and my mind struggled to make sense of it. Names.

"He got what he wanted, didn't he?" Midge said sadly. "Beheaded her. And now he's back. Seems he's paid the whole block so much money no one will turn him in. No one ever listens to us anyway, sure not the police. They want nothin' to do with these acres of hell. But a beheading, shouldn't that count for something? Aren't we human? Don't we deserve better than that?"

I nodded my utmost agreement.

And then it came to me. Barbara. Beheaded. There was a girl back at the asylum obsessed with Catholic saints. Mary O'Donnell had relished telling of all the awful, ungodly ways in which they were martyred. Saint Barbara was beheaded. Jonathon had said that the beast mentioned the forty martyrs of England before overtaking him. Mary had listed those martyrs to me all in a torrent that was quite impressive. I recalled that several of them were named John...*Jonathon*. But the beast had wanted to call him John, like the saints.

"What's in a name"...indeed. The beast was going to kill as many saints as possible. They were offerings to his mad quest. Sacrifices. Martyrs.

My eyes widened. The women were staring at me.

And then the proprietor pounded on the door. "Cecilia!" he cried. "When yer done in there—and with a boy that young, I daresay it won't take long—ye've got another one who's taken with ye. A right British gent."

Cecilia's eyes grew wide.

Poor Saint Cecilia, how did she die?

I desperately tried to recall the other names Mary had imparted to me. As Lutherans, we're not as enamored of the saints, but such gruesome deaths were ingrained in me. Saint Cecilia had withstood many death attempts—suffocation, beheading, crucifixion. I could only imagine how Denbury would try this in a brothel room.

"*You must get her out of here*," I scribbled furiously, and Midge read my note aloud to Cecilia as I wrote. "*She has the name of a saint. It's about the saints. Tell any woman who has the name of a saint to change it, until he's caught.*"

Cecilia looked as if she was going to faint.

Midge pursed her lips. "Boy, we're all named for saints. There's a hell of a lot of them," she retorted. I gave her an exasperated look. "Well, we've nicknames too. Best use those. Come, I've a place we can go," Midge murmured, gathering Cecilia. "I'm not letting anything happen to you, girl. I swore to protect you, and I mean it."

Midge turned to me. "Thank you, lad. I don't know who but God sent you. May heaven and the saints be praised indeed. I'll tell any girl I know." She opened the door cautiously. Stepping outside, she grabbed Cecilia and hid her tiny frame in front of her as they moved quickly to a rear door. I followed, not wanting to face that beautiful demon again. The reality of how closely I had flirted with danger was overwhelming, and I felt sick to my stomach.

We were out the door before I heard the proprietor's yelp. Midge and Cecilia didn't wait or say another word. They were off into the shadows down alleys they knew far better than I did. I was between tenement buildings, a pile of wood scraps on one side of me and a stinking pile of trash on the other, rats squeaking between the two.

I was wondering how to get back to the front of the building and the carriage I hoped was still waiting where the streets opened onto a grim open space as the five streets came together, hence the name Five Points.

And that's when Mrs. Northe's man clapped me. The dread of the situation had begun to take hold once I saw panic on faces other than my own, so I'm surprised I did not have a fit right there when I was seized. I think the saints were with me after all.

I related all of this to Mrs. Northe, who was incredulous, but she commended me so highly for my deduction about the saints that you'd have thought I'd cured some disease with my brilliance. I couldn't stop blushing. Once I was presentable as a lady again, she seated me in her study and we discussed the matter.

"This is the key!" she cried. "Not only to the victims, but perhaps to even more. Well done, Natalie!"

She took her seat opposite me and leaned in, speaking

excitedly. "Naming has great power," Mrs. Northe said, "despite Shakespeare's protestation, a phrase our devil was all too eager to quote. Countless instances in works of folktale and faith invoke the power of the name. Poor Hagar, banished when she was about to give birth, is unnamed in the Bible until God calls her by name and establishes her for the ages. There are times when names are avoided, as in the case of something very evil, when things or persons shall not be named. Speaking the name is thought to give the unspeakable some power. Other instances may occur to you."

I grinned and a small sound of amusement came from me. I signed out many letters. "Rumpelstiltskin."

Mrs. Northe laughed.

I gestured to my forearm, thinking of my dream, Denbury's arm, and Barbara's corpse.

"It would seem carving the names is part of harnessing that power. I can't piece it together yet, and that may speak to greater spell-crafting. I can't think this only has to do with poor Lord Denbury. This devil has a bigger game afoot." She scratched her head. "Runes. Allusions to many faiths mixed with base signs of witchcraft and paganism, the stuff from which all faith was born. It has no one ownership. And that frightens me."

"Why?" I signed.

"Well, if it were just full of the telltale signs of the Golden

Dawn, theosophy, or some sort of subverted Masonic rite, we could just adhere to that for our answer, couldn't we? Just find the right restricted, scandalous book? But this is something new, and like I'd said, all those jealous gods pitted against one another in this ragtag assortment of religious weaponry. Jealousy makes sane men mad and gentle persons into murderers. Who knows what demons may do with it? Now how do we turn that very power back upon the beast?

"Let's think through the procedure Lord Denbury related. It's that phrase the demon said. I know that's the key, but it's not complete enough to send him back." She pointed at the phrase, running her finger over it and tapping one particular word. "This word does not make sense. It is not Latin. Part of it, but not the whole."

I cringed as she said a few of the words aloud, but she did so in English, rather than Latin—so that any power of the word was hopefully dispelled in translation.

"I send the *soulren* through the door…" She made a face. "In Latin or English, it doesn't make any sense. But once we wrap our minds around that final piece, we'll have the spell. Perhaps with the name thrown in—do you recall if he used the name Jonathon or John in the midst of the incantation? Because I find it hard to believe the beast wouldn't have been specific about it."

"John," I signed. "But the fiend gave no name. Without his, can we reverse the spell?"

"I don't know, and how could we gain such access? How do we lure and keep him close without his suspecting?"

An idea began to form like a ghost in the back of my mind. It terrified me, but the moment I began to dream it up, much like following the fiend, I knew it was right. I could speak in Denbury's world. It was time I started speaking in this one. No one would suspect me. Until it mattered most.

I took a deep breath and tried to speak, ignoring how much I hated the sound. The words were rough, and they came at great cost, amid tears, and it took a long time to wrestle with each sentence, to muscle each word. Mrs. Northe took my hand, patiently encouraging me.

Something supernatural had cured my voice. I had to imagine it possible here.

I thought of the press of Jonathon's spirit, a helping and encouraging hand, from one heart to another. I tried. And I spoke, though it seemed to take years to make my point.

"I spoke in Lord Denbury's world," I said, my voice slow. Dull. I struggled against my distaste. But I thought about the ease of my voice within the painting. It had grown strong there, and that helped me now. "I need to speak...in *this* world. If the devil comes...in ritual...*I'll* lure him close enough...to reverse the spell. He saw me. At the Art Association. And...I do not flatter myself to say that he liked what he saw." I shuddered. "He made that quite clear. But he won't suspect a woman he thinks mute, will he?"

Mrs. Northe watched me, worried, as if she wanted to fight this but couldn't.

"The longer we delay…the more women will die," I said.

We sat in silence for a while before Mrs. Northe said, "You must go to Denbury once more. Keep up his spirits. We need him whole. He'll need to be a strong anchor of soul and conscience if this can be reversed well. You bring hope into his darkened world. And he'll need every shred of it. Do you love him?"

I was unprepared for the question, but there was no use fighting it. "Yes." The word came out very clearly.

"Good. That will help."

Mrs. Northe did not agree to my plan, but she did not argue against it. The struggle on her face told me she wasn't sure she could. Then she arranged to take me home, and I crept in here to my bedchamber to relate all this.

I shall begin practicing, softly and in English, the phrase that must be said. Mrs. Northe and I will puzzle over the word we cannot make sense out of—I dare to use the Latin—*animusren*. A word that is and isn't Latin at once. But if I don't know what it means, then I have no power. But once I do…I will take the magic. And wield it.

Facing the impossible seems to be what I was made for, and I only pray my courage matches the boldness of my plans. I pray for Cecilia and all her kind. May they be safe this night. May Providence grant them a way out of a life that few would choose to live.

# June 18

The *Herald* appears to have missed the irony that it has included in its paper today. On the page opposite the text I have included is another hasty sketch of an infernal-looking Denbury, with an upside-down pentagram, which I learned from Mrs. Northe is oft used as a Satanist symbol, though right-side up the pentagram is a symbol of luck and prosperity and remains a fine talisman.

The irony occurs to me in regards to the symbol and the place. A five-pointed star. The Five Points.

The Devil is full of homage.

But here is his damage, from the *New York Herald*:

June 18, 1880

FIVE POINTS DEMON SLAYS AGAIN

The reign of terror continues. The tortured body of Laura May was found in a squalid room at 13 Orange Street late last night, her head at an odd angle and burn marks all over her body. It's said the method of the burns has not been determined. And once again, witnesses tell of seeing a well-dressed gentleman before the attack.

Though police have extensively questioned area residents, officers have no leads on any suspect and will not confirm whether they believe this is the same killer who struck at Cross Street. It seems the Five Points is the very Devil's playground, and he abuses his own home with impunity. Perhaps we can hope that the district may simply cannibalize itself and thus eat its way out of existence and the city will breathe a sigh of relief.

The opinions at the end anger me. The Five Points and the people living there aren't to blame for this; they could have hardly asked for such terrors to be theirs. I recall my father's friends speaking out on the behalf of the ward—that people there needed to be taken seriously, not treated with derision. My heart goes out to Laura and all those who live in such fear as to be silent, their lives bought and sold for a price.

But really, if newspapers are only going to mock rather than seek justice, why talk to a reporter at all and try to fight for the truth? Poor Laura. Saint Laura. Would that I had known her and could have saved her, as I hoped I'd been sent to save Cecilia…but in turn, her life was traded for another.

"Saint Laura."

You see, I put her homage in quotes because I'm forcing

myself to say things. I can whisper in this world better than I can speak. Last night I went to sleep murmuring the dread phrase over and over again, the Latin, the *spell*, hoping a ghost of a voice will be voice enough when it comes time to use it.

I am shocked I did not dream last night. But then again, the mind is not always predictable. Still, I would have liked to be warned of Laura. Or would I? It isn't like I could have found her. Being wrapped up in this madness has given me such a sense of responsibility for what occurs.

What if we can't determine the last piece of the word puzzle?

I pray it's a small enough omission that will not render the entire magic useless.

Any spare moment that I'm not watched, I practice the alphabet quietly and aloud. As if I were a child learning a skill I'd long since sworn off. And while my speech hardly sounds as effortless as my words did when I was within the portrait, I think about things that are just and good. I think of angels. I pray. I muse on Mother. I think about Jonathon, and my heart swells. At this, speaking comes easier.

I knew I had to go to him during the day, and thankfully Father said he'd be in meetings but if I wanted to come and sketch, I was welcome to it. And so I did, making one sketch in case Father asked what I'd done, and then I made my way to where I was needed most.

# LATER, AT MY HOME

*(Ignoring dinner* again—*oh, but how could I eat?*
*My stomach is all in knots.)*

I gritted my teeth on seeing the painting. It was like a
punch to my stomach. Jonathon looked gray and sunken,
with nearly all the gorgeous vitality sucked out of him.
Another scar, this time upon the opposite cheek. Not only
would more innocents die if we could not reverse this
curse, but Jonathon would wither away into nothingness.
I'd give anything to see his perfection once more.

I stood before him for a moment, took a deep breath,
and then stepped through.

"Oh, Natalie, you're safe," he said as I fell into his arms.
"When we didn't meet in dreams—I didn't know…" He
stroked my hair and clutched me tighter, his relief making
him bold. And I let him. In fact, I clutched him in turn. I
held him to me. He moaned in pleasure, a delicious sound.

"But you were there with me. I felt your hand on my
shoulder. My angel."

"Did you?" He lit with pride. "I wanted to be with you
so much."

Then he drew away, racked by a violent cough. He was
a ghost of himself, pale and sickly. The cuff of his sleeve
was bloody—likely the carved wounds on his arm had
been reopened during the murder. I moved to caress his
cheek, and as I did, a crease on his face eased again into

the smooth picture of youth I so admired. I had an effect upon him, and it was for the better.

"Do I look as terrible as I feel?" he asked with a worried laugh.

"Yes," I replied. It was the truth. I had no kerchief, but I ripped at the lace of my sleeve to dab at his wound. We both winced. I led Jonathon to the window. Even if it was false sunlight, we would let it warm us as it would.

"What happened? All I saw out there were swirling madness, smoke, and laughter, a mad jumble. I heard more screams…"

"Do you want to know? I warn you it isn't pleasant."

He nodded, wincing again, not from pain, but in bracing himself for the news.

"It was the same as the first. He did strike. I managed to save a Cecilia, but he found another unfortunate woman."

Denbury turned away, seething, his fists clenched. "Take that beast down! If it means killing me, so be it! Kill my body, then. I can't let this—"

I grabbed him and turned him to face me. "No! It doesn't have to come to that. We have information now! Mrs. Northe and I believe we have figured out the structure of the counter-curse. We hope. Save for the one word that doesn't quite translate. But we hope that one word won't render the whole phrase useless. We have a plan."

His pained expression filled with anxious hope.

I spoke evenly and described the mission. "The phrase he used on you will be used against him by someone he would not expect, someone 'accidentally' in his path, someone he would see as an easy target, an offering from the gods, as it were."

Jonathon's eyes widened as he watched my face. I was sure to keep it defiant and proud to hide my fear. "You?" he breathed.

When I nodded, his face clouded. "It's too dangerous. There has to be some other way."

I spoke to reassure him, more confident than I felt. I had to be strong for him. "I can speak here with you. Somehow you gave me that gift. I must believe that I can speak beyond this place. But not until I've made him believe otherwise. I need you to answer me something—"

"Natalie, it's insane for you to be in his presence—"

"If we delay, more girls will die and there will be nothing left of you to save!" He opened his mouth to protest, but I continued. "I will need your help—"

"Anything, tell me."

I gestured for him to sit at his desk, and I perched on the side.

"I need you to recall *exactly* what was said to banish you here. As it stands, the spell is incomplete. When the beast struck you with that phrase, did he attach a name to it? This creature is driven by names. The power of the name is the oldest magic of all. He's collecting something he's attached meaning to, targeting victims with the names of saints."

Jonathon clenched his fists. "That's why he liked to call me John, all that forty martyrs of England nonsense! There was something else. After the Latin phrase he added, 'John the Doctor,' but my mind was fixed upon what I thought were 'soul' and 'door.'"

"You see, this is a door," I explained, gesturing to the window portal that was the picture frame by which I'd come and gone. "A door he created to separate your soul from your body. Mrs. Northe had the good sense to pry beneath the nameplate outside on your frame. Below the nameplate was written the word 'ba.'"

I snatched a pen whose slender length struggled against me, this physical world wanting to rebel, and wrote the word upon the blotter.

"Ba?"

"It's Egyptian. Mrs. Northe sorted it out. Otherwise I'd have been lost. That pendant of yours is an Egyptian cartouche. The pendant names you as a vessel. The ancient Egyptians believed there were seven parts of the soul, all of them small words like 'ka' and 'ab'—each has a different name. "Ba" is the part of the soul that flies in and out of the tomb, sometimes as a bird—"

Something struck Jonathon. "Small words, you say? What are the others called?"

I thought about Mrs. Northe's note where she wrote them all out. I had been so intrigued by the words that they had lingered in my mind, but I didn't recall them precisely. "They're all brief, one-syllable words, like those I mentioned—"

"Ren? Is one of them 'ren'? If the devil entwines his spells among so many traditions, perhaps the part that confused me, the Latin *animusren* is actually 'soul,' *animus,* and *ren* as separate words—"

"Yes!" I cried. "Yes, *ren* is one of them—that must be it! I wonder which of the seven soul parts that refers to. Mrs. Northe will know. Oh, Jonathon, you're a genius. That's it!"

He flushed. "You're the genius here."

But it was like he was a whole new man, having empowered himself with knowledge, with deduction. He'd seized the bars of his prison and rattled the cage. He looked almost entirely himself again. I couldn't stop smiling.

"What a team we've made, you and me and Mrs. Northe!" I exclaimed, and he grinned with me. "Mrs. Northe will help us make sure *every* word will have power we can use! And 'Doctor'—that's yet another piece. Naming as power is starting to make sense."

"How so?"

"He called you 'Doctor' because it's what defines you. It is something important to your soul, your essence, your conscience, and that's what he banished here. He needed to separate you, your higher being, from raw materials."

228

Jonathon took in a sharp breath as if he'd seen something wonderful, but he was looking around me, not at me.

"What?" I asked warily.

He took me by the arms, leading me into the center of the room where things seemed most sharply in focus.

"Colors, Natalie, when you speak of the counter-curse! A flurry of green and purple light, like a garden full of life. Freedom. If the red, sulfuric fires of Hell crackle around the demon as he speaks, and the opposite happens when you talk of curses, it must mean you're right, and the magic is telling me so."

This gave us both immeasurable hope. We could feel it as if it were a humming vibration in the air. Our hands reached for one another. But there was still one missing piece in the way. With so many little pieces to keep track of…my head spun as they danced just behind my eyes.

"But what name do I reverse upon him?" I said, turning to pace around him, thinking. "He deliberately left it out…"

The words "left" and "out" clicked for me, and my eyes widened. I stopped in my tracks. "Oh!"

The final piece.

"The poem!" I cried, turning to him. "The fiend wrote a poem, carved in runes, on the back of your portrait frame! A poem by Baudelaire—"

"I hate Baudelaire."

"All the better for your captor," I muttered. "The poem is 'The Possessed'—fitting, don't you think? And as it was carved, a word was deliberately left out. A word that in the original French is '*Belzébuth*—'"

"Well, Beelzebub! The Devil. If he had a name, he'd aspire to call himself Beelzebub!"

"Yes! Surely, in homage. That creature would like to think he is Beelzebub the Devil, though I wouldn't give him as much credit as all that—"

"I agree," Jonathon said, nodding. "The Devil can't only be one entity. Too many terrible things happen in separate places." He shuddered suddenly. "The beast has frequently mentioned a society, a new day and new world order, that the likes of him have already taken hold. I'd hate to think the Devil has an institution."

"Indeed, but that is a problem for another day. First, we need to reverse your spell."

"Now that we have the whole of it, it actually seems possible by evoking those Latin and Egyptian words and then naming him in turn." A great weight was lifting from Jonathon's shoulders. He would not waste away here, trapped in a canvas. "And look, I see your light again, telling me we're correct! The mystery solved!" He picked me up and swung me around. "You are absolutely, unequivocally, incredibly brilliant, my beautiful, *exquisite* Miss Stewart!" he cried, and lowered me again.

In that moment, time slowed. The way his head was tilted, and mine...and then his lips met mine.

How can I begin to describe...explain...*rhapsodize* about this single most glorious moment of all my life? I am not being overdramatic. For once.

He tasted of a hint of bergamot, residue of his favorite Earl Grey tea upon his lips. This scent would compel me, surely, for the rest of my days. His lips, soft and full, gently shifted to cover mine, to leave no part of my mouth untouched. He was reverent and gentle, and the press of his lips was followed by the press of his hands, slowly closing over my shoulders and anchoring me to him. He tasted my tongue with his, and his fingertips danced across my collarbone, shifting the lace ruffles of my dress as his hands quested, perhaps still hoping for confirmation that I was real.

We breathed and gasped in unison. My body trembled in his hold, and I didn't bother to hide it. I didn't want to deny how much he affected me. I wanted him to know and to rejoice in his power over me. We sank to the ground, our kiss deepening and then migrating to travel over cheeks and brows, all with soft cries of wondrous abandon. I'd always dreamed of finding such passion as I'd read about in books. He breathed against my neck, kissing it gently, trailing his tongue along my earlobe, and whispering, "There is magic in your kiss indeed, Natalie Stewart."

"Jonathon…" I breathed, blushing and tucking my face against his neck. I'd had no other kiss to compare to, and I couldn't guess the level of his experience, but nothing was more amazing in all the world and nothing else mattered in that moment.

It was magical indeed, but…perhaps not magical enough. "If this were a true fairy tale, my kiss would release you from this prison."

He shifted, cupping my cheeks in his hands, his eyes holding the power to stop my heart, to cleave my heart, or to make it race. "But if I can't have you, *this*…" He brushed his lips over mine. "Then I don't ever want to leave."

I drew back, his words striking a chord. "That's a dangerous thing to say. The demon would wish you to say so. You'll leave this prison," I insisted. "We have the counter-curse, and I will free you. We cannot live like this—"

He sat back, his brow furrowing. "Of course…I…"

I grasped his hands, desperately trying to maintain focus. The pleasure I felt destroyed my sense of time. I was moved to confess: "I was lost to you the moment I saw your portrait." I touched his lips with my fingertips. "And now…I cannot imagine not having you with me. But this place has its dangers, and we're so close to freedom. Mrs. Northe demanded I tend your spirit.

"Speak of something other than death and spell casting, Jonathon. We need ironclad souls for what's to come.

You've seen what's in my nightmares. Give me something else to dream of. Tell me of England, reclaim life beyond this prison." I moved toward the bookshelf, to that place hidden from the frame's view.

"Where are you going?" He called from the center of the room. "Stay, sit with me." His murmur was like a purr. "I can think of many more pleasant things than talking."

"From here, I can't be seen. It's safer, should someone notice the painting changed." I took a seat against the shelf and gazed up at him. He maintained his position but shifted so that he could see me. "Stay there and tell me of England. I've always wanted to visit!"

"Only if you'll tell me all about your great city that awaits us beyond this frame," he countered, offering a look that thrilled me head to toe. "So we two may dream of it."

"Of course!"

Jonathon spoke of his country estate in Greenwich (the pale imitation of which we were currently inhabiting). I told him of Greenwich Village downtown and what I found lovely there. We compared the bustling streets of London to those of New York, what new inventions were where, how many of our streets were lit by gas lamp and how much of the riversides were industrialized. I regaled him with the glory of Central Park and he did the same about Regents and the gardens in Chelsea. I confessed how many New York neighborhoods had borrowed British names, and he joked that Americans were child imitators.

We laughed and shared, dreaming up schemes and planning a future together. It was *thrilling*. A world existed outside this peculiar circumstance, and the more we talked about it, the more real it became. It was only a matter of time. Warmth fought his devilish contagion; every laugh and joke brightened him; and he complemented my wit at every turn, his just as sharp and engaging. Our limited world was aglow with appreciation.

And all I wanted to do was kiss him more. Of the same mind, he moved to stand over me.

"You say you can't be seen here?" he asked, his voice low.

I looked up. "No."

And suddenly he dove upon me with a flurry of action, kneeling over me, scooping me up to himself with a rain of kisses, and seizing caresses roving across my body. I gasped, arching myself to him and acquiescing to his exploratory touches, unable to help myself. The sensations were heaven.

"If it's our *spirits* here, Natalie, beyond our coil," he gasped, "what could be more glorious than the coupling of two spirits? The joining of our hearts and souls by the spirit of our bodies—"

"Coupling? Do you mean—"

"I want you so terribly," he said, shifting to look at me, his eyes wide and his hands trembling on the buttons of my blouse. "It's all I can think of." He breathed me in deeply, dragging his nose and lips up my cheek. "You're the only thing that's real in this hell." He'd managed to undo a few buttons of my high-collared blouse, and his lips were instantly at my throat as he moaned, "Good God, you've given me my *senses* again. I'm *starving* to feel alive…"

He tore at my blouse, and I couldn't say that seductive abandon wasn't appealing. I could still claim chastity. These weren't *actually* our bodies, though we felt every sensation as fully as if they were; these were our souls. How beautiful was that? Here the laws of propriety were only as we made them. But still…I felt flush with furious desire, but my mind reeled with apprehension. "Lord Denbury, I don't wish to deny you, but…is this truly the place for such liberties to be taken?"

"Jonathon," he insisted. "You *must* call me Jonathon, and I'd never ask more of you than you wanted to give, Natalie." He cupped my cheek in his hand. The apprehension on my face stilled him as if it were a slap or a douse of cold water. He drew back. "I am too bold, surely—"

"It isn't that," I breathed, touching his cheeks gently and knowing mine were similarly hot. "I want to be everything you need…But not like this, under mad circumstances." I struggled to regain my sense, my focus, my power; the dangerous mission that was mine alone lay yet ahead of me. I straightened myself against the bookshelf and tended to my buttons.

The truth was that I hesitated because he hadn't yet said he loved me.

And a girl could give herself only in love. Mutual love. Otherwise she'd ruin herself for nothing. A girl's body was a prize. It had to be more than asked for. It had to be earned, worshipped, and avowed. Generally, rings and other oaths were a part of the bargain. Supernatural circumstances being what they were and with my life potentially on the line, I certainly felt I deserved a vow. A ring would be nice too.

"I'm sorry," he murmured, discomfort overtaking him. He jumped up. "I must seem the animal. Surely you've seen too much of that. Perhaps you think me too much like my other half."

"No, you mustn't think that," I scolded, straightening my dress as I moved away from our private corner. "There's been so much upheaval in my life in so short a time...I just can't give *everything* so soon—"

I noticed movement across the frame, signaling our time was at an end.

I rose and moved toward the image of my body beyond, turning to offer him this: "Before I met you within this portal, your other half accosted me at the Art Association.

While I admit *he* was too bold, he did say one thing that's true: that we'd be beautiful together."

I didn't wait for his response. Tumbling back into my body, I startled a poor maid who must have begun to think I was an uncanny statue added to the exhibit room.

"Are you all right, miss?" the matronly woman said, steadying my dizzy form while I was reeling to regain my balance from the cross between worlds I alone could feel.

I nodded, blushing, and moved to pick up the pad of paper I'd left on the wooden bench at the side wall. She continued her cursory cleaning, looking at me warily as I sat to sketch as if nothing out of the ordinary had happened. Alternately she'd turn to gaze at the painting. Jonathon's magnetism affected everyone, it was true. He didn't look nearly as bad as when I'd found him. He looked refreshed, even vibrant now, and the fact gave me strength and courage.

As did his kisses.

Nothing could ever take away that exquisite bliss. I keep reliving it.

We dined early that night at Mrs. Northe's home. She'd had the good sense to invite a man with whom to entertain Father, a British colonel who had more stories from around the globe than Scheherazade had in her Arabian nights. Plenty to keep my father entertained, and Mrs.

Northe and I, as usual, took to our tea while Father and the colonel took to the den.

I asked about Maggie, and Mrs. Northe said her niece had been pouting lately so she simply didn't have the patience to extend an invitation. I pledged that once this madness was settled I'd make great efforts to regain our friendship.

Mrs. Northe then relayed that at some point in the morning, guards had called on a local mental alienist to "assist"—or rather, escort—Crenfall out of the Metropolitan, where the man had been distressing others as he shambled along—*limping*, she was proud to note, proving he'd been in her home the night of the break-in to receive her bullet.

He was seen muttering to himself from one wing of the museum to the other. He's currently being examined at a local institution. I doubt he'll be released. I wonder. If we are successful, will the dark hold over that wretch cease, or will his last shred of sanity snap? What lured him to such a fate in the first place? Will we ever know?

But no more distractions. The exciting thing (aside from kisses), the *important* thing was that we had the answers!

To share my discovery, I again tried speaking in halting words. My face burned at the discomfort of it, but I fought for each syllable. Mrs. Northe signed to me that it was all right, that I didn't have to tax my voice if I didn't want to. Frustrated tears rolled down my face. I did want to speak. But I still hated how I sounded and wondered when that burden of shame would go away. There were many more inelegant pauses in my speech at the time than I've written here.

"I...need to practice," I said aloud. That simple phrase seemed to take ages to utter. My mind was a thousand times faster than my tongue. It was unbearable. But while I may lure the possessor with my disability, I would not trap him unless I overcame it and spat back at him the evil he'd dealt.

"Of course, dear, and I'm honored that you do so around me."

I reminded myself that magic was flowing through my veins, magic that allowed me alone to share in Jonathon's secret prison. Perhaps it was not magic but a miracle that allowed me to help restore him. Faith. I just needed to have faith, something that had been serving me well of late.

I told her of the spell phrase, *animus ren*, of how they must be separate words, Latin to Egyptian, and she jumped up to consult her book. Her eyes widened.

"Soul Name. *Ren* is the *Soul Name*. How fitting, of course! Good work, Lord Denbury! Why didn't I think of that?"

"I'm glad Jonathon did. It was like he was a whole new person. Here we have been trying to solve a mystery for a man. Men seem to like to figure things out for themselves."

Mrs. Northe laughed. "You are frightfully insightful, Natalie. Oh, and he's *Jonathon* now?"

I blushed. I went on to tell her about how the demon had called Denbury "John" and how surely the title "Beelzebub" would fit the bill for the counter-curse.

"Oh, Natalie, that's it!" she cried. "Of course. Answers are always in the space between. Well done, you two!" Then her tone became more serious. "And now, Natalie, it will be up to you to deliver the final strike."

I nodded gravely, accepting the task. Accepting my fate. And then we began to formulate our plan.

I'll detail the plan of course, but for now I need to set these pages aside.

I'd like to sit and take a cup of tea with Father. I've neglected him of late, amid this obsession. And if something should happen...I want him to feel loved and appreciated, for nothing would have been possible without him. My life has meaning because he allowed me to be who I am. I've lived in safety because he did not cast me off. I owe him time and affection before I go and put myself in danger. I shall write "I love you" upon a little note card and hand it to him before I leave him. There could be no better parting words.

# June 19

3 A.M.

*(Awaking)*

One last nightmare before I face the living nightmare and demand a reckoning.

But this time...My nightmares might be learning...

Running again. Pursued again. Perhaps by the demon Denbury, perhaps by only my own perceptions of shadows. Again the same dark, dank alleys in the struggling corners of New York that did, quite truly, terrify me. For good reason.

Again the door, again tumbling into Denbury's study and swiftly being caught up in his hold, as if he were always waiting for me. I suppose he was.

And only in my nightdress.

I don't recall what I'd been wearing in previous dreams, but our heightened awareness of one another's bodies had us crossing further boundaries. He most certainly noticed.

"Hello, beautiful," he said, low and aching. A kiss was inevitable. And wonderful. To feel him against me without the boundary bones of my corset, able to arch to him in ways prohibited by all the trappings of female fashion…it was exquisite to say the least.

But as he turned me so that I was cradled even stronger and deeper in his hold, breaking from me to sear my neck with kisses, I made the mistake of opening my eyes, there over his shoulder, and looking at the door from which I'd come and had been foolish enough not to close.

I pulled back with a gasp. Jonathon did not turn around. "What is it this time?" he asked quietly.

"The corpse, there on the threshold."

I could not see her face for the mussed auburn hair obscuring it, but she was in the same lacy white shift, her gray-white arms exposed. And on the forearm, a name carved into the flesh dripped congealing blood down her wrist so that it fell on the threshold with a faint, tapping rhythm.

"Arilda."

Jonathon turned to face the phantasm. "I suppose there's a Saint Arilda."

"There is," I said quietly. "I need to stop this. No more women will die, because it stops with me. Now."

And then the apparition lifted its head.

I choked back a scream.

It was me.

The corpse was me.

Jonathon was instantly on the move. He pushed me behind him, trying to shield me from a sight that should've undone my senses.

The eyes of the corpse—*my* corpse—stared straight ahead: vacant, dead, and yet still my body bled precious blood. My face was ashen, my lips were tinged blue, and the sight was everything one would expect in death, save that the lips *moved*.

Worse, it...*I*...began to murmur. I recognized the words. It was the phrase. The spell. The spell I'd been saying, practicing over and over again privately. The lifeless eyes, the blue mumbling lips, and the dripping arm were more than I could bear. I'd had enough. Denbury didn't need to prompt me this time.

"Enough! All of this. I am *done*. We will win. I renounce thee!" I cried. "I tell you, I renounce thee!"

My corpse-self turned to me, its eyes suddenly as alive as if I were looking into a mirror. She seemed filled with relief, and that body began to fade, to step backward, all the while murmuring the spell. The corridor behind lit up with shafts of light.

One by one, pale and much like the white-silver halo I'd seen coming from Jonathon, glimmering threads surrounded my corpse-self and illuminated the corridor to make it an open, vast expanse. Out of that sparkling transformation came a familiar, stirring sight: Central Park, built by an engineer with the soul of a poet, my sacred place...

We gasped at the vista that had replaced my dead body. It was a view that I'd rhapsodized about when we had regaled each other with our cities; there was my angel of Bethesda, sanctifying the waters and gently touching down upon the fountain at the center of that beloved Central Park terrace, the boat pond and lush greenery beyond. My cruel mind had willed something beautiful for us instead. "That's my park. That's my angel!"

Jonathon pressed against my back, his breath warm on my neck. "Yes, Natalie. Banish the darkness and show me angels instead."

I melted against him, grabbing for his hand. "Now I've an abundance of angels..."

Drawing him closer to that doorway, I yearned to make it reality, to bring him into that romantic place where we could promenade, blessed beneath those precious wings...

But on the edges of that beautiful terrace hovered darker threads amid the trees and shrubbery. Cords of light shifted amid the utter absence of light, and countless thin, vertical masses moved inside a fabric. The threads were like people, souls, moving energy, raw materials...They almost seemed to wrestle with one another like a jostling crowd fighting for space on New

York City streets; they entwined, merged, parted, and disappeared—like brushstrokes of a painting come to jumping life, the picture never static but in progress.

Jonathon watched with intense fascination, drinking in something other than his prison. I drew him still closer to the door, testing the boundaries. The threshold crackled and snapped like a whip. The cuffs of Jonathon's sleeves singed. I frowned, easing him back a step. Yet the aura about him was palpable, a coiled thread of silver light reaching up from him as if he were tethered there to something divine. It made him even more magnificent—which I'd hardly thought possible.

At the edge of the door, the shadows clung, trying to encroach on those places in my mind that had been so totally theirs. Yet the more we wanted that angel before us as we stood hand in hand, the clearer her statue became. But it was a struggle. The image began flickering, those lively threads swarming—as if a battle were being waged.

I closed the door. As wondrous as the view might be, it was all illusion. We needed to begin staring at reality.

But what of me? What of my own corpse lingering somewhere in that hall?

A sudden sharp and burning pain seized my arm. Gasping, I pushed back my sleeve. My arm was bloodied, carved with the name Arilda.

I was the next victim. But the beast did not have my name. That was the trick.

"Saint Arilda," I murmured, blinking back tears of pain. Jonathon snapped his cravat from his neck and calmly began binding my arm. He was a doctor, after all. Even in a haze of pain I still managed to revel in how his undone collar offered me a glimpse of his naked throat.

"What of her?" he prompted with a smirk, noticing I'd drifted off in staring at him.

I coughed. "Of all the saints," I explained, "my friend Mary and I were fondest of Saint Arilda. She refused to give her body to a tyrant of a man who would lay claim to her."

Jonathon cleaned his fingers as he tied off the fabric and reached out to touch my cheek. "And so you shall."

"Yet she died upon the tyrant's sword," I replied. "She was run through." A new pain took me, and I doubled over, gasping and pressing my hand to my abdomen. It came away bloody. Dreaming. I had to remember I was dreaming.

"I renounce it," Jonathon countered vehemently, his aura brightening with angelic fury.

I awoke with a shot, a pain at my abdomen. But no wound. No blood. No carved arm.

Only worry.

The dread thought that none of this will work, that this will fail miserably and a reversal may not occur, sits in my stomach like a rock. I may never be able to see Jonathon or touch him again. I may be harmed. I might be killed.

No.

I must not leave room for fear, for the shadows of my mind will only feed on it. I demand angels on my side.

## LATER...

I'm just back from an afternoon at the museum.

In desperate, strange times like these, the heart must be honest—or live to regret it. Lord Jonathon Denbury is a worthy man to be passionate about, and I'd best tell him so. Words wield power. Names have power because they are words. And there are three powerful words that I needed to speak.

I entered the painting, Father thinking I'd taken to sketching yet another wing of the museum.

I was caught in Jonathon's arms as usual, and his pallor brightened at the sight of me. His smile was delicious as he said, "What a shame, I rather liked that nightgown. Now you're all properly dressed."

I blushed and laughed. "At least I'm not in men's clothes."

He didn't let go as he continued: "You're lovely no matter what. Ever since I first touched you, you're the only thing that's made sense. It's as if we've always been friends or..."

"Lovers," I supplied. He looked wistfully at my lips.

"Mrs. Northe said when someone is meant to be in your life, it feels like that."

"You are. Meant to be in my life. Was there ever a time when you were not a part of it?"

"Well, there won't be from now on, if you'll have it—" I nearly blurted my words right then and there, my oath, my declaration. But instead I spoke of the task at hand. "Tonight is the night. Be ready. And if something should happen…" I took a deep breath. "Please know that I…I care for you deeply."

I was too nervous, too embarrassed to use the word *love*, even though that's what I'd come here to say. How could I be so bold in some ways and so cowardly in others?

I had no idea how he would react to the declaration. The words might seem like another curse—like I was trying to wield more magic over him. Though powerful words were the best ones in times like this: words meant with care, hope, and affection—the opposite of the terror that could overcome us. Just as I'd sat with my father the night prior and wrote the words "I love you" on a note card, a gesture that had seemed to touch him more greatly than I'd expected, this was the time for such honesty.

"The Devil can't win," he rallied, touching my cheek. "We've angels and saints on our side."

"I do hope you're right."

"I am right. In every fairy tale, love conquers all. Why should this be any different?" And here he took hold of me and stopped my breath with: "For I do love you, Natalie Stewart…"

I gasped, hearing those desperately hoped-for words. Tears sprang to my eyes.

Our lips met in a kiss full of promise. Promise for a brilliant future…

I breathed against him, a soft sound matched by his responding sigh. We had just made the vow I needed. I withdrew and saw that his cheeks were flush with health, his blue eyes never so piercing, and his scars lessened by our love. But not gone entirely. Still visible were signs of wear and aging, and strands of silver glistened in his youthful mop of black hair.

His eyes narrowed a bit and his jaw tensed as I pulled away. "And…you? You said you *cared*, but do you—"

"Oh! Yes, of course I love you too," I gasped, giggling, a bit silly and certainly inelegant. But we kissed again. Fervently. His hands again roamed freely over me. Heaven.

"But it's more than loving you," I murmured. "It's fate."

He touched my cheek. "You are the angel your colorful light predicted," he mused. "I wonder if I will continue to see such fateful omens outside the painting."

"Perhaps it might give us an idea of whom to avoid in the future."

"I'll be grateful if I never encounter another supernatural event as long as I live." His expression turned worrisome. "When, Natalie, when are you going to attempt your plan?"

"Midnight. Tonight. The ghosts of dead girls will haunt me forever if we delay."

I shuddered. I now knew enough of ghost stories to fear far more than whispers and white lace.

I glanced at the door within the room, the one that should have led to the rest of the Denbury estate in reality, but that in my dream world revealed only the dark and unpredictable emptiness of my mind. He followed my gaze.

"That door opened onto a magnificent park, onto the New York you so beautifully described. You can change what haunts you. And you'll show me that breathtaking view."

"Yes," I murmured, knowing he was right. I felt that the world could be ours, any world, real or imagined, that I had the power to turn my shadows into golden fields.

Overcome with emotion, I dragged him to our private corner of safety. "Touch me," I said. It was my turn to reverse the demand he'd asked of me from the first, the demand that had drawn me in. "Give me another taste. Anything to forget the fear."

Jonathon accepted his mission fastidiously, unbuttoning my blouse carefully. As each button was parted, he placed a kiss upon my bare skin. He slid the shoulders of my chemise aside, his fingertips on my bare shoulders sending coursing shivers of delight between us. The rigid bones of my corset made my already heightened gasps of breath even more difficult to capture. Though he was gentleman enough to keep my corset in place, I could still feel the press of his lips through the thin fabric, his breath gracing the swell of my bosom.

We sank to the floor, his body over mine, my head lolling to the side as he devoured my neck with kisses, supported fully lest I swoon in his covetous hold. His cravat, vest, and shirt lay open by the fumbling work of my fingers seeking his skin, brushing over the fine dusting of black hair and edging toward his heart. I needed to press my lips to his bare and pounding heartbeat. When I did, he sighed. "If I had ten hearts to give, I would. You've worked so hard to earn them all."

We were a tangle of limbs and fabric, patches of bare skin and mussed hair. Waking raging fires, our curious touches crossed into foreign, hidden territory. I'd never been so gloriously undone; this exploratory passion was its own new world. This wasn't how an unmarried lady purported herself. But if I was going to try to tempt a demon, I wanted the evidence of true, loving passion on my skin. To tell the true Denbury from the false one.

It was an unspoken knowledge that we both wanted as much as we could possibly have of one another, but we both knew we could not cross boundaries. To undo all my laces would have been to undo me entirely, and I did not think it wise to leave the whole of my carnal innocence, even the entwining of loving spirits, upon a foreign, magical threshold.

"Jonathon…You know I could lie with you like this indefinitely. But my body awaits beyond, as does our plan."

"I'll be with you. Just like the last time when you felt my hand on your shoulder. Promise me you'll come back before—" he said.

"I'll try."

He helped me to my feet, his arms around me as we shuffled toward the portal wall. "Natalie, I…" He seemed to think further words were best offered physically so he gave me such a parting kiss so as there was no question.

I was Juliet bidding Romeo good-bye as I waved, stepping to the frame as if it were that famous balcony. "What's in a name" indeed. His name was my quest. Two star-crossed lovers from two separate worlds. I'd bring him into my world again.

Or I'd die trying.

As I tumbled back into my whole body, I slumped down on the floor. I touched my lips and still felt him there.

"Hello, dear," came a familiar voice that made me jump. Mrs. Northe awaited me in the room, and I was surprised but glad to see her. She helped me to my feet. Tumbling from one world to the next, thankfully I had two dear souls to help me up again.

I did not tell her of kisses, vows, or sacred touches. Those were my glorious secrets. She may have guessed from my flushed cheeks, being perceptive, to say the least. But she was rightly tempered by the gravity of the situation, and I could not revel long in girlish rhapsodies.

She closed and locked the exhibition door behind her and we were all business.

We discussed the plan, how I might appear within the basement of the Metropolitan. She insisted that "her man," a Mr. Smith—the one who had dragged me up to meet her after my foray into the Five Points—would be on hand in case of emergency, there to deal with any of the beast's entourage, though Crenfall was conveniently out of the way. Smith would remain hidden but on hand, and she herself would not be far. This was not negotiable, she said.

And so I would be at the mercy of the fiend until Mr. Smith came to check on me as she had demanded and, should it come to it, he would retrieve me back to this world if I'd gone too long into the painting or lend his hand in a brawl. The fact that Mrs. Northe trusted a grim person like Mr. Smith with something magical was shocking. But she said she paid him well and he never raised an eyebrow. Though it was disconcerting to entrust my life to a stranger, I did feel some relief in not having to be completely alone.

"Don't think I'm being casual about your being put into danger," she stated. "But I shouldn't be the one there with you. Not if the fiend can sense…people like me."

I raised my eyebrow.

"I have clairvoyant tendencies," she explained.

I stared at her, wondering why she hadn't told me, though I could have guessed as much.

"My gifts are very unpredictable, Natalie, and inconsistent," she explained. "I didn't dare tell you of them until I had something concrete to offer. When we met, I told you I knew you were important, but instinct is not clairvoyance. We've had to deal with this situation one step at a time. What if the beast sniffs something on me that he doesn't like? He may have senses we do not; I can't know. I could inadvertently put us all in danger."

I furrowed my brow. But wouldn't I set off some sort of similar alarm? Why was Mrs. Northe eager to see me do this?

"Why…if you know it is dangerous, are you not stopping me?" I asked, again hating how my voice sounded so different here than it did so softly against Jonathon's cheek. But still, I muscled on. "You look at me knowingly. What do you see? There are things you've not been saying. Now is the time to tell me *everything*."

She was reticent to speak of her gifts, as I suppose all

persons gifted with something the world cannot accept seem to be. But my own fate rested in her hands, in a painting, and in an unpredictable, possessed body with a penchant for murder. I deserved answers.

"Do you really want to know?" she asked. Something in her tone indicated that perhaps I shouldn't. But curiosity is a fierce creature. "Knowledge is power. Not all knowledge is welcome. I must be very careful what I say and when. I told you to steel your mind."

I gulped. "It is steeled. My heart too. Tell me, please."

She cleared her throat, her face masking deeper emotion. "I'm not stopping you because your mother told me not to."

I stared. I felt my hands start to shake. My eyes watered, as they always did when Mother was mentioned, which is why our household never, ever, spoke of her. I could do nothing but wait for Mrs. Northe to continue.

"I didn't...seek her out, Natalie. It doesn't work that way for me. Every medium...every *person* deals with these...situations differently, and spirits deal with each medium differently."

I let the tears flow. I was too afraid of missing a syllable to even reach up to dry them. Mrs. Northe paused.

"Is it all right to continue?" she asked. "These are delicate matters, surely, and I never know exactly how to broach them."

"Please," I murmured, gesturing for her to continue.

"I awoke one night, and there was a shimmering, transparent specter at my bedside, beautiful. You look just like her. She spoke your name and told me that I was to let your destiny unfold as it would." Mrs. Northe smiled. "She was adamant, passionate. You must get that from her."

I smiled and more tears dropped onto my hands.

"She said that the great and the magical, the mysterious and the wondrous, and yes, the truly terrible, would be laid at your feet. And that it would be best if the world left you to it. I know. It's a bit vague. I thought she may give me some insight into our current problem, but it seems she speaks more grandly of your future."

"With Lord Denbury?" My untried voice was hopeful.

"She didn't say. But you're meant to help him. You are meant for great things. I'm sure of it, and it's confirmed from beyond the veil by your very own. Great things may not change the world, but they will change the lives around you. I think it has begun with him." She gestured to the painting.

"You think we'll be all right, somehow?" I said, staring up at Jonathon's portrait, my body flooding with heat as I thought of how he'd just touched me in his alternate world. "Do you think luck might be on our side?"

"I don't know that I believe in luck, Natalie. Of all the things that may be at work here, I'm not sure luck is one of the factors. You see, life is one grand transaction, a constant exchange of energy and purpose. Your mother gave you a weighty gift. A boon." And here Mrs. Northe paused, and for the first time ever, she looked uncomfortable. "Do you know how she died?"

"A runaway carriage. Run down in the street," I replied softly.

Mrs. Northe nodded. "Are you prepared for one more detail?"

"Yes. I've always wanted someone, anyone, in my house to speak about it, but no one ever has," I muttered.

"She was pushing you out of the way."

I felt as though I had been slapped. A sting upon my face, inside my heart, my lungs—I blinked slowly, heavily, as if trying to clear the fog of this news. It was no mere detail.

It changed everything.

Mrs. Northe allowed me the necessary time to catch my breath, and when I could look up at her again she calmly continued. Her measured control encouraged me not to get lost in a drowning tide of sentiment. For now was not the time.

"This imparted an energy to you. While some dare call this magic, it's not spell casting nor witchcraft. It is the simple transference of sacrifice to your life. And that boon then indebted you. Your mother's spirit lives on, in part to hope you'll return that favor for another worthy candidate.

And you have done so. You saved young Cecilia down on Anthony Street, and now Lord Denbury's fate lies similarly in your hands. You were born for this, Natalie Stewart."

"And my mother died for this," I murmured. The tears would not stop.

"In that terrible moment she was not thinking of passing a burden or gift on to you. She was thinking only of the survival of her child."

And so the trauma of my not speaking was far worse than I'd thought, more than anyone had dared say. I was surely too young, waddling along at the age of four, to remember—or else I'd blocked it from memory. But it had been shock enough to cut my voice right from me. Only now, with Jonathon's help, was I able to find it again. He gave me gifts too.

"But how did I not know this?" I fumbled at my memories. "Did Father tell me and I merely forgot—"

"Your father *adores* you. Once the trauma robbed you of your voice, how could he add further guilt to your burden? He refused to allow himself or anyone to think the accident was your fault."

I yearned to run to my father immediately, to reassure him and be reassured by him. But I'd promised Mrs. Northe—and Jonathon—that I'd steel my soul. I could not get sentimental now. I had to keep seated and calm the riptide of emotions that threatened to pull me apart.

"Forgive me for not telling you the moment I understood," Mrs. Northe continued. "But these things unfolded in pieces the more time we spent together, not all at once. And the sad knowledge would do you no good unless you understood the debt and how you are to repay it. It isn't about luck. More than luck, there are angels on your side that seek to enlarge your gifts. Exponentially. Instead of seeking to help one, they hope you'll help many, while darker energies would seek to cut you to the quick."

Mrs. Northe seemed to wrestle with something.

"What else?" I prompted, despite the fact my heart couldn't take much more.

"When someone dies for someone else, a particular energy releases, a bond both mortal and ghostly. A kind of magic is tied to your body and to the spirit who gave herself for you. When someone dies because of malevolence, though, a different exchange is released. And that will tie the perpetrator to a darker coil. But still, both energies are powerful."

"I am the former. The demon is the latter."

"Indeed. And while he has his powers, angels are on your side, Natalie. You have their sort of magic. Lord Denbury sees your magic as light and colors, and this may yet be his gift. You have been granted gifts in your life, the two of you. Whether you make them gifts or burdens is up to you."

I swallowed hard. I wanted my mother to come to me. I suddenly resented Mrs. Northe for explaining what I'd rather have heard from my mother, declaring her sacrifices in *her* voice. But Mrs. Northe deserved my love, not my frustration, and so I posed questions. "You believe in angels, then?"

"I believe in good spirits and evil spirits," Mrs. Northe replied confidently. "I believe in God, and I believe that there are beautiful things I cannot see and terrible things I dare not see. And I believe in a space between where all might be glimpsed."

Somehow, even if Mrs. Northe appeared to dodge a question at first, she always managed to answer it more sensibly than if she had merely said "yes." I thought of those swarming threads of vibrancy and shadow from my recent dream and nodded. The world had ceased to have clear yes or no answers; the world was gray scale. Save for my mission—that was black and white, survival or failure against evil.

My heart was heavy but my duties were clear, and there was, frankly, no point in belaboring the issue further. I embraced Mrs. Northe and dried my eyes, and Father took me home. I gave him a very long hug good night that he seemed to awkwardly appreciate, chuckling softly and likely wondering what flight of fancy had made me sentimental. Part of me wished to tell him everything, to unburden myself of my fear, but that would have done him more harm than good. My fate was sealed, and no one else could help or stop me.

## LATER...

The strangest thing has just happened. Bessie ushered Maggie into our parlor. Father was holed up in his study, so I received her with a smile. I opened my mouth to speak but was too nervous I'd sound inelegant, and I didn't want to have to explain my "cure." It was all right because she clearly planned to do all the talking.

"Oh, Natalie, dear, I've only a moment. I'm expected at the Bentrops' but I just wanted to invite you, this weekend, to my house. She leaned in and in a whisper said, "Fanny and I are staging a séance."

I raised an eyebrow at her. She continued, giddy.

"I was given a book as a gift. It's *fascinating* and full of incantations! Mr. Bentrop's niece and I became acquainted at a ball. She had me over for tea, and we got on famously. Mr. Bentrop says that I might have particular talents, provided I study hard, but that I mustn't ever let that book out of my sight because it's one of a kind. It's good to be in his favor. He's richer than anyone can quite tally!"

I gave her a warning look. This sounded like the sort of thing Mrs. Northe would never have approved of. And how did I know that name? But in her rush, Maggie was off to her engagement in a whirl of turquoise taffeta before I could place it. When I did, a chill crept over me.

Bentrop. He was one of the men in line to buy the Denbury portrait. One whom Mrs. Northe had described unfavorably.

I'll have to tell Mrs. Northe that the man was meddling with young, impressionable women. But later. I must now prepare myself for tonight's dread deed.


## LATER...

I'm sitting at the desk by my bedroom window, waiting for the pebble to strike the pane to indicate that the hired carriage awaits me below. Then I shall slip away and to the task. I write this so I may again go over the plan, for in writing I find calm, focus, and purpose. Perhaps someday I'll try fiction. Or, perhaps, I'll merely publish this account instead. No one would believe it real.

I've dressed in a fine gown fitted to accentuate my femininity, my best dress from last year. I'm not fond of it anymore; it has too much lace around all the edges. I have altered the neckline so that it might plunge a bit too low. I have dabbed lavender oil upon my wrists and behind my ears. My hair is done winsomely, up but with a few stray locks curled around my ears and neck to suggest a style that's nearly undone. Men seem to find undone hair a delicious tease. I need not practice blushes or looks of surprise, fear, or innocence. Those will come naturally enough, I don't doubt. I needn't hide my apprehension either; the demon will likely feed upon it.

I'll act as though I am lost and think myself locked inside the building, yet am drawn to the painting, just as I was from the start. The demon knows he's compelling. I will lock several of the floor's exits from the outside, leaving less-known passages open. (I dare not block every means of escape.) But I think it hardly out of the question that a girl with no voice might have wandered below stairs and found herself lost, trapped, and without recourse to call for help. I would appear the trapped little lamb to Denbury's possessor, a girl already associated with the painting. An offering.

I will scribble the plea of my situation upon a note card, and this will surely ensnare the fly—for I will declare my name. As foretold.

Arilda.

This should seal his interest in me as quite an unexpected catch. Arilda is an uncommon name. An uncommon saint. For an uncommon purpose.

Dear Saint Arilda, fighting to be taken by love, not by force. Mary and I agreed that the only way to give oneself to a man was to love him, and that the claim, while a man may suggest it, is ours to make and no two ways about it. Naming has power. So does the body.

However, I hope not to follow in young Arilda's footsteps as a martyr slain on a tyrant's sword. It is bold to use such a telling name, but Mrs. Northe and I are wagering that the demon has grown too proud not to think me a fortuitous gift rather than a trap.

Oh! I am startled. The pebble strikes! Mrs. Northe's hired help is at the door. The hour is at hand. I'll need all the prayers I can muster.

## LATER...

*(Upon the bench in Denbury's exhibition room)*

Dear God.

Imagine my surprise when Mr. Smith escorted me down to the exhibition room and there I found Maggie staring up at Denbury, the curtain of his painting drawn to reveal him. She was murmuring up to him, a black book in hand and with a pentagram marked on the floor in chalk.

"Maggie," I choked. I actually spoke her name.

She whirled to face me. Her face flushed furiously, and her jaw dropped. She glanced in horror at Mr. Smith and then again at me.

"What are you doing here?" We both spoke at the same time.

"You're speaking!" Maggie cried.

"I work here," I declared, ignoring her exclamation. I

glanced at Mr. Smith. He was expressionless, but if I wasn't mistaken, a part of his mouth curved as if he was amused.

"This late at night? Who's this? Isn't that one of Auntie's servants?"

Mr. Smith raised an eyebrow and walked away. I'm sure he didn't consider himself a servant; that much was clear. Maggie rushed up to me. I pushed her inside the room and closed the door.

"Maggie, what are you doing?" I demanded.

"I had to do this," she blurted. "I hid upstairs in the museum until closing. I've been studying. This is what I've been given." She lifted the book, which bore a golden goat's head on its black leather cover. I didn't recognize the volume offhand from Mrs. Northe's library, and I was fairly sure that she and Bentrop didn't share the same reading list.

"I can't get him out of my head or my dreams!" Maggie exclaimed, rubbing her head as if it ached. "I'm trying a summoning spell to bring Denbury's spirit here, to talk to him—"

"Maggie, this is dangerous, a man like Bentrop and a book like that. You don't know what you're doing. That pentagram—"

Her eyes flashed. "And what would you know about it? All the time spent with *my* aunt…Has she been teaching you all the things she's denied me? What makes you think you're so special? Tricking me into thinking you're mute—"

"No, that isn't true," I said. My voice, nervous, was inelegant. Surely Maggie could see I wasn't entirely cured. I blushed furiously, ashamed at the sounds. "I could speak all along, with some work. I just suffered trauma when I was young so I never did. Your aunt has been helping me regain speech." It was partially true.

"Because she likes you better than me."

"That isn't true. Maggie, listen to me. Something very bad is about to happen, and you need to get out of here."

"Why? What do you know? Why do you keep things from me?"

"I'm here because I'm helping the museum with a problem. And you need to go," I stated.

I had to clean that pentagram off the floor. I threw the exhibition-room door open again and stalked to a nearby supply closet. Maggie followed me as I grabbed a towel. Mr. Smith was standing patiently in the hall. His fiercely sharp eyes and quiet manner made him a man not to be questioned. Maggie gestured to him.

"Why is Mrs. Northe's man here then, and not your father—"

"Maggie, please…"

I reentered the room, knelt, and began to rub the yellow chalk off the floor.

"What are you doing? I made that for the spell—"

"Maggie, listen to yourself. You sound mad. You can't go

around drawing on museum property. And certainly not something like this."

"Something's going on, and you're going to tell me. I'll tell Aunt Evelyn *you* drew the pentagram. I can make her take my side!" It was incredible how an entitled, wealthy girl could rely on threats. I stared up at her.

"I'm sorry. I really do like you, Maggie, but you have to go home." I moved into the hall. "Mr. Smith, I desperately need you to make sure Miss Hathorn gets home safely. She is not part of the equation."

"Natalie," Maggie called, "what are you—"

"And please keep her quiet," I added.

Mr. Smith advanced to the open doorway with a look on his face that made Maggie take a step backward.

"You'll be sorry, Natalie. I could ruin you in society." Maggie was such a pretty girl. But ugly when angry.

"I'm not trying to be in society," I replied. "I hope to explain one day, Maggie. I really do."

"Don't touch me," Maggie hissed at Mr. Smith as he reached for her arm and exited. "I have a driver outside."

I watched as Mr. Smith followed her anyway, to make sure of it.

It hurt to lose the only female friend my age I'd managed to gain.

Flustered, I was shaking horribly as I wiped the floor clean. But I had a task to do. Lives depended on it.

After securing every obvious door to make it seem as though I truly was trapped, I stowed a small bag with a few amenities and every piece of my jewelry—the only valuables I had—in a darkened alcove just past the exhibition room. I pulled out a small vial. Oil used in blessings. Mrs. Northe had given it to me. I took a dab onto my finger. I wanted to counter the pentagram. Its marks were gone, but anxiety still hung in the room. While I knew a pentagram could be used for a sign of luck and blessing, I couldn't credit Maggie for knowing which direction to draw it, as the direction changed the meaning from good to ill.

And so I countered the pentagram with a small mark of the cross upon my forehead: an act of blessing and forgiveness, of cleansing, hope, renewal, and the power of the Holy Spirit. I needed angels on my side tonight, and so I called upon that sacred vow granted me as a baby, a vow I renewed now as a woman in this moment, a vow to reject the Devil.

Of course I had to go in and see Jonathon. Just one moment. We'd said good-bye earlier, but it was not enough. Not that I would ever have enough of seeing him. Even from looking at the portrait, I could tell he was in fading health. He was pale, and his fine cheekbones looked even more pronounced. The beauty that so enticed me was turning harsh.

He was loath to let me out of the embrace that I fell into, as I always did when I fell into his world.

And I was loath to let him go as I watched him brighten. Some of the pallor reversed, to my great delight, as he caressed my cheek.

"You look so lovely, too lovely," he murmured.

"No I don't. The lace is absurd." I chuckled and gestured to my neckline. "You like that it's cut low."

He tried to offer a smile, but his flirtatious nature was fading. Only weariness remained. "Natalie, someone was here. I think it was that friend, the girl—"

"Yes, Maggie. She's out of the way now, not a trouble. She was being foolish and…well, trying to summon you as if in a séance. She's quite…taken with you."

Jonathon sighed. "Even now? I'm sure I look quite the fright."

"A ghost of yourself, but still, even the Devil can't take the beauty out of you," I exclaimed.

"So you are then too?" Denbury asked.

"What?"

"Taken with me?"

"Oh, helplessly," I breathed. This compelled him to seize me and to steal one last kiss. I was addicted to them.

"Natalie," he murmured against my cheek, "you know you don't have to do this—"

"Too late," I replied, "You and I are in this madness

together, thick or thin. This must be done. The women of Five Points—or wherever he strikes—will bear his torment no more."

His expression was complex, but he murmured, "God be with you."

"And also with you," I replied, as in my Lutheran liturgy, a comforting structure amid the events that had torn our realities apart. "And he will be. He's on our side, you know," I replied with false bravado. Our eyes were honest; we each knew how terrified we were.

"I'll be on guard, ready to drag him in here forever," he growled. "I beg you to be careful. If you are in too much danger, leave. We will find another way."

I moved to the edge of the frame, hand outstretched toward my body in the museum.

"Natalie, look at me."

I turned.

"Swear you'll abandon this course if you're in grave danger."

"I swear," I said to assuage him. "I love you," I murmured, wanting *love* to be the last thing we said before facing battle.

"And I you," he replied, his voice shaking a bit. I stepped out and down into myself again, trying to hide my own fear.

I sit now upon the bench, practicing the phrase upon which lives hang. Lives should never be down to mere words, but I suppose they always are. Whether declarations of war, law, or treaty…words ever determine lives.

I hear noises above. Subtle, quiet noises. Likely the fiend is in the building. I cannot pretend I am not terrified. I *am*, most assuredly, terrified. I feel Jonathon's phantom hand at the small of my back, bolstering my courage and reassuring me that I am never truly alone. I yearn to feel that touch in this life, in *this* reality. It is the only thing helping me keep my wits. The sounds grow closer.

I must look distracted, unaware. I've closed the curtain, having given Denbury a kiss upon the air as I drew it. He could not move to acknowledge it but kept staring at me until the last. Forgive the trembling, telltale jagged edges of my writing that betray my fear.

I hear a slow and sauntering step down the hall. I'll turn the page and write something benign, lest he see damning script. I must act surprised…demure…everything he expects. Dear Lord, be with me now. Steady my resolve to do what must be done. I shall turn the page and fold the cover over. The fiend closes in!

And I think, dear diary, I'd like to travel to Italy, where I could see fine art and where perhaps the men are as beautiful (and perchance as scandalous) as legend would have them…

I must pause, someone seems to be at the door of this

chamber where I sit, trying to pass the time while locked away. Am I saved at last?

## HALF AN HOUR LATER, IF THAT
*(Oh, Time, you are unreliable, and Terror, you affect it.)*

I write this as the visage of Lord Denbury is being cut into pieces. Oh, gruesome sight, oh, harrowing night—a poet of such unnerving talent as Baudelaire could not even begin to pen an account of this. I can hardly believe it as I sit here to recount it. I begged Jonathon's leave to write this, to sort out the tumbling mess of my thoughts and my senses, struggling to comprehend these last moments...

The demon was dressed as a lord every bit as beautiful as mine, but with that darkness, that pallor, that hollow-eyed terrible mask, those reflective eyes that make him not my dear Jonathon but a devil. He slid into the room like a snake.

His lowered head fixed me with a gaze I thought might asphyxiate me in the instant. "Oh! Hello, pretty thing. Why, you look familiar..." His voice was a terrible purr. "What on earth are you doing after hours in the basement of a museum?"

I bit my tongue and gestured to my ears, nodding, and to my mouth, shaking my head.

"Oh, that's right, my mute beauty!" he exclaimed. Now for the next snare…

I shook my head. I ripped a page from the diary and scribbled a plea, placing myself entirely in his hands…

I tucked the diary beneath the bench and held the paper out to him. He read. His eyes widened.

"Arilda? Lost and locked in? Your name is Arilda?"

I nodded and gave him a quizzical look—as if why on earth should that matter? Though I knew very well why it did. I tried to appear as if I was falling into his trap when in fact it was the other way around…

I practically could see his mouth water. "Perfect," he said, in a tone that made me shudder. "Oh, you are a treat indeed." I suppressed a violent shudder and instead smiled with what I hoped was a look of charming enticement, rather than a grimace.

"I don't have to go out hunting tonight, Denbury," he called in delight. "The prey has come to me!"

My eyes flickered to the curtain, to the painting, to the man inside. Thinking of Jonathon, I was bolstered. He loved me. *He loved me*. And this…form…before me was not my love.

The demon advanced. "What a rare and succulent gift. My powers increase. Subjects laid at my feet, my quest opens unto me! Have you ever been with a man, fair one?"

Now I did allow myself to shudder. Part of the act, I

looked appropriately horrified. The demon wanted to defile a lady. I wanted to spit in his face. The look on my face seemed to satisfy him, for he laughed. I didn't need to fake or stage a blush; my cheeks were scarlet from his forward talk.

"No, of course not! You are a virgin saint..." He approached closer. "Perfect. Do struggle, will you? Act your part. It will add to the effect. And who knows, perhaps someday they'll canonize you too!"

Horrifying, so terribly horrifying, yet he was mesmerizing, it was true, for he still *was* Denbury—in the flesh. Something of his otherworldliness, something of his demonic nature had a sort of intoxication, a drug to it, beyond his handsome trappings. I recalled how Jonathon had been immobilized, and I watched the demon's hands to see if they contained some weapon.

The fiend's eyes were now luminous with an eerie quality beyond their animalistic bent and clouded. Reddened. Blood pooled in the tear ducts. I took his untoward approach as my cue and backed away.

I prayed that his base nature would not make him hesitate in coming closer to the painting. How could he know our plan? He was so clearly focused on how my violent death would aid his power. The devil hadn't remembered how the real soul of Denbury, my hero, had been watching me from the first.

I reminded myself of the knife tucked at the edge of my bodice and knew that if worse came to worst, I would defend myself. I would not go easily into that good night. Opening my mouth, I demonstrated my inability to speak with a small squeak of protest.

"I can be as rough with you as I please. You can't make a noise. And so the powerful preys upon the helpless. You and countless others…I will carve your names in blood on your own flesh. Names written in the Book of Death. And when your name is called, you will follow me. The society will rest upon the shoulders of the restless…"

He grabbed me by the throat, just like the first nightmare featuring him had foretold. My breath choked out. Good God…a society. Seemed the Devil had an institution after all.

As he scraped his thumb along my collarbone, his breath was hot against my neck. I loved nothing more than being held close by Denbury. But not like this. Again, this was not Jonathon.

His tongue traced the hollow of my throat, and it felt like the forked kiss of a snake. I shuddered again. He snickered. "Like that, do you? A shiver of delight, perhaps? The angel of a girl will fall to her demon, and I grow ever powerful in the depths of our sin. The more I take—" He raked a hand over me. A cold, deathly hand. Hardly the caress of the lover I knew and cherished. He stepped back so that he could watch my body react. "The more I gain."

His hand had released my throat to fumble at his clothes, at his pants. I felt hysteria tickle at my nerves. I'd practiced the words. I prayed then, harder than I'd ever prayed in my life. I reached out and took his face in my hands, as if begging his mercy.

His eyes lit with delight. I struggled a bit closer to the painting. I needed our weight on my side...

His eyes looked into mine, deeper. I stared into cold-blooded inhumanity, into sulfur, hell, and death. I stared into eyes that would see me dead, if they could, and I feared his very stare might kill me. But my panic overcame his dread gaze and made my body leap to action.

In a fluid, violent motion, I threw back the thick red curtain over the portrait. Then I spoke. My voice had never been so authoritative. The angels were on my side, surely...

"*Ego transporto animus ren per ianua*...Beelzebub the Devil!"

In the moment that his horrible eyes widened, he stared up at the painting, now revealed, and then back at me. He began to snarl and gripped me painfully tightly. I did not fight the violent momentum of his grasp. Instead I threw my weight to the side as if we were on the edge of a cliff and I intended to take us both down, the watery sensation of a trip inside the painting washing over me like a cool wave. His surprise allowed for my slight frame to succeed in dragging him into the terrible magic of his own making.

I heard Denbury—both of them—cry out. I felt hands clambering over me. I was on the floor of the study. I couldn't tell at first which hands were which. But I gasped as a hand reached beneath my skirts, pawing with claws and scrabbling to get at me. My God, it would seek to take me even in the agony of defeat. It was an animal…Red and gold light crackled all around us, the throes of his hellfire.

The demon became a morphing form, shifting and flickering like a candle, one moment wearing the handsome face of Denbury and the next a gray and horrid shifting silhouette of ghastly forms from legend and nightmare. It was too terrible to describe, and I turned away from it lest I go blind or turn to stone, like in ancient tales.

The struggle over me continued. The beast was gurgling things in other languages—foul, terrible things, surely—and his clammy hands were suddenly on fire. A claw against my bosom scalded me.

In a shriek I repeated the curse and took my chance to spit in his face. The demon threw his arms up as if my fire had countered his. I could now see the colors Jonathon had described: my green and violet halo fighting back the flamelike light of the enemy, while other threads of light swarmed over us like helping hands. Glancing at the portal that was the painting's frame, I could see that it was no longer cloudy. It was crystal clear, and I prayed this meant the space was literally open for us to retake the world as we knew it.

Denbury, *my* Jonathon, had never been so full of life and force. He threw the demon off me, lifted me into his arms, and did not hesitate at the frame's threshold. He leaped with me out and down just as the most horrific cry sounded in the air, a swelling, keening cry of every death knell and warrior's wail, furious and devastated.

While I wanted to know what the beast meant by "society," wanted to know if we'd yet be cursed and haunted by more such terrors, there was no time to inquire of the beast. There was no chance to see what else it may be connected to, to investigate if its works of evil were a coordinated effort, or even how it might be an omen of a new dawn of terror upon our land. Having these questions answered might have been good, but in the moment, most importantly, only our lives were at stake. The rest, I shudder to think, may yet be revealed.

The threshold separating body from soul seemed unstable. There was smoke as if the whole painted study was about to ignite, the red and gold light swirling and sparkling, the magic and devilry a potent, unwieldy force.

One might think that after having just been accosted by a nearly identical man, I'd hardly want similar hands to be upon me, seizing and holding me protectively close, but these were the hands and the arms of the man I loved, and they carried me away from destruction.

We lost our balance and fell out into the empty museum room, onto the floor together, Jonathon turning and falling so that his body hit the floor first and I landed safely atop him. His breath was knocked from him in a whooshing swoop, but after a wince of pain and a moment to regain himself, he breathed deeply, relieved.

And then all was silent except for our ragged breaths. Silence meant triumph.

And then Jonathon kissed me. It was gentle and he cradled me fondly, erasing the touch of hell with a touch of heaven. He kissed my whole face, part by part.

"Natalie, my angel. My salvation. My brave, brave, dear one…You have won me back. I am forever in your debt. I love you, dear girl."

Terror was overcome by joy. All Jonathon's imperfections were gone, his hair no longer graying, the wrinkles of aging vanished. His eyes regained their brightness and his color was restored. He was just as intoxicating as ever, all youth and vigor, as he should be. And now our two worlds were one.

But what of the demon?

We turned to the painting, and my hands clapped over my mouth to stifle the cry that was strangling my throat.

In that golden frame now stood a monster. He wore the suit of Denbury, but his beautiful face was disfigured, as if melted, scarred and horrible—his eyes a demonic red and black, his teeth jagged and fanglike, his lips curled back in a snarl. His face was cracked, and bone shone through. His hands were giant claws, meant for tearing flesh. The picture was somehow even more terrible than the shifting creature that had held me within. Sometimes a picture of a moment captures more than the moment itself. Horror made manifest.

"My God…" I murmured. My voice was awkward, but it was present and accounted for. And it had withstood the greatest test. I would speak more often. I had spoken to a devil and my voice had not failed. I would speak more to the world, and I would never stop.

"Indeed. God most certainly blessed us." Jonathon plucked my diary from beneath the bench and handed it to me. My shaking hands took it and clutched it to my chest. "I have a feeling your accounts will do us both great credit"—he looked at the devil we had trapped—"for I'm sure we'll wake tomorrow hardly believing any of this. I stand here having lived it, and I cannot believe it."

He took the painting from the wall and flipped it over, and we gasped again. All the markings on the back were wet, as if the carved runes dripped paint. But the red paint had become like blood, spattering onto the floor. I didn't hazard to pick up the substance in my fingers; the vague coppery scent told me that there was, indeed, blood in this infernal mixture.

I withdrew the knife from between my corset and bodice and handed it to him. He smirked, taking it. "Good girl…Thank you."

Grimly, Jonathon accepted the gore dripping onto his boots as he leaned the top of the painting against the wall, pierced the top with the knife, and tore at the corner of the canvas. Slowly, painstakingly, cutting every few inches, he tore the canvas from top to bottom. There was still a bit of hazy red and gold glow, the magic still ripe and fresh, and I feared for him.

"Jonathon…the light…" I murmured, gesturing to the veritable halo the painting wore. "Be careful."

He nodded. "But we cannot leave it whole. We cannot leave this as an accessible doorway."

I could not argue with him. He set to work ripping apart the two-dimensional object that had inexplicably held his soul prisoner.

I wish I could describe the sounds that came from the canvas, but they are too wretched to put to paper. I know that sound will haunt me to the end of my days, so I needn't immortalize it here. Imagine the terrible. Then give it soft whispers. And it is more terrible still.

Mr. Smith ducked his head in, glancing and narrowing his eyes at Jonathon, taking stock of him before turning to me. "I didn't hear you call or cry out, Miss Stewart, though I did hear some mighty awful noises of animals and such…"

"Indeed," I replied, my voice still breathless. "All is accounted for, Mr. Smith. We are victorious, and all is well. I thank you for being on guard."

If Mr. Smith had seen the particulars of the dreadful tumult, and if he had an opinion about it, he didn't show it. His face was, as ever, impassive. He nodded to me and then to Jonathon with formal politeness. "I'll be in the carriage out front when you're ready, Miss Stewart, Lord Denbury. Mrs. Northe is desperate to see you."

"Thank you kindly, Mr. Smith," Jonathon said, bowing. "I am blessed to have such friends. I'd take your hand but…mine is a bit soiled."

Mr. Smith nodded again and made a face as he turned away. I had to clap my hand over my mouth. An ungodly stench had begun to waft from the frayed threads, as if putrefaction was setting in immediately. And the slats of the painting that remained showcased a face that was rotting away. Terrible upon terrible.

We laid the waste in the center of the room, piling it in the middle of the frame laid upon the ground. The red fluid that had begun to drip from the runes was now a thin film of greasy liquid that smeared and streaked the floor around where the remnants were laid.

"I'd like to set fire to it. But it is too much of a risk to the museum."

"Indeed," I said. "Just let it be. We can undertake only so much risk. Lock this horror behind a closed door. There's beauty outside. While you may need a while to regain art appreciation, I could give you a tour. I know this place intimately."

Jonathon looked at me, and his striking face was full of apprehension. "Oh, Natalie, I want to revel in my newfound freedom, but how much freedom can I have if everyone suspects me of committing those horrible murders? Surely, I cannot stay in this city, but if I'm dead in England…" He raked his hands through his hair. "I don't know where to go."

"Mrs. Northe first. Plans later. She'll want to know everything, and she's the most sensible woman in the world, so she'll know what to do." I then indicated my diary. "And I must continue this dread retelling. These pages are my friend, and nothing calms me or engages me as much as writing in them. Except…" I gave him a beguiling look.

He grinned and we even forgot the disgusting particulars at the center of the room, forgot what he would do with himself again in the world as we indulged in a particularly questing embrace. His hands were bolder than ever before and I rejoiced that in this outside world, he still seemed to find me lovely in every way. Our passion managed to cross the threshold and still live. I pulled away, gasping.

"Now *that* I have to write down."

And so I do.

## LATER...

I sit in Mrs. Northe's study, her being better than her word, as always.

What on earth will the museum do when they discover what remains of their troublesome masterpiece? Will I be blamed? Will Mrs. Northe? But I couldn't worry about that at the moment. The more troublesome fact was that Lord Denbury was a wanted man. He'd have to flee. No jury would believe this.

The only account of the truth lies in these pages. As much as I commend my narrative style, I can hardly believe my own eyes, let alone trust a jury to take the words written here as fact. But I swear upon my mother's grave—a thing I would not do lightly as my mother's spirit yet lives—this is our truth.

Mrs. Northe was wonderfully kind to Jonathon, better than I'd hoped. She greeted him like a long-lost son and indicated where Mr. Northe's old room and his clothes remained.

"You might think it morbid for a woman to keep her

dead husband's clothes at the ready," she told Jonathon with a winning smile. "But I have learned that having spare clothing on hand, of every kind, comes in frightfully useful in times of crisis."

Indeed, no one is quite as useful as Evelyn Northe. I brought my small bag with me, not making mention of it and stowing it unobtrusively by the door.

"Surely, if for nothing but dear Miss Stewart's sake," Jonathon began, "you'd like to hear the events. Please trust me that I never meant the girl harm, though you see those bruises—" He grimaced, examining marks I'd yet to see. "It was a demon, I assure you, though that sounds utterly mad—"

Mrs. Northe hushed him with a wave of her hand. "You've been through harrowing experiences the likes of which I have never seen. I expect you, Lord Denbury, to tell me all about them over tea, coffee, or hard liquor, whatever your preference, once you've changed and refreshed yourself. Natalie, the same."

I checked my face in the nearby foyer mirror and was in for a shock, having not realized that I bore such telltale signs. There were little burn marks around my throat, likely where the claws had gotten me. I shuddered, violated. My torn skirts were enough to remind me that a demon's hands had been where only Jonathon's bold caress had gone during one bout of mutual passion, and I burned with sudden shame. My emotions were as tumultuous and unwieldy as a thunderstorm.

Mrs. Northe was studying me. She noticed my blush and the tears that threatened to spill down my cheeks.

"Lord Denbury, would you mind helping yourself? I didn't keep my staff on tonight as I expected we'd be in for odd fortunes and I hate countering housekeeper superstition. But I do believe our valiant Miss Stewart needs a bit of tending to," she said, coming closer.

"Of course." Jonathon approached me and held out his hand, his questing, gentle eyes asking permission. I gave him my hand. He kissed it gently. "Miss Stewart was a heroine like I've never seen. I tell you, Mrs. Northe, there is not a more incredible woman upon this earth than her," he said quietly, as he released my hand and bowed.

The tears fell from my eyes. I found that in his gentle stare, I could smile, though the terrors of the night were gnawing at me, the rush and shock of the moment fading into a cold chill.

"I don't doubt it," Mrs. Northe replied. "Come, sir."

Once she showed Denbury to his refreshment, she came back to lead me into a boudoir to get out of the torn clothes. She brought a cool ointment to ease the sting of the burns left by the demon's touch and said nothing, but her face was warm and gentle as she waited for me to speak when ready. Everything I didn't want to have to say was explained by the physical evidence that Mrs. Northe examined like any good detective.

"The wretch didn't get far," I spat, my voice hard and sure. The night's events had emboldened my words like nothing before could have done. I indicated the torn bloomers Mrs. Northe held as I slipped fresh under-garments onto my legs. "But it was far enough," I added, and there my voice broke.

I fell into helpless sobs, trying to exorcise the terror with a good cry. Mrs. Northe held me and made no effort to stop the flow. She let it run its course. Her empathy was genuine. Likely her gifts had her feeling exactly what I was feeling, and that was a blessing, for my mind was a complex knot I was having difficulty untangling.

"Would you like to speak privately to me? Or will you and Lord Denbury give me an account in the parlor?"

I wiped my eyes, my muscles willing themselves back to control again, their helpless tremors abating. "I'd like to have his hand to hold while recounting the horrors, if you don't mind…" I blushed suddenly. "Unless you find that inappropriate. These events have taxed all propriety—"

Mrs. Northe smiled her best sister-conspirator smile. "If what I've sensed is any indication, you and he will do far more than hold hands in time to come, and I'd hardly begrudge you the contact. My, he is quite breathtaking in person."

I chuckled. My blush reignited and I wondered what sort of psychic glimpses Mrs. Northe had seen of us. I would have pressed her for details of our future, giddy like a girl at her first ball, had the night not so sobered me.

A new wave of sadness hit me, and I clutched at Mrs. Northe's arm. "Maggie was there when I arrived. She… somehow stayed on after hours. She drew a pentagram on the floor in chalk and she had a book that I believe came from one of those men you despise—"

Mrs. Northe's eyes flashed. "The fool," she hissed. "Forever tampering with what she cannot grasp. Mr. Smith had her marched right to my waiting carriage. I gave her quite the talking-to and threatened her with the histrionic ward. Our friendship might be damaged, that of the three of us, but she knows her mother would kill her if she found out about her little stunt, so I maintain leverage. I will have to ask about that book, though. Here, I've a dress I can adjust to fit you. Step in."

I'd never been in so fine a dress, and when I glimpsed Jonathon awaiting us in the foyer below, looking perhaps more dashing than I'd ever seen him, we smiled broadly at each other. Though tired, he looked as if fresh clothes and fine toiletries had renewed his spirit and made him feel human again after being trapped in his portrait clothes, marred, torn, and unkempt. Before me now was the portrait of the lord whom I wanted forever in my mind.

We both stared at one another, drinking in our freshly composed selves, and I do believe he liked what he saw of me as much as I did of him.

In our stares was such relief. It had been as if any time that we weren't present with the other, we were convinced we knew each other only in the dreams we shared. But here he was, fully in the flesh and still pulling on my heart. What did Mrs. Northe see for us? Would we marry? That's what people our age did; they found love and married. My heart raced at the thought. No, what was I thinking: he'd have to flee; he was a wanted man. I most certainly couldn't go on flights of fancy at this time. Most likely, I had to prepare a good-bye. But I loved him...

My heart careened back and forth as we were ushered gently into the sitting room. Mrs. Northe bade us sit side by side so that he could take my trembling hand in his steady one, as I'd hoped.

As we told our tale, Mrs. Northe was patient and grim faced, as if she were reliving it with us and seeing it with her own eyes. Our hands were white from grasping one another too tightly. As our tale came to a close, Jonathon voiced the fresh horror.

"And now, Mrs. Northe, what am I to do? No one knows that demon as Lord Denbury, but Lord Denbury is dead and I wear the face of a killer. I would hope my solicitor was sensible enough to maintain some sort of provision—if I could simply get hold of him without alarming or alerting—"

"Allow me to intervene on your behalf in terms of your estate. As for who may take the fall in your body's place, I have my ideas. I think we'll find a dead French artist in your crypt in your stead. I have contacts in London who will find out. But you should, for safety's sake, go into hiding, not only because of police pursuit but because of evils that may yet seek you out as a vulnerable vessel. Magic will hang about you both. I can see and feel it, a paranormal aura like a perfume that can attract those gruesome muzzles that sniff out the most revolting of odors and pounce like hungry animals..."

Mrs. Northe's eyes were cold, and in that moment, I wondered if she had seen more darkness in her circles than she cared or dared tell. "Do you have any contacts, Lord Denbury, say, out West—as suitable a place as any to wait out a storm?"

He thought a moment before nodding. "I do. I have a dear friend, a man I'd trust with any life of value. I met him in England at medical lectures. We bonded because we were often the 'children' in the room."

"Then you should go there. There's no better time in one's life for good friends than when one has been lifted from the jaws of hell. In the meantime I believe we may implicate Crenfall in this insidious matter. The timing would suit, and he *was* an accomplice. He must be brought to justice, though the real culprit remains trapped in shreds of canvas."

While I wanted to see Jonathon safe more than anything, the idea of him going away, now that he was real for all of us, was a knife in my heart. I'd dreamed of adventures by his side here, showing him all the glory of this greatest of American cities, of coming out from the shadow of tragedy and into the light of courtship, just as I'd dreamed there beneath the wings of an angel...

My face must have given away my sentiment. Jonathon and Mrs. Northe turned to me.

"I'll not forget you, Natalie—I mean, Miss Stewart." He glanced at Mrs. Northe. "Forgive the familiarity—"

"I expect us to be on familiar names here, all of us. The inexplicable breeds familiar family," Mrs. Northe stated, absolving any impropriety.

"I-I'll write. I want you in my life—need you in my life. I'll come for you..." He trailed away and I saw how overwhelmed he was, as if his instinct to flee and his desire to stay at my side were equal.

"I want what is best and safest for you. You..." I stared into my lap. "You know my heart."

"And you know mine," he countered. He turned to Mrs. Northe and embarked upon discussions of business, and I felt flattered that he did not wish to keep me from them.

After they had spoken of solicitations, attorneys, and other matters, Jonathon turned to me again, a bit sheepishly.

"Why is it, Mrs. Northe, that out of all the impossible things, here we sit, the three of us, new friends. Yet Natalie is so familiar to me, like an old friend—full of light, color, and magic that she didn't even know she possessed. You have such a way of accounting for the strange, Mrs. Northe, can you tell me why us?" He reached toward me, touching my cheek.

"Is it past lives?" I breathed excitedly.

Mrs. Northe rolled her eyes. "Don't put stock in past lives. It's *this* life that makes the difference. And in this life there may be certain destinies, people you're meant to meet. We three have been meant to meet. But there is no sole person for another's heart. Souls cannot be broken and then completed by another. That's not healthy, nor wise. There are infinite possibilities as there are infinite people and some matches better made than others. Your magic was what was called for at *this* time in your current pass around the globe." She made a face.

"Just don't say that you'll die without the other one or that you'll never love again or that you're not whole—" She batted her hand. "That's the stuff of *Romeo and Juliet*, hasty nonsense, and you know how well that turned out. There's magic about the two of you, yes. Just don't be desperate about it. That's where souls go wrong, when they think they don't have choices. The heart must make choices."

She looked to both of us, as if waiting for us to affirm that we understood. We nodded.

"Tell me, Lord Denbury, do you see other colors?" she asked. "Other lights around persons, other auras?"

He nodded. "Yes. You, for one. I sometimes see you with a slow and steady white haze about you, up from your head, almost like a thread. Calm, unruffled." He smiled but his smile quickly faded. "The girl, Maggie. Red and a bit of yellow. Natalie, green and violet. But not everyone."

Mrs. Northe nodded. "Likely you're sensing abilities or picking up on those whose energy might have an effect on you. It will be interesting to track your progress or to see if the ability hones itself. Did you see these things before your…incident?"

Jonathon shook his head. "No, but I've always been an uncanny judge of character. Save for the demon. He took me utterly unaware." He blushed, and I knew he was again regretting the opium den. There was no need to mention it.

"Part of his magic. Put to rest. Good work, friends, and now on to your next adventure." Mrs. Northe turned to me, a curious look in her eyes. "Natalie, you and I have discussed many things. I've laid treatises at your feet, and you have listened patiently. I have done so to lay a foundation. The things that we've discussed will not pass as easily out of your life as they so suddenly came into it. And so it's my duty to arm you as best I can. For I believe you two have been drafted into a most uncommon war. There is, after all, a 'society' to attend to," she said ominously.

There was an awkward silence as Jonathon and I shuddered. He was going away. Yet, what of me? Were we, as Mrs. Northe indicated, soldiers meant to fight side by side or separately? Was our joint magic now to go two separate ways?

I would have followed him anywhere. And he knew it, surely...Mrs. Northe cleared any chance for further discussion by rising. "We'd best get you to the depot, Lord Denbury. I'll pack you a bag. I had Martha make some soup. Go into the dining room and have some. You look hungry and cold, the both of you."

We did as we were instructed and said nothing. *Please kiss me*, I thought, yearning for some reassurance. But this was Mrs. Northe's home, and privacy was not ours. Nerves, exhaustion, and worry for the future had taken a grievous toll and we kept silent.

Dazed, he and I were trundled into a carriage, Mrs. Northe beside us. Looking at Jonathon, so elegant and dashing despite the night's terrors, made me ache, but I couldn't force my eyes away. He was in my world now. My world was bursting at the seams. Mrs. Northe gave him some money, tucking it quickly and firmly into his palm. "I know you'll repay me when you can, but don't refuse my gift."

His eyes poured volumes of thanks upon our gracious, incredible benefactor.

He turned conflicted eyes on me and I had no words, only the widening ache in my heart. I felt with hard certainty the knowledge of what I would have to do. His hand would clutch mine and then pull away. A maddening cycle.

When I saw Grand Central Depot, a behemoth mass of tracks and steam engines, my heart leaped to my throat and I had trouble breathing. I couldn't say good-bye to him; I just couldn't. It would be wrong if I did. All my life I'd had keen instincts. And my instincts said it was wrong to part—not yet, not so suddenly free. I had taken pains to make sure that when we'd left the museum, my small bag was with me. I knew what I had to do. But he'd likely not accept my coming along, as he chafed at my making sacrifices for him. I had to make an argument, but I had no words.

"This isn't good-bye, Natalie," he reassured me. "I'll come again. I'll write to you sooner, via Mrs. Northe."

I opened my mouth, and it was as if I were as mute as I had been before I'd met him.

He hopped out of the carriage, just north of the depot's platforms. The steam and the noise of the rails were intrusive and maddening, the air gritty and unpleasant.

He reached for my face through the carriage window. I leaned out to him. "Pardon me, Mrs. Northe, I must—" he murmured, and kissed me passionately. He murmured in my ear that he loved me. I clutched his forearms as if I could hold him to me by force.

After an interminable moment he pulled away. "Thank you for everything, Natalie. You will hear from me, and I will be whoever you would wish me to be, anything you wish of me…" He fought tears in his eyes and walked away before either of us could exchange more vows or even before I could manage a word.

I couldn't keep the tears at bay as I watched his figure, striking in a greatcoat and wide-brimmed hat, disappear into a crowd of passengers.

Mrs. Northe was staring at me with a curious expression as my feet nudged the cloth bag I'd stowed behind my heels.

"I know that's a bag you're fiddling with," she stated casually. "I assume since he didn't invite you that you're too proud and stubborn to invite yourself along. So instead you'll steal into a separate car and announce yourself only when it's too late to turn you back around."

I blinked at her. That was exactly what I was planning to do.

"Clairvoyant tendencies ruin all the fun of surprise," she pouted. "But they are most certainly useful, just like changes of clothes, in times of crisis. I didn't think you'd be able to bring enough without making a show of it so I packed another bag and had it waiting here for you," she stated, sliding a small case from beneath the seat.

I knew my mouth was agape, but I couldn't seem to shut it.

"I think I know your heart sometimes before you do." She chuckled. "That, and as I told you, I've premonitions. But let me be clear, I'm speaking not in the interest of young love, but in the interest of your safety. I'd never recommend a hasty trip such as this, because it seems desperate. However, there's something else. There's residual, powerful magic lingering about him, as I'd warned. And it's most certainly lingering on you too. It will be there hanging about the Metropolitan, perhaps even about me. What I'm saying is this residual echo may make you a target as well—"

"But are you safe?" I gasped finally.

"I'll make sure I am. And I'll have to convince your father this is for the best, for now. But you might want to catch that train."

"Good God, how I'll miss you! Please tell my father that I'm sorry and I love him—"

"I will, don't worry. And you'll not get rid of me easily." She grinned and descended from the carriage to help me out and hand me the bags.

"I should hope not. I adore you," I cried, throwing my arms around her once my feet hit the cobblestones.

"And I you, dear girl. There's an extra bill in your case. With that, be sure to get a sleeper car and ally yourself with a few respectable-looking women until you're brave enough to confront Denbury on that train," she instructed, pointing a finger. When she pointed her finger, I knew it was of grave import. I nodded.

The train's whistle screamed.

While surely we both could have listed thousands of reasons why what I was about to do was a terrible idea, I was a woman of decision and I'd made mine, though Mrs. Northe had managed to say it before I did.

"I'll write. And I promise to pay you back for everything, somehow," I called as I retreated. Out on the air, the words on my tongue were still heavy and awkward, still getting used to themselves. Mrs. Northe was again inside the carriage and at the window, her face betraying the first conflict I'd yet seen. While she knew the situation and knew she wouldn't have been able to stop me, she, like any good substitute mother, would think that getting on a train unbeknownst to the young man you loved might be a terrible idea, all supernatural events aside.

And still she let me go. Just as she had let me stare down death and the Devil. Likely because whispers from my real mother had told her that my present destiny lay with Jonathon and that I was, perhaps, safer with him. Or so I hoped. Now to convince him of it.

I sit now at the back of the train, and here is where I've been relaying all of these events.

When I boarded the train, I helped myself into a seat next to three generations: a grandmother, her daughter and granddaughter. The Wills family took instantly to mothering me so that I needn't have worried about being without a chaperone. I've learned that if you just look a little lost and appeal to well-dressed older females, and you yourself are well-dressed, they generally are a beneficial, generous species, if not a bit opinionated.

New York is rolling away from me in all her massive mess and glory. Beloved and familiar lanes, clutter, congestion, and horse dung. Gorgeous palaces of homes, churning industry, smoke, fire, and gaslight. "I love you," I whisper to my city as it chugs away and the steam engine gains speed, my breath on the glass and a new darkness ahead as the train veers west.

Onward! What an adventure! It is not every day that a young woman runs away from home after a handsome man and sees the country by rail. My nerves are mixed with a growing excitement. However, exhaustion sorely tempers me.

"Pardon me," I said to the ladies around me. I laid my head upon the glass, not even bothering with the sleeper car, as I've never been so exhausted. I'm sure I'll be asleep in a mere moment. A new world will await me when my heavy eyelids open at dawn.

## LATER...

I slept. And I dreamed.

In that dream was a dark, long, smooth corridor. Much like the corridor of a train aisle.

Somewhere in the distance was a pale light, like dawn. Moving. Perhaps that shifting movement was from the threads of light that were so like people, as when I'd dreamed of such tumbling, shifting forces against the backdrop of my city. Perhaps this is what Mrs. Northe meant by there being another existence entirely...

There were doors at intervals on each side of me, with beveled glass knobs like the one on Jonathon's painted study door.

Out from one of those doors far ahead walked Jonathon.

He turned and looked at me. There was a long silence.

"You're on the train," he said, raising an eyebrow.

"Yes."

He laughed and then held out his hand. I bit my lip, hardly able to contain myself.

I moved forward, reaching out to he who is my angel in waking and in dreams.

I opened my eyes.

There, awake, at the door of my train car, was Lord Jonathon Denbury, real and in the gorgeous flesh, holding out his hand for me. I stared at him. I was the girl he'd asked for.

"Yes, you," he murmured with an irresistible grin.

And here I conclude.

Dear Father,

By the time you receive this diary, likely you will have already seen to the odd business of the painting, or what's left of it, anyway. The answer lies within these pages, and while I realize you'll hardly believe them, please be content in the fact that I am safe and that I am following my destiny. Please do not read the part(s) about kissing and such. You don't want to know, and I don't want you to.

I send this to reassure you I have not been abducted and so you'll have a testament to the strange events surrounding the portrait of Lord Denbury. (That very man himself has vowed to send me back to New York City unless I assure you of my safety and give you the full story.)

Whether or not you believe that Mother told Mrs. Northe that this was my path, I believe it. I was not coerced; I am here of my own free will. I pursued the innocent man I love because we will be safer this way. We shall be in contact, and none of this is permanent. I am still a lady, and Lord Denbury is a consummate gentleman. It is my hope that you and Mrs. Northe can come visit. I will write you often.

I am so grateful for your love, your support, and all the gifts you've given me. I cannot express that enough.

Please respect this path, however strange, and know that I endeavor to make you proud. Jonathon and I want to do the public some good, and we shall do so.

Through the unusual circumstances of the last weeks, I have once again found my voice. I cannot wait for you to hear it. To converse with you, Father, will be such a gift! And that's all due to Lord Denbury.

He is convinced I should make sure I'd rather not have any other suitor—but here is the only area in which he is a fool. I want no other, and when he asks for my hand, I do hope you'll give your blessing. I daresay a better match could not be made. I love him. Again, please skim over the kissing part(s), and we'll both be far less embarrassed.

I cannot mention where we're going. While Denbury is innocent, I can't expect the police to believe a word of this and must protect him until he can be absolved of any wrongdoing.

Please keep in mind that Mrs. Northe suggested that lingering traces of the magic may still be upon us, a beacon, if we remained in New York. Please realize we have both taken ourselves from the area in the interest of safety. While you may not believe us on account of magic, I hope you will believe that we mean you no disrespect or harm. As for public opinion, as an "unfortunate" anyway, I daresay this won't ruin anyone's expectations of me as I had none to begin with. Please do be careful around the Metropolitan. It unwittingly housed a curse. We're sorry we brought it upon you.

Mrs. Northe will corroborate as much of this as she may

see fit, and she is attending to the loose ends of this odd case so that all may be put to rest.

I love you always,
Natalie

Dear Mr. Stewart,

While I imagine you may hate me for all that has transpired and are surely as baffled by the turns of events as I am, please believe that I am a gentleman, and upon my life, I shall do right by your daughter. While you've never met me, I look forward to meeting you in the future and proving that I deserve the kindness and bravery your daughter has shown me.

She is the most incredible young woman in all the world. Surely you know this. I promise you that she will be well cared for and provided for. I intend to live out my life in the service of others, and there is no better partner in this than your daughter, a gift from the heavens who saved my life. I am more than indebted to her, I love her. We shall make you proud, we promise.

With utmost sincerity,
Jonathon Whitby, Lord Denbury

June 20, 1880

New York City Police Record Case File: 1306
Missing Person, Vandalism

Report of missing person, described to and taken down by
yours truly, Sergeant James Patt, on this day, June 20, at one
in the afternoon.

Reported missing: One Natalie Stewart, age seventeen.

At noon on June 20, Mr. Gareth Stewart came into the
precinct and asked to speak to an authority, as his daughter
had gone missing the night prior. Mr. Stewart is a lean man
of average height, with hazel eyes, close-shaven beard, and
russet hair. He is of average means, an employee of the
Metropolitan Museum of Art with no criminal record. Mr.
Stewart reported that his daughter was not in her room, not
with another guardian with whom she had been close, a Mrs.
Evelyn Northe, nor was she at the Metropolitan, where she
had been apprenticed.

Additional concern: Mute status of Natalie Stewart. Adept
at sign language but no known vocal capacity.

Behavior of late: No different from average for a girl her
age—save for her voice. Mr. Stewart grew red in the face as
he described a certain obsession with a painting. A painting
he described as now lying in shreds in a downstairs storage
room of the Metropolitan Museum.

Case development: Case of vandalism of painting of one Lord Denbury, portrait. No museum guards expressed anything out of the ordinary but confessed to having been present only at front entrance, and other entrances might have admitted the vandal.

Mr. Stewart here concluded that there was a connection between the painting and his daughter's disappearance but that he could not, "for the life of him" imagine what.

I questioned him about this friend of the family, Mrs. Northe. Here Mr. Stewart's face again grew red. My suspicion of both Mr. Stewart and the widow Northe was piqued. He said that while he knew Mrs. Northe would never harm the girl, she may know something he did not as they had grown "close as mother and daughter."

It was around this point in the narrative that the very woman in question, Mrs. Evelyn Northe, was escorted into the room.

"What the devil's gone on, Mrs. Northe?" Stewart stated before anyone could be properly introduced. "Where the hell is my daughter? The guards report that Denbury's portrait is grotesque and all in shreds!"

Mrs. Northe turned to me then and said, "It's a domestic matter, Sergeant, not a criminal one, and there's much to explain to Mr. Stewart." Here she turned to him. "Your daughter has confided in me, but I think it best to discuss her future elsewhere."

"You'll tell me right now—"

"Your daughter is safe, Mr. Stewart. A criminal investigation would prove fruitless as there is no harm or threat involved, save for a case of young, impetuous love."

"Young love?" he cried. "With whom was she in love?"

"All will be explained," Mrs. Northe stated.

Here Mr. Stewart appeared confused and began to protest that Mrs. Northe should have stopped his daughter. But Mrs. Northe stated that no matter what, Natalie would have done what she wanted. Mr. Stewart seemed unable to argue this point. Clearly he trusted Mrs. Northe, and it did seem she cared for the girl. But the two were undoubtedly odd. Northe in particular. She put me in mind of some gypsy fortune-teller, even though she was dressed as any fine lady might be. She kept staring at me with odd scrutiny. It was uncanny and I didn't like it.

She blamed Mr. Crenfall—whom her agents had been spying upon ever since he and an unidentified man broke into her home—for the destruction of the painting. (Refer to case file under Northe for reference to this breaking-and-entering charge.) I shall have him brought in for questioning and call upon Mr. Stewart and Mrs. Northe next week to see if there are developments in this case.

July 5, 1880

Mr. Stewart immediately assured me all was well, and I caught him tucking into his pocket a little note card that read "I love you" in feminine script. There was something nervous in his voice as he tried to shoo me out the door.

"Glad to hear you are well, Mr. Stewart, but I've a few more questions. Due diligence and all. I'm sure you can understand, sir," I explained.

"Of course," Mr. Stewart said, glancing about. "But the matter is resolved."

That's when I noticed the diary upon the desk with the subject's name upon it. "What's this? I think I'll have to examine this, sir, if you don't mind."

"There's really no need," Stewart said quickly—which increased my curiosity. "It was sent to me just this week from Natalie herself, proving she's fine." He flipped through the pages and took out the separate letter addressed to him and, with cursory inspection, I saw that the penmanship did match. "You can see that she's still alive. And that it didn't come from New York. The postage bears a seal of Chicago."

"Indeed, so she's not dead. But I'm still taking this diary

into the station. There's a file for her, you know. Just in case something else comes up."

The man's nerves made me not trust the situation. Mr. Stewart was loath to let it go, which I suppose is understandable, but it remains with us nonetheless.

"And do you approve of your daughter's actions?" I had to ask.

"No...but...but I've been overruled."

I raised an eyebrow.

"My late wife...she...well..." Mr. Stewart coughed uncomfortably. "Well, she told me she quite approves of the situation and I need to let it be for the time being."

"And just how did you find this out from your *late* wife?"

"Séance, Sergeant," Stewart murmured, flushing.

"A séance?"

"Yes, sir."

"I doubt words of a dead woman would hold up in court," I retorted. "But it doesn't look as though this is going to court, so go ahead and have fun with your magical parlor tricks," I stated, having had quite enough.

I will peruse this diary, though, in case there's something I should attend to, or if it may indicate that Mr. Stewart is lying and the girl is being kept somewhere against her will.

July 6, 1880

Sergeant James Patt, New York City Police
Notes on Stewart Case/Five Points Murders

Good God.

After having read this mad account, I must now turn
the diary over to the detective investigating the Five Points
murders.

I spoke with the Five Points detective, and he told me they'd
nabbed a man named Crenfall for the crimes—got him out
of a local madhouse after he'd been reportedly wandering
the Metropolitan Museum like a mumbling bum. Seems he
killed an artist in France, too, before committing murders
in England, some young lord, and then here in New York.
He confessed to all of it, though I'm unconvinced he has
enough wits to speak to a woman, let alone kill her. Mrs.
Evelyn Northe brought his name to their attention. Seems
she shot the man in the leg when he broke into her house after
a painting. What a lot of fuss over brushstrokes and canvas!

Crenfall. I recognized the name from the diary pages, and I
now saw it was all connected. I'm going to pay a visit to Mrs.
Northe then. This very afternoon.

I will say this; the woman is charming.

"Mrs. Northe, I have no jurisdiction to arrest you but I'm almost inclined to."

"Yes, I was told you took Miss Stewart's diary. Since you're here, I assume we all look guilty in your eyes because you don't believe the girl."

"You do?"

"Wholly."

"Crenfall did it, did he?"

"Well, he assisted. The possessor did the rest, sir. And I'd be wary. This is only the sign of more to come. So don't waste your time following a young girl and her lover. That's not the problem. There's a society of people calling upon forces of evil and amassing dark magic practices. What you read in that diary was only one instance of a host of bad omens. The society is who I'd worry about. You need to think about a different sort of battle on a different sort of battlefield."

"Whom and what should the precinct employ, then, Mrs. Northe, a battalion of mediums and fortune-tellers?"

"That would be a very good start, sir," Mrs. Northe replied.

I shook my head and begged her leave.

I stand by my decision to give these materials over to the Five Points detective, who likely will see it closed, satisfied enough to have a conviction in Crenfall. I want nothing to do with the case; it makes my head hurt.

Should you be curious about devils, societies, séances, etc., please call on Mrs. Evelyn Northe, Fifth Avenue. I'm sure she'll be glad to oblige you. If there is such a thing as a society of devils, then I hope to God they stay patrons of the arts and leave the rest of us regulars alone.

Should anyone who has followed this narrative to this conclusion regret doing so, don't say I didn't warn you.

# Acknowledgments

My dear Oscar Wilde, thank you for Dorian Gray and for your genius. I'd like to think that if I had the privilege of knowing you, we'd have gotten along famously. Regardless, I am eternally your fan.

Thank you, Biz Urban, for going through this book line by line with me; your presence in my life has been so helpful in so many ways.

Thank you to Lexie for your time, care, and insight. This book goes out in particular to you.

Thank you, Christina, for your valuable thoughts and many windows onto communication.

Thanks to amazing author and friend Sarah MacLean for spot-on advice and support.

To my dear writer gals—Hanna L., Sammi W., Lizzie W., and Akasha H., don't you ever stop writing or dreaming, girls. You're talented, and don't you *ever* forget it.

Marijo, it's your turn.

Thanks to my angels in the book blogging community who have been so thrilled about the prospect of this series. You're more valuable to me than you can ever know.

Thanks as always to my hero of an agent, Nicholas Roman Lewis; and to my fabulous editor, Leah Hultenschmidt, for the opportunity of this new adventure and the joy that is working with you; and thank you, Dominique and Sourcebooks, for being as excited as I am.

# About the Author

Leanna Renee Hieber aims to be a gateway drug for nineteenth-century literature. Having graduated with a theater degree and a focus on the Victorian era, she's adapted works of Victorian literature for the stage, and her one-act plays have been produced around the country.

*The Strangely Beautiful Tale of Miss Percy Parker*, the first in Leanna's Strangely Beautiful quartet of Gothic Victorian fantasy novels, hit Barnes & Noble's bestseller lists and won two 2010 Prism Awards (Best Fantasy and Best First Book). Option rights have been sold for a musical theater production currently in development.

A member of Science Fiction and Fantasy Writers of America, International Thriller Writers, and Romance Writers of America, she's the RWA NYC 2010 Author of the Year. A member of actors' unions AEA, SAG, and AFTRA, Leanna occasionally works in film and television. A devotee of ghost stories and Goth clubs, she resides in New York City with her real-life hero and their beloved rescued lab rabbit, Persebunny. Visit her at www.leanna reneehieber.com, and follow her @LeannaRenee.